Wounded Warrior Hearts

Book 1 - Steven

Book 2 - Amy

Book 3 - Russ

Deborah Wallace

Deborah Wallace

Wounded Warrior Hearts: Steven, Amy, and Russ

Published by Deborah Wallace

Copyright © 2020 by Deborah Wallace

All rights reserved.

ISBN: 978-1-951457-06-8

Cover Art by Raymond and Deborah Wallace
Photographs:
Guardian Darrah by Jonathan Borba
Bell Rock by Collin Rose
Motorcycle by Salvo Rubino

TABLE OF CONTENTS

Wounded Warrior Hearts: Steven

Deborah Wallace

Wounded Warrior Hearts: Steven

Published by Deborah Wallace

Copyright © 2019 by Deborah Wallace

Cover Art by Raymond and Deborah Wallace
Photographs:
Guardian Darrah by Jonathan Borba
Bell Rock by Collin Rose
Motorcycle by Salvo Rubino

Chapter 1

"Goddess, I have an Intervention." Darrah hovered in the doorway, afraid Goddess Eva would tell her to work with another guardian before presenting the Intervention.

Eva looked up from her glass desk. Every blonde hair was tucked into a twist on the back of her head, her flowing forest green robe matching the green of her eyes. "Guardian Darrah. Is this the first Intervention you're submitting?"

Darrah swallowed a lump and nodded, her loose blonde curls bouncing. She stepped past the amethyst wall, and glanced out the window. Clouds almost always obscured the view of Earth far below, and today was no exception.

She'd studied many interventions by other guardians, and felt ready to take on one of her own. Others had told her she was ready, but no assignment had been given to her. She'd gone searching where no one else had and found her own.

"How long has this veteran been stateside?"

"Two weeks."

Goddess laced her fingers on the desktop. "You know we wait longer than that."

Two months was the usual wait time before interceding with a veteran. "I know, Goddess, but in three weeks, he'll have an event he won't recover from. I thought you would need time to intercede." She bowed her head and held out a two-inch, flat, black onyx square with the veteran's information.

Goddess took it and closed her eyes. After several

seconds, she sucked in her breath. "You are correct. We don't want a returning soldier to take his own life. Do you have a plan for First Lieutenant Steven Halloran?"

"Yes, Goddess." She held out a stack of nine pale peach squares. "I believe the right woman could save his life." She was embarrassed that she'd chosen so many, but she wanted to make sure the right candidate was in the group. In her observations, the people who survived suicide were the ones surrounded by those who cared. The Lieutenant was about to lose the only one he thought did.

Goddess took the disks and fanned them across her desk. The flat of her hand hovered above the first square and slowly glided across to the last. She plucked one out, about two-thirds through the row.

"Angelina Carrera." The square rested in her palm.

Darrah held her hand over it.

"Have them meet tomorrow and two days after the event."

Darrah let the scenes flow through her. She'd never put scenes in motion before. She couldn't fail this soldier. Failure for her meant death for this man.

She picked up the square. "Yes, Goddess."

She slipped the two squares into the pocket of her yellow gown, gathered the rest and headed for the door.

"Darrah."

She turned back, afraid Goddess had changed her mind and would give another this assignment.

"You did well. This one would have slipped through the cracks. If you need assistance, see Guide Rayah."

"Yes, Goddess." She bowed her head and left.

~~~

Steve hobbled out of the diner, his cane clicking on the

concrete with every other step. As he reached the empty parking space beside his truck, a small Honda touring bike pulled in. The rider removed her helmet and ran a hand through short, brown curls. The bike was smaller than his Harley that he hadn't ridden in two years. It sat in his friend's garage.

The painting on the black gas tank caught his eye, a sunset over Bell Rock in Sedona. Maybe he'd get that painted on his if he rode again.

He nodded at it. "Nice picture. Who did it?"

The woman jumped. He hadn't meant to startle her.

A grin lit her face. Her brown-green eyes didn't seem to have a care in the world. She had a cute little upturned nose. "It is nice, isn't it? My cousin finished it a month ago. She does cars and bikes...and tattoos."

He smiled. "You got one of those, too?"

"A tattoo?"

He nodded.

"Yeah, but I'm not showing it to you."

He held up his hands and chuckled. "I'm not asking." His gaze traveled over her motorcycle. "Nice little bike."

She glared. "Hey, it's the biggest I can handle."

"Sorry. Nothing wrong with that." He envied her. He wasn't sure if he'd ever ride his bike again. He craved that free feeling. Go where he wanted, feel the wind on his face, perfect control of the machine under him through turns and over hills. He sighed. If he could ride again.

She waved at his lower body. "Are those real?"

He lifted his brows. There was no way she could see the prosthetic through his pants.

She narrowed her eyes at his legs. "Military issue fatigues?"

He didn't know why he should feel relieved a stranger hadn't noticed his missing extremity. "Yeah. I got my

discharge two weeks ago. It's been hard to get used to jeans."
And it was difficult getting them over his foot. He needed to
buy boot-cut jeans.

She stared into his eyes. "Thank you for serving."

He'd been told 'thank-you-for-your-service' many times
when he came home on leave, but her exclamation was
heartfelt. Most times, he gave a nod, kind of embarrassed at
the attention, but she made him remember why he'd served.
"You're welcome."

"Hey, you want a ride?"

On the back of a bike? He'd never ridden on the back
before, never wanted to, but it might be the only way he'd
ever be on one again. It wouldn't be the same as him having
control, but what the heck.

"You don't mind?" He hoped he didn't sound too keen.

"No. You look like you could use a ride."

"Uh, thanks, I think." Maybe his face was too revealing,
too eager. He hefted his cane. "Let me toss this in my truck."
Fortunately, they stood beside it and she wouldn't see him
struggling for more than a few steps without it.

She pointed to the small trunk on the back of her bike.
"Open the case and grab my spare helmet."

Steve clicked the latches, and lifted the top, retrieved the
helmet and closed the trunk. The woman backed around as he
shoved the helmet onto his head. A tight fit, but it worked.
He'd be lucky if he didn't end up with a headache, but it
would be worth it.

"I'm Steve."

"Angel."

"Angel?"

She gave him a wide, beautiful smile. "I always get that.
Angelina. Angel's my nickname."

"Both are beautiful names." As beautiful as the owner.

He stared at the seat. Now he had to figure out how to

get on. He couldn't balance on his left leg, so he was going to have to mount on the wrong side. Since she'd turned the bike around, he circled it.

She raised her eyebrows.

"I can't put weight on my left leg right now."

She nodded.

It was the most he'd give her about his disability. He rested a hand on the small trunk for balance and lifted his bad leg over the seat, settling his butt into place. He eased his lifeless left foot on the peg, and kept his other foot on the ground. He leaned against the backrest, glad he wouldn't have to manhandle her. He rested his hands on his thighs.

She glanced over her shoulder. "You ready?"

Steve nodded, grinned, and drew his right foot up. "Yeah. Let's do this."

She laughed, gave the bike gas, then leaned as she pulled onto the road. She was competent cruising the road and passing cars. They weren't far from the edge of town and soon, buildings dropped away. If he'd been in control, he would have taken the last right onto Payton Road, the curviest drive in the area. But he wasn't in control of the bike, and might never be again.

Instead of stewing over what couldn't be, he needed to get into this. Angel was nice enough to offer a ride to a stranger, so he'd better enjoy it.

The landscape flew by, sand, cactus and low shrubs. Most people would call this a desert, but life grew here and it was beautiful compared to the deserts in Afghanistan.

All too soon, Angel returned to the diner. Steve scrambled off her bike, and stood beside her. He couldn't tell how tall she was since she remained seated. "I can't thank you enough for the ride. I can't ride my own bike, so it was a real treat riding with you." He gave her hand a squeeze on the handlebar grip.

She grinned. "You're welcome. I would have made it longer, but I've got to get back to work. Maybe I'll see you around."

She roared off and he stared after her until the bike disappeared around a corner.

He assumed she'd originally come to the diner to eat lunch. Instead, she'd somehow known how much he needed that ride and gifted him with it. Now, she headed back to work hungry, apparently without regret.

~~~

Steve had been trying to get a hold of Tiffany since before he arrived home from the hospital, to no avail. The last few days, he left two messages a day with no returned call. He'd driven by her apartment at all times of the day and night, and she was never home. She'd answered so few of his calls when he'd been in the hospital in Germany for three months, and he hadn't talked to her in more than a month. It was frustrating. He needed to hear her voice, get reconnected.

Back in town for two weeks, and he'd yet to see or talk to his fiancée. He'd try once more to call, and then he'd call her mother.

He waited as the phone rang. It would be voicemail again.

"Hi, Steve?"

"Tiff, finally." He let out a breath. "You haven't returned my calls."

"Sorry. I'm on a business trip and cell service is spotty. I'll be back day after tomorrow."

He hadn't seen her in six months. Many of the messages he'd left told her when he was due home. She might have been able to postpone her trip, or at least let him know she would be away. And she could have returned his call when she got a signal, or from the hotel phone. "Okay. How about if we go out to dinner the night you get home?"

"I'm going to be tired after all the traveling."

He closed his eyes. There were so many times he'd gotten home after traveling clear from the Middle East, and she'd taken him straight to bed. And it wasn't to sleep. She couldn't sit and have a meal with him?

"All right. How about if I pick up take-out? Say about six-thirty?"

Her breath huffed across the line. "Okay. I'll see you then. I have to go."

"What? You can't talk? We haven't talked in almost a month."

"Steve, I'm between meetings. I've got to go." He couldn't tell if she was rushed or annoyed.

"Fine. I'll see you on Thursday." He ended the call and set the phone on the kitchen counter. If he had two good feet, he'd go for a run to work off the frustration. Anger boiled up inside, and he roared, swinging his arm, sending his coffee mug to the tile floor, smashing it into a hundred pieces and flinging coffee across the floor and up the front of refrigerator.

He roared again, snatched his cane from the table and headed out the door. With his hand on the truck door handle, he closed his eyes and sucked in and blew out long breaths. He couldn't drive like this. He'd likely cause an accident, and be devastated if someone got hurt.

He spun around and lost his balance on his unsteady left foot, falling against the truck. He'd go for a walk. He was supposed to do it for physical therapy anyway.

For the first half block he concentrated on his steps, keeping the cane off the ground.

The hospital had given him a number for a local physical therapist before he left. He hadn't called yet. He was so done with doctors and hospitals and all of it. Maybe in a couple of weeks, he'd call if his progress was stalling.

He reached a spot where the sidewalk was raised and broken from tree roots, and had to use his cane. Just his luck, he'd fall and a little old lady would come out of a house and help him up.

By the time he'd completed two blocks and was in sight of his apartment, he was putting weight on the cane, not just using it for balance. His stump ached and probably had blisters.

Time to go in and clean up the mess he'd made. At least it wasn't his favorite mug.

Everything would be normal again once he got to see Tiffany. A new normal.

Chapter 2

Steve had ordered Tiffany's favorite meal from *Il Camino*. He'd chosen her second favorite for himself in case she wanted that instead. On his way to the restaurant, he'd stopped at the liquor store and bought a bottle of wine.

He rolled into the parking lot of her apartment building at precisely six-twenty-eight. He juggled the food bag and the bottle in his left hand so he could still use his cane. He didn't want to fall and drop the food all over the ground. He'd refused a handicap placard, so had to hobble through two rows of parked cars.

Steve slipped into the building when a couple came out the door. So much for a locked outer door. He used to run up the stairs to Tiffany's second floor apartment, but now had to take the elevator and was grateful the building had one.

He knocked on her door, and a few moments later, it opened. And there she was. Despite looking tired, she was the most beautiful woman he'd ever seen.

"Tiff." If he had a free hand, he could pull her close and kiss her, but he was afraid he'd whack her with his cane if he tried. Instead he leaned forward, but she twisted her head so his lips landed on her cheek. She only did the head turn thing when she was mad about something. Maybe she was annoyed he'd insisted on getting together on the day she returned.

Normally, when he came home on leave, she'd grin from ear to ear and throw her arms around him and not let go until the next morning. He'd never minded skipping dinner. But it wouldn't happen that way tonight.

He sighed. "Let's eat while this is still hot." He led the way to her kitchen, placed the food and drink on the empty table. He got out plates and silverware, and carried them one handed, then retrieved the wine glasses.

He removed the containers from the bag. "Veal Cacciatore and Chicken Napoletana. Your choice." He gazed at her, waiting for her answer. She stared at him and he got a very bad feeling. Whatever it was, he wanted to delay it. "Let's eat first."

He poured wine, then sat and opened both boxes. "Which one? Or we can have half of each." They'd done that many times, but by eating off each other's plates.

She sat. "I'll take the veal." She picked up her glass and took a sip, her engagement ring twinkled in the light from the overhead fixture.

He dished the chicken onto his plate. "How's work? Must be going good since they're sending you on long business trips."

Tiffany cut multiple pieces of veal before putting one in her mouth. She chewed while twirling her fork in the spaghetti. "I have been on a lot of trips the last few months. The start-up I joined a year ago is exploding, partly because I've gotten really good selling it."

"I'm glad for you. It must be exciting that your effort has contributed so much to their growth." She'd been really nervous about jumping into such a new business, but it seemed like it was paying off.

Her eyes sparkled. "It is. It's still a small company, and they don't have stock, otherwise they would have given me stock options, but I've got a tiny sliver of ownership."

He wished he had his work life figured out like she did. He'd expected to be in the army for a few more years. "I'm not sure what I want to do. I think I'll go to college. Take some general classes while I decide what to major in."

She squeezed his hand for a moment. "That's great." Then she told him more about her work.

They finished eating and Steve stood, picking up his plate.

Tiffany grabbed his hand. "Leave it. I'll take care of it later." She stood and filled their glasses then carried them into the living room. His had been empty for the second time and hers was barely touched. Tiffany waited for him to sit on one end of the couch before setting the glasses on the coffee table and taking the other end.

He should have sat in the middle. This evening was going nowhere near how he expected it to.

"I need to tell you something."

Her words chilled him. He didn't know what she'd say, but he wouldn't like it. He guzzled the contents of his glass, then slammed it onto the table.

He stared at her as she fidgeted, her eyes downcast. She lifted her gaze to him and bit her lip, then slipped his engagement ring off her finger, and held it out to him. "I'm breaking our engagement."

He would have thought he heard wrong, except for the ring she held out. His body numbed, but not his heart. It ached with an intensity suggesting a heart attack. "What?"

Tears glazed her eyes, as if it hurt her to break up with him. She had nothing on him.

He was the one in pain. "You waited for me while I was enlisted and you're giving up on us now?" He couldn't understand. She was the only good thing about his medical discharge, being with her all the time and not a few snatched weeks here and there.

She dropped her hand, still holding the ring. "I couldn't take it when I was told you'd lost your leg. You were perfect before…and…"

"And now I'm not?" His anger rose. "It was my foot.

The most important parts of me are still here. I'm still me. Isn't that enough?"

She wouldn't look at him. "I-I kept remembering how you'd wake me with kisses and tickling my feet with your toes. And now…it's gone."

He rubbed a hand down his face. She acted like the rest of him wouldn't be in bed with her. "Tiff, I still have one foot I can do that with. You'll get used to the missing one. I had to." It had to be ten times worse for him than her.

"I was a mess when I found out. And I…" She rasped in a breath and let it out, staring at her lap. "I'm pregnant."

His gaze dropped to her stomach. She should be as big as a basketball. If it was his.

The numbness was gone, replaced with a heated rage, but the heart attack pain increased. He sprang to his feet, momentarily forgetting he only had one good foot, and nearly fell on his face. Yeah, that would prove to her she made the right decision to eliminate him from her life.

He grabbed his cane, and Tiffany jumped up. "I'm sorry. I wish it could have been different."

She tried to take his hand, but he yanked it away. He hobbled to the door, his leg aching more than it had in weeks. Slamming the door behind him was less than satisfying.

He made his way to the elevator, down and to his truck, all thoughts revolving around his lack of a foot. Is that all he was? A man with a missing foot? Couldn't people see the big picture? He was still Steven Halloran. A smart, caring man. And eventually, he'd walk without a cane and no one, but the people closest to him, would know about the missing foot.

~~~

Angel showered, thinking about the hike she'd planned with her brother at Bear Sign Trail. There'd be just enough time to eat breakfast before leaving. She dried off, and ran a comb through her hair, then fluffed it with her fingers. She dressed in shorts and a t-shirt and headed to the kitchen.

An image of Bell Rock popped into her head, along with a dull pain in her stomach. Strange.

She plucked two bottles of water out of the package in a lower kitchen cabinet and set them on the counter.

Her cell phone rang, and she frowned at her brother's name. "Hey, Alex. What's up?"

"Sorry to do this to you at the last minute, but I have to cancel this morning."

Worry twisted her gut. Alex never cancelled. "What's wrong?"

"Nothing's wrong. You know that job interview I've been waiting for?"

"Yeah."

"They called this morning and want to see me at eleven. Can you believe it? Last minute and on a Saturday."

The pain in her stomach eased. "Maybe that's a good sign. We can hike next weekend."

"It's a plan. Wish me luck."

She laughed. "You always have my best wishes. Let me know how it goes."

"Will do."

Angel had been looking forward to the exercise, and would have to come up with a new plan. The image of Bell Rock entered her head again. Okay. That was doable. Plenty of times she'd hiked it alone. Decision made, she scrambled eggs and wolfed them down, somehow feeling she was late for an appointment.

She grabbed the water bottles and a couple of protein bars from a drawer, stuffed them and her wallet into a small backpack and headed outside. The bag fit into the small trunk behind the seat of her bike, since she didn't want a sweaty back before starting her hike.

She buckled on her helmet and jumped on her bike. It would feel wonderful for the wind to blow through her hair, but her uncle owned a bike shop, and had told her of people who were messed up or dead because they hadn't worn a helmet. Yeah, and she should be wearing leather chaps, too, but only did when she was climbing hills on one of her uncle's dirt bikes. And jeans? They wouldn't protect her from road rash.

She revved the bike and roared out of the driveway, feeling again she was late for something. A half-hour later, she entered the parking area at Bell Rock next to a familiar black truck. Like there weren't a million black trucks on the road. She removed her helmet, fluffed her hair, and got off the bike.

A man limped to the front of the truck. It was him.

Angel gravitated toward Steve as he threw his cane letting it fly in a long arc. A glance down didn't find the dog she'd almost expected waiting to run after it.

"You don't need it anymore?"

"Jeez." He jumped and spun around, catching his balance on the hood of his truck. "Where did you come from?"

She laughed. "You didn't hear me drive up?"

He shook his head. "I was lost in thought."

She nodded toward the spot where the cane had landed. "What's with the cane?"

"I don't need it." His hand touched the gun strapped at his waist, but dropped back to his side.

She wasn't getting a good feeling. "So, the leg's all better?"

He glared at her. "No. It's not all better. It will never be all better." He yanked up his pant leg, and shoved down his sock, revealing a prosthetic attached just above where his ankle should have been. Anger filled his face, his shoulders tensed.

"It's not so bad."

He slapped his thigh. "Not so bad? I lost my fiancée over this."

That's what this was about. "If she couldn't live with a missing foot, she doesn't deserve you."

He roared. "No one deserves the likes of me."

She put the pieces together. Rejected by the woman he loved. The cane he didn't need anymore. The motorcycle he thought he couldn't ride. The gun he reached for. He'd come here to kill himself. He could have done it at home where, possibly, no one would find him for a while, but he'd chosen to do it here. Maybe it was a favorite spot he wanted to see one more time. He had commented on the picture on her bike.

If she had anything to say about it, he wouldn't die today.

She pointed at his foot and glared. The anger mounted. "What? You're going to take your life because you lost five-percent of your body? My cousin was in Afghanistan. He lost five-percent of his body, too." She blinked the tears that always erupted when Tony entered her thoughts, but one slipped out and she dashed it off her cheek. "Only his five-percent was his head. He came home in a box, and my aunt and uncle would have been overjoyed if he arrived home in a wheelchair." She poked his chest. "Get over your pity party."

She stalked back to her bike, and buckled on her helmet. She lifted her secondary helmet, and held it out to him. "Get over here."

He stood his ground, fists at his sides.

She shook the helmet. "Take this. And get. On. My. Bike."

He nearly fell, trying to take long strides, and snatched

the helmet from her hand. She climbed on the bike and pulled out her phone while waiting for him to mount, and sent a text to her uncle. *Meet me at your shop.* Most Saturdays, an employee covered.

"What about my truck?"

"I'll bring you back later."

It was almost a surprise when Steve climbed on behind her. She started the bike and took off.

Angel was reasonably sure Steve wouldn't kill himself by falling off the bike. Being a biker, he'd know it might throw her balance off, and cause a crash. He wouldn't do something that might hurt her.

Twenty minutes later, she arrived at *Carrera Motor Sports*, parked in the lot, and removed her helmet.

Steve removed his helmet. "What are we doing here? You know I can't ride."

She got off. It was harder with him still on the bike. She'd had to swing her leg over the front. "Shut up and come inside."

They entered the shop and Angel spotted her uncle talking to Terry behind the counter. He glanced their way and a smile broke out across his face. He circled around the counter. "Hey, my Angel." He wrapped her in a huge hug.

Whenever she needed some extra love, this was the place she'd get it. She leaned back. "Hey, Uncle Rick. I brought someone to meet you."

Steve stepped forward and held out his hand. "Steve Halloran."

Angel's uncle grasped it. "Richardo Carrera."

"Uncle Rick, Steve was in the army."

Pain pinched Rick's eyes, and he added his other hand to the handshake. "Thank you for serving."

Steve pulled his hand back. "I'm sorry about your son."

Rick nodded and raised an eyebrow at Angel.

She took her uncle's hand. "Can you show Steve your leg?"

He studied her for a few seconds. "Sure, Angelina." She wasn't surprised when he unbuckled his belt.

She kept her eyes on Steve, wanting to see his reaction.

Steve's eyes were glued on Rick. They widened. "Y-you have a prosthetic."

She'd seen her uncle's leg many times before. He lost his left leg above the knee. He didn't hide it, and often wore shorts.

Rick's zipper rasped and his belt buckle clinked. Show was over. "Yeah, I lost my leg five years ago while riding my bike. A car ran a red light."

Steve's gazed darted to the motorcycles lining one wall. "So, you don't ride anymore?"

Rick chuckled. "Oh, I ride. I learned all about adaptive gear shifts for my bike."

"Adaptive?"

"I'll show you." Rick strode across the room to one of the bikes along the wall. Most people wouldn't notice the hitch in his step.

Steve followed, his gate uneven and slow.

Angel leaned an elbow on the counter as her uncle explained and demonstrated how the adaptation worked.

Steve straightened from his inspection of the gear shift. "Can you put one of these on my bike?"

Rick slipped a hand in his pocket. "Sure can. I could send a truck to your place and pickup the bike. I'd have to check the model before ordering parts, so I should have it done in a couple of weeks."

The sparkle was back in Steve's eyes, like after the ride they'd shared the day they met. "It's not doing me any good the way it is, so let's do this."

Rick hurried to the counter and slipped to the other side.

He grabbed an order slip and started writing. "Tell me your address and what day you want the pickup."

Steve gave the address for his friend's house. "How about Tuesday morning?"

He planned on being alive then. Angel shivered at the morbid thought he might not have been.

She hugged her uncle. "Thanks for coming in for me."

He whispered in her ear. "Always willing to help a vet."

Angel gave Rick an extra squeeze. "More than you know."

His brows drew down. She gave a quick nod. His eyes widened, and he hugged her again.

"Steve, I'll take you back to your truck now."

Steve held his hand out to Rick. "Thanks. This is giving me back a part of my life I thought I'd lost forever."

Rick hauled Steve into a hug and patted his back. "Glad I could help."

Chapter 3

Angel stopped the bike on the driver's side of Steve's truck, thoughtfully giving him a short few steps to his door. He got off and removed his helmet. She did the same.

Staring at her, he couldn't believe what he'd almost done. He'd been so deep into his pain, he hadn't thought about anything but ending it. Nothing but his Angel could have brought him to his senses.

He wrapped his arms around her and blinked back tears. Men didn't cry. "Thank you."

Her arms squeezed tight, then released him. Tears shimmered in her eyes when she stepped back. "I was supposed to hike somewhere else today with my brother. He cancelled at the last minute. I had an urge to come here." She shrugged. "Divine intervention?"

"By my Angel." He stared at his hands. "Thanks for not telling Rick what I'd planned to do."

"If I leave you alone, you aren't going to…"

He shook his head. "No. You completely changed my thinking. I thought I had no one because I lacked a foot. But you showed me people do care. And your uncle is an amazing example of learning to cope with his disability and thriving. Today has been an awakening."

Angel bit her lip. "Have you talked to a psychologist?"

"I did when I was in the hospital." He huffed out a breath. "I guess I should talk to someone again."

She squeezed his hand and released it. "You'd probably find it helpful." She glanced at his prosthetic. "What about physical therapy?"

"I had it in the hospital, and they gave me the phone number of a local physical therapist, but I haven't called."

"You should call. Who did they suggest?"

He shrugged. "I don't know. It was just a phone number." He extracted it from his wallet, found the hospital appointment card and flipped it around to the number on the back.

She grinned. "That's my number."

"You're a physical therapist?"

"Yes. I teamed up with another student, and we opened an office here. I was in high school when Uncle Rick had to drive two hours for his therapy, and it made me determined to make it easier for other locals."

He lifted one corner of his mouth. "Okay. I'll call and make an appointment on Monday. Two appointments."

"Can I have your number so I can check up on you?"

Excitement raced through him, until hearing she only wanted to check up on him. He'd just been rejected by his fiancée, and he was already reacting to another woman. Maybe crazy should be added to his list of deficiencies.

She fished her phone from her pocket and entered the number he recited.

She glanced toward the trailhead. "Want me to get your cane? You might need it for a little while longer."

He leaned against his truck. "That would be wonderful. Thanks."

She stalked into the brush and cacti. When she found the cane, she lifted it triumphantly over her head, hands spread about two feet apart, like a capital Y with a line across the top. Angel flipped the cane down and raced across the uneven ground. Twice, she used the cane to pole vault over short bushes.

She stopped in front of him with a grin and held the cane

toward him.

"Show off."

She shrugged. "You could do it eventually. You'd have to push off with your good foot and land on it, too, but it's doable."

He shook his head. "I just want to walk normally without this cane." He twirled it.

He talked to her like nothing momentous had happened, as if he hadn't planned on being dead by lunchtime.

He'd read somewhere that most people who failed at suicide were glad they hadn't succeeded. They'd hit bottom and their lives improved after. Probably through mental health visits.

If Angel hadn't arrived, he would have been one of the successful ones. He wouldn't have found out there were people in his corner rooting for him.

Air huffed out of her when he hugged her too tightly. "Thank you for following that urge."

She kissed his cheek. "You already thanked me."

"I know, but it's really sinking in what I almost did. The permanence."

She stepped back. "Let's go to lunch."

Great change in subject. "Okay. I'll follow you."

~~~

Steve strode to the receptionist's desk, the cane taps muted on the commercial carpet. "Steven Halloran. I have a one o'clock appointment."

The woman squinted at her screen and typed. "Ah, with Dr. Farrell." She handed him a clipboard with a pen stuck through the top. "Could you fill this out, please?"

He sat, crossed his ankle over the other knee and propped the clipboard on his leg. He answered the normal get-to-know-you questions, medical questions and a couple mental health questions.

He'd called Monday morning and told the receptionist of his close call on Saturday, and they'd given him an appointment for Wednesday. His physical therapy appointment with Angel was the following day. After he'd returned from lunch with Angel, he'd spent the next four hours going through his apartment, throwing away anything remotely reminding him of Tiffany, which included clothing she'd said she liked on him. He breathed a bit freer when he tossed the two bags into the dumpster.

Steve completed the paperwork and deposited it on the receptionist's desk, then resumed his seat.

He glanced at the inner door as it swung open. The receptionist stood in the doorway, a folder in her hand. "Mr. Halloran?"

He pulled in a breath and followed her along a carpeted corridor to the third door on the left. She stepped inside and handed the doctor his folder.

The woman behind the desk accepted it and tipped her glasses down. "Have a seat, Mr. Halloran."

The other woman left, closing the door behind her.

"You might as well call me Steve. I have a feeling you're going to know me better than anyone by the time we're through."

Dr. Ferrell glanced at him and back to his file. Steve studied her. She appeared to be in her late forties, brown hair raked back from her face with a few strands of gray. Her brown eyes were a few shades darker than her hair.

She set the folder down and picked up a notebook and pen. "What brings you here, Steve?"

"I almost killed myself Saturday."

"And what stopped you?"

"Angel."

Her eyebrows rose. "An angel came down and talked to you?"

"Angel Carrera roared up on her motorcycle and talked to me."

Dr. Ferrell smiled. "She's a force to be reckoned with."

Steve laughed. "That's for sure. How do you know her?"

"My son broke his leg. She was his physical therapist after the cast came off. He probably wouldn't have made it back on his basketball team, if not for her brand of therapy. I sure couldn't get through to him."

He hadn't expected a psychologist to share anything personal, but he wasn't surprised by her description of Angel.

The doctor straightened her shoulders. "Anyway, let's get started. What brought you to the decision you were better off ending your life?"

Steve sat forward, elbows on thighs, and told her what he'd told Angel. The doctor drew more out of him, and made him realize subconsciously he'd suspected Tiffany was pulling away before he got stateside. He'd ignored the signs because he needed to cling to her.

They talked longer.

Dr. Ferrell closed her notebook. "We covered a lot of ground today, Steve. I'm a little surprised."

He'd barely met her eyes the entire time they'd talked. Now, he stared into them. "What I almost did scared me. I don't want to be in that position again."

She smiled. "That's a huge step. Let's schedule another appoint for next week, and be thinking about where you want to go from here."

He stood, feeling a little awkward after spilling his guts. Did he just walk away? Say good-bye? Nice meeting you?

He held out his hand.

Her eyebrows quirked, but she took his hand in a firm shake. "Have a great week, Steve."

"Likewise, Doc."

~~~

Steve parked in front of the building his GPS led him to. It shared a parking lot with a strip mall. High windows lined the front of the red brick building, letting in light, but no prying eyes. He wondered if anyone walked into *Get Physical* thinking they were entering a gym.

He got out, passed four parking spaces designated as handicapped, two with cars, and stopped in front of the glass double doors. To the side, three brass plaques displayed names. Angelina Carrera LPT, Carole Wilson LPT, and Roland Rodriguez LPT. It appeared Angelina had added another therapist after teaming up with her friend.

He opened the door, announced himself to the receptionist, and sat in a comfortable chair in the waiting room. Several real plants—at least they looked real—sat on tables and hung from the ceiling on hooks. The purple-gray wallpaper was covered with silver, black and burgundy geometric shapes, wild enough to distract a worried patient.

He bounced his right leg, would have bounced both of them if he could. His surroundings didn't distract him from the nerves that set in over seeing Angel again. She knew almost as much about him as the psychologist he'd spilled his guts out to the day before. He didn't want her to see him as needy, but it couldn't be avoided when she was the reason he still breathed. Now, he needed her help to walk properly.

"Steve?"

He hadn't seen or heard the door open, but Angel stood with her hand on the doorknob, a chart in her other hand.

"Angel."

Her dark eyes sparkled, and the upturned nose gave her an almost pixie appearance.

He grabbed his cane and stood. He hated having to use it, but it would be worse to stumble and fall. In front of Angel. He stopped in front of her and their eyes met.

"How are you doing?" It was more than a casual question. They both knew it.

"I'm doing okay. I talked to a psychologist yesterday. I'm still angry at my ex, but I'll get through this." There was one thing he'd told Dr. Ferrell that Angel didn't know. Tiffany had cheated on him before breaking their engagement.

The engagement ring sitting on his dresser entered his thoughts. He'd found it while emptying his pockets that horrible night. He'd considered flinging it into the woods, but that seemed a waste. He certainly wouldn't give it to another woman. There were too many memories attached to it, picking it out, proposing and slipping it on Tiffany's finger. Maybe he'd donate it to some organization. They'd probably get more money for it than he could.

Angel lifted her folder. "Thanks for sending your records. I've set up a plan. Come on back." He followed her into a room with various types of exercise equipment.

She closed the door. "Did Alice ask you to bring shorts?"

"Yeah. They're under my pants." He reached for his buckle, Angel turned away, setting the folder on a table and adjusted a setting on the closest machine.

Maybe she was embarrassed, but she must see men in shorts all day. He took off his shoes with his pants. "Shoes on or off?"

She faced him. "Off. And socks, too. I want you to have good footing."

She had him demonstrate the exercises he'd been given in the hospital. He hadn't done them consistently since he'd been home, and it showed. She corrected him on some of the movements, then added two more exercises to his routine.

Angel sat on a bench. "Okay, now put your socks and shoes on. I want you on the treadmill."

He narrowed his eyes at the piece of equipment. It was hard enough walking on surfaces that didn't move, how could he keep his footing on a moving belt? "Are you trying to kill me?"

She gasped and her eyes widened.

"Sorry. Bad choice of words."

She closed her eyes for a second and nodded, then stood. "We'll take it slow. On the treadmill, you can hold on with both hands and keep your body more upright. The cane gives you some confidence, but it's not doing you any favors. It's keeping you slightly off balance. You'd do better using a walker."

"No. I don't want to look like a little old man. I used one for a short time in the hospital, but no more." Just thinking about a walker reminded him of the early days when he shuffled and stumbled.

"Okay. So your goal is no walker, no cane." She patted the bar on the treadmill. "Hop on. I've got it set slow. I want to study your gait."

"You want to study the whole fence?"

Her eyebrows dropped down. "What? That's not even funny."

He shrugged. "I tried." He stepped on and grabbed the bars.

Angel started the machine and stepped in front of him. "You're practically waddling. Concentrate on being a debutante."

"What do you mean with that?"

"Pretend you have a book on your head and you don't want to lose it."

"Riiight." She was correct about hanging on. He could

concentrate on his steps without worrying about his balance. Before his injury, he'd never thought about how he walked. Now, he had to think about every step. He paid attention to what he did with his right leg, and hoped it was what he always had done with it, then tried to copy the move with his left.

"You're doing pretty good." She touched the speed button. "I'm going to up it just a bit."

He picked up the pace with ease.

She studied his legs, then shifted to the side. "Your right stride is longer than the left. Try to even it."

He hadn't noticed, but he did seem to lift his left foot sooner. He concentrated on evening it out.

"Okay. You did great today." Angel pushed the stop button.

He swiped a forearm across his forehead, and she tossed him a towel.

She sat on the bench and patted the seat beside her. "Come sit."

He joined her. He'd worked harder for her than any of the therapists in the hospital. Of course, she would have said he'd done it for himself.

"Besides walking without a cane, what are your other goals?"

"Goals?" He shrugged.

"What did you do before that you miss?"

"Run? I used to run twenty to thirty miles a week." Yeah, like that was going to happen.

She stared at his foot. "I'll have to check the specs on your prosthetic. If it can't hold up to running, we'll have to see about getting another model."

"I can run?"

"Sure. I've got other amputees who are running now. What else do you want to do?"

"Play racquet ball."

Her eyes traveled over his body. "That doesn't seem like it would be one of your sports. I'll have to research it. I'm not sure if you can handle the sideways explosive bursts. What else?"

"Ride my bike."

She waved her hand. "You'll be able to do that as soon as the adaptive gearshift is installed. Unless you mean a bicycle."

"No. My motorcycle. What about paintball?" He used to play, when he was home on leave.

She tipped her head. "Maybe once you've mastered running, you can do it."

"Wonderful. Do you want to have a paintball experience with me?"

"I don't know how to shoot."

She hadn't turned him down yet. "I can teach you. By the time you're competent with a gun, hopefully, I'll be ready to run."

"I don't know…"

"You know you want to. I bet you've always wanted to try paintball. We'll start on Saturday."

She bit her lip. Probably thinking how she shouldn't date a patient. "Okay."

He beamed. "What's your address?"

She rattled it off.

"I'll pick you up Saturday at ten." She wouldn't change her mind now she'd agreed.

"I can't. I'm hiking with my brother on Saturday."

He stood. Maybe this was her way of telling him she'd changed her mind. "All right. Maybe ano—"

"Sunday?"

He grinned. "Sunday it is."

"Steve, schedule another session for Monday. We're

doing twice a week for a few weeks."

He'd almost forgotten where they were. "Yes, Ma'am."

Chapter 4

Angel surveyed her body, hoping jeans and a t-shirt were standard wear for a shooting range. She couldn't believe she was going out with a patient. Steve wasn't the first patient to ask her out, but was the first she'd said yes to. She'd almost called to cancel, but what swayed her to keep the date was that they'd first met outside the office. And she had an attraction to him that hadn't been present with anyone else in a long time.

She was glad he'd waited to ask her out because any sooner, it would have been a resounding no. She'd rescued him from suicide and hadn't been a hundred percent sure when she left him that he'd be all right. If he'd asked then, maybe it would have forced him over the edge again when she turned him down. She didn't want to be involved with someone only because it kept him alive.

At her office, he seemed like a normal guy. He understood the need to get his head straightened out by talking to a psychologist, something not everyone would be willing to do. That made her more comfortable accepting a date.

He was right about paintball. She'd always thought it would be fun shooting splats of paint at other people. Without learning to shoot first, she'd probably be the only one not covering everyone else in paint.

The doorbell rang. She filled her lungs and let the air whoosh out, hurried to the door and opened it to his grinning face.

There was a sparkle in his eyes that hadn't been there before. "Hi. You ready for this?" He wore a light blue t-shirt and jeans. Perfect.

"Just as soon as I get my shoes on." She found her Nikes in the closet, slipped them on and tied them, then grabbed her purse from the hook on the closet wall.

He stood with one forearm propped on the doorframe and the other hand on his cane. Casual, but the way his shirt stretched across his chest did crazy things to her heart rate. Athletes checked into her practice every day and she hardly noticed, but this man could draw her attention in a crowd.

He ran a finger down her cheek. "Your eyes."

She squinted. "What about them?"

"They're green today. I thought they were a mix."

She shrugged. "It depends on what color I wear."

"Not affected by your mood?" Maybe his were. The blue-gray seemed a warmer blue today.

"Not that I know of."

He stepped back. "I was going to take you target shooting at a real gun range, but decided it would be better for you to practice with actual paintball guns. If you decide you really like shooting, I can teach you how to use a real gun at a later time."

He was planning ahead. She liked that suicide seemed far from his mind. She wished it was far from hers, too. What would happen if this attraction fizzled, or whatever it was, between them? She wouldn't want him to fall into depression and try again. She thrust the thought away. That kind of pressure was no way to go into this.

His gait seemed smoother as he paced beside her to his truck, parked in the driveway behind her bike. "Looks like you're doing your exercises."

He wagged his finger. "Uh-uh. No patient-therapist talk. This is a date." He squinted at her and tipped his head. "Yes.

Definitely a date."

Maybe he'd thought about his ex-fiancée and that she'd broken their engagement a little over a week ago. Maybe Angel was a rebound date to prove someone could be interested in him with his disability.

He opened the door and she scrambled into the truck before he could offer assistance.

He came around to the driver's side and scooted in, starting the vehicle. "Do you enjoy being a physical therapist?"

"Hey, I thought we weren't discussing that."

He dropped the truck into drive and headed onto the street. "We're not discussing my physical therapy. I'm asking my date about her work."

She chuckled. "Okay. I see the difference. And yes. I love my work. I enjoy helping people get to a level they didn't think was possible. What are your plans?"

He wasn't working yet. "I've been checking out college classes. They start in a month. I don't know what to major in, so I'll take general classes the first semester."

"What did you want to do when you were a kid?"

His mouth tightened and he let out a long breath. "I seesawed between wanting to be a soldier and a fireman. Neither are options now."

She squeezed his arm. "There's still a lot you can do. Even what I do. One of our physical therapists, Roland, is an amputee just below the knee. Most of his patients don't even know it."

"I'll have to meet this Roland."

"We're thinking of hiring a massage therapist. Their training is about a year."

"Hmm. That's interesting. I've had a few massages. Not sure I'd want to give them, though."

Steve turned into a parking lot with several cars lined

along the building. Its previous life appeared to have been manufacturing, and it had to be as long as a football field.

The graffiti style mural on the building contained the name, *Urban Jungle Adventures*. Half the painting was a jungle, and the other half high-rises.

She waved her hand at the wall. "Does it really have a jungle and city in there?"

"Pretty much, but you'll only see the practice area today."

"You've been here before?"

"Yes. I'd come in and join teams that were a member short when I was home on leave."

Steve escorted Angel to the door and to the front desk. "Hey, Gabe."

The man behind the desk glanced up and smiled. "Steve, haven't seen you in a while." He checked his computer screen. "I don't have any short teams today."

"That's okay. I'm teaching Angel how to shoot, so we just need the practice range."

"Two markers?"

"No, just one."

Gabe disappeared through a door behind the desk.

She frowned at Steve. "What's a marker?"

"That's what paintball guns are called."

Gabe returned with a marker that resembled a machine gun with a huge bubble on top. He set it on the counter with two sets of safety glasses and ear protection. "There you go."

Steve used his credit card, then signed the receipt. He handed Angel one set of glasses and ear protection, gathered the rest and she followed him to the shooting range.

He set everything on a small shelf way too far away from a person shaped target, and slipped on his pair of safety glasses. She copied him.

He explained how the marker worked and how to aim.

Steve put on his ear protection, and so did she. They didn't totally block out all sound, but muffled it. He picked up the marker, and shot off three rounds. Of course, all except the first one hit within the circle around the heart on the target. She'd be lucky to hit the target, but wouldn't be the only one to miss, considering all the colored paint splatters on the back wall.

He lowered the gun. "These aren't as accurate as real guns. Even if you had this on a tripod aimed at the target, each shot would hit a different spot."

He handed her the marker and she placed her hands like he had. She thought she had, anyway. He stepped behind her, his arms coming around, and covered her left hand on the gun, shifting it a bit, and grazed the right. His hard, hot chest at her back made her head spin, his arms lay against hers. It was like a warm cocoon enclosing her. She closed her eyes and leaned back.

He laughed. With the ear covers, she barely heard it, but his chest vibrated into her soul.

She dragged her eyes open, only to see his hand wave in front of her face. She glanced over her shoulder at his grinning face.

His arms tightened around her for a second. "We going to do this?"

She bit her lip and gave a quick nod, deciding he meant shoot, not kiss. She faced the target. He called out instructions that she was pretty sure he repeated from when she'd totally ignored his voice for the feel of his body against hers.

She squeezed the trigger. Squeeze, not pull, but wasn't sure what the difference was. A new blue splat appeared to the right of the target. "I thought it would kick more." She'd raised her voice to be heard through the ear protection.

"It doesn't need as much force as a real gun."

She shifted the gun a bit and tried to compensate for how far she'd been off. She closed one eye, but remembered he said both should be open. She pulled—no—squeezed the trigger again. Her person target now had a blue hand. No shooting back for him.

More adjustments and more shots, and she finally struck the heart. The marker almost fell out of her other hand when she pumped a fist in the air. "Yes!"

Steve stepped to her side and she missed the warmth at her back. He waved at the target. "All on your own now."

She hadn't realized how much he'd steadied her until she pointed the marker at the target, and it wavered.

"A wider stance, and stiffen your upper body."

She glanced at him. "This was a lot easier with you holding me."

He smirked. "I won't be holding you next time when we're shooting at each other."

Her mouth dropped open and she snapped it shut. "I thought we'd be on the same team."

"I don't want you on my team until you figure out what you're doing. Next time, it's just you and me."

"Oookay. Competitive aren't you?" She faced the target and sighted it.

Steve pushed the gun down, yanked off his glasses and slid back one side of her ear protection. He cupped the side of her head, turning her face towards him. "I lost that for a while. A long while where nothing mattered to me, but you helped me remember who I am."

The intensity of his gaze caused a hitch in her breathing and then her heart pounded. Angel licked her lips. Inch by slow inch, his head drew closer, his gaze never wavering. His lips touched hers and then they didn't. That couldn't be a kiss. She pursed her lips and moved closer, finding his lips again. His hand slid to the back of her head and made it a real

37

kiss. Tentatively, she slipped her tongue out and he moaned, opening to her. She'd never thought dueling tongues could be as sexy as this.

He set his forehead against hers, his breathing labored. "I forgot where we were. Why don't you resume shooting?" He backed away.

She was supposed to shoot after that dizzying kiss? She slipped the ear protection back into place, and sucked in a steadying breath. She tried to remember all the rules, and squeezed off two shots. Hit the target, but not even close. She kept firing until the marker clicked on empty, then laid it on the shelf, and removed her muffs and glasses.

He smiled. "That was better than some of the guys did at the beginning of basic training with real guns."

She bounced on the balls of her feet. "Really? I did all right?"

He wrapped an arm around her shoulders. "You did fantastic. Now, you want to schedule an hour in the urban landscape for next Saturday?"

She popped her eyes wide. "Do you think you'll be ready?"

He shrugged. "Maybe. Certainly more ready for that than the rough terrain of the jungle." He grinned. "It'll give me a goal to shoot for this week. No cane."

He was driving himself too hard, but if she said anything, it would be the therapist talking, and he'd made that off limits. She had Monday and Thursday to check his progress and could veto the plan if she didn't think he was ready.

Chapter 5

Steve found a space in front of Angel's apartment on a rare rainy Saturday. Hers was in the middle of a row of five townhouse style units. He sauntered up to the door without his cane. A first. His cane was in the truck, and he was pretty sure he'd need it by the time he finished paintball.

He should have pushed off this activity at least a week, but he'd promised Angel, and he wanted to get his life back as much as he could.

His motorcycle was returned the day before by Rick with an apology for taking so long. His supplier had the gear adapter on back order and they had to wait a few extra days. Steve might have suggested a ride instead of paintball, but the weather was against him. It was for the best, since he wanted to be comfortable on his bike again first, and familiarize himself with the new gear shift.

He rang the doorbell and in moments the door swung open. Her grin lit her face. She seemed to be more beautiful each time he saw her. Her gaze dropped to his empty hands and her eyebrows arched.

He held his hands up. "I practiced yesterday without it. I can't use it and carry a gun."

She bit her lip. "I hope this doesn't cause any damage."

He wanted to touch her, but held back. "I'll call a halt if it's too much."

She nodded. "Okay. Let's go do this." She grabbed her purse from the doorknob and closed her door, following him to his truck.

Once settled inside, Angel tipped her head back and closed her eyes. "I stayed up too late last night. I wish our paintball session would've been later."

He hoped it wasn't a date that kept her out late. Maybe she was seeing several guys.

He glanced at her. "You did agree to eight o'clock." He immediately regretted the sharpness of his words. It was the only open time slot where they could have the space to themselves.

"I know. Kind of grudgingly, if you remember. I just should have closed my book at ten, instead of telling myself I was almost done."

He chuckled, relieved a book and not a man had kept her awake. "I've been there. What were you reading?"

Her eyes flicked to him and back to the road. "A romance novel."

"I've read a few."

Her eyebrows shot to her hairline.

His face warmed. "Um. Yeah. One of the guys in my unit used to buy erotica and they got passed around when he was finished reading."

She turned her head away. "That stuff's too steamy for me."

Maybe too steamy for her to read, but he'd bet she would enjoy what he'd gleaned from those pages. Like he'd start with kisses. Her mouth, her cheeks, her eyelids. He'd tease her earlobe before nuzzling her neck and...A subject change might be good before they got to the paintball place. He needed to cool off, so he could get out of the truck without embarrassing himself. "So, what types of movies do you like?"

"Everything, but horror."

Picking out a movie to watch with Angel might be easy. "What about old Westerns?"

"And old westerns."

He chuckled. "What about superhero movies?"

"Some are better than others. There are a few I'd never watch again."

He entered the parking lot for *Urban Jungle Adventures.* "We'll have to discuss this more later. Maybe we can do a movie marathon sometime."

"That would be fun." She opened her door and hopped out, and he met her at the corner of the truck.

He had to concentrate to minimize his limp, not wanting Angel to veto their plans.

They entered the building at seven-fifty, plenty of time to suit up before their time slot.

"Hey, Gabe."

"Hi, Steve." The man scrutinized Steve's date. "And Angel, right?"

"Yes. Hi."

Steve pulled out his wallet and rested his arms on the counter. "We need all the gear."

Gabe totaled the rentals and Steve handed over his credit card. Once the transaction was completed, Gabe pointed to a door beside the one he'd used before. "Go pick out your gear."

Steve led her into the room, sort of like a huge closet. Along the left wall, padded one-piece jumpsuits hung on a bar in a range of sizes. He waved his hand. "Pick out something that fits you."

He stepped farther along, found his normal size, sat on a bench and removed his shoes. He slipped into the suit, zipped it up, and put his shoes back on. While Angel donned her suit, he selected two neck protectors, and wrapped one on his neck, sealing the Velcro and did the same for Angel.

"Let's find you a mask." The masks were size organized like the suits, so near the door he selected the smallest one.

41

"Try this."

She took it. "It's almost like a motorcycle helmet, except lighter. I thought we'd wear safety glasses like last time."

"Last time, paintballs weren't coming at you. You don't want to get hit in the face or back of the head with one of those."

"Okay." She slipped the mask over her head and clipped the chin strap. "How's this?"

Steve checked the fit. "Looks good." He tried on a couple of masks and chose the best one, then they returned to the main room.

Two markers sat on the counter. Gabe handed him a bag. "Here are the extra balls. Have fun."

"Thanks. Let's go, Angel." He picked up one marker and she grabbed the other.

"How do I add extra paintballs?"

He held the door open. "I'll help you when you run out."

She marched past him and lifted her brows. "You won't shoot me?"

"No." They stopped inside the door.

Her gaze took in the room. "This is so cool."

Apartments, small stores, cross streets, and a few cars lined the single street.

He set the extra balls near the door. "Okay. Here are my rules."

"Your rules, huh?"

"Yes. When you run out of ammo, yell, 'Break', and I'll help you reload."

"Good."

"Normally, you're out of the game when you get hit, but since it's just the two of us, we'll keep playing so you get more practice."

She nodded.

"When one of us gets hit, the shooter will count to five,

so the other one has a chance to get away."

"I like that."

"The winner is the one with the least amount of paint on them, and gets to choose where we eat, and the loser gets to pay for lunch."

She poked her finger into his chest. "You think I'm going to lose."

He grinned. "There's a good chance of that." He strapped on his mask. "Ready?"

She checked her marker, not that she knew what to check. It looked like the one she'd practiced with. "Yes."

"Okay, go hide."

"Hey, that makes it sound like you're chasing me."

He suppressed a grin and shook his head. "No. I'm going in the opposite direction."

"Okay." She raced off.

He wouldn't be running, more like slow and methodical. He needed to protect his leg.

Angel disappeared around the corner of a building. His excitement mounted. He hadn't played one-on-one before, and his normal opponents were experienced. Angel had the advantage she could run and was steadier on her feet, but he was a better shot and wouldn't panic. He would enjoy covering her in paint.

He realized he'd never done anything exciting like this with Tiffany. She'd go on the occasional hike with him and complain about bugs, or go to a bar where he could sometimes talk her into shooting pool. She enjoyed dancing, but pretty much the only real excitement they'd had was in bed.

He shook himself. He was on a date with Angel.

With his watch timer set for fifty minutes, it was time to go hide-and-seek. A fast walk took him to the back of the buildings on the left. Some of the buildings had open doors in the back and front, about half, only in the front. No windows opened to the back.

At the end of the first building, he peeked around the corner, and not seeing Angel, hurried the four feet to hide behind the next. The third building had a back door and he entered a mock corner market. Empty shelves added cover from the doorway, but not from the large Plexiglas windows lining the front.

He crouched and crept to the door. The street was clear, so he hiked across to the building directly opposite. No door in back. A quick check outside, and he did an awkward near sprint to the space between buildings. There. Angel's leg disappeared to the right. He grinned and stalked to the end of the alley, stepping out. He lifted his marker and shot, catching her in the hip.

She squealed, and faced him.

"One, two—"

She squealed again and raced into the nearest doorway.

He chuckled. "Three, four, five." A fast shuffle took him back down the alley, only to watch her scoot into another building.

He worked his way from doorway, to alley to doorway, until he stepped into the one she'd entered. And took a hit to his shoulder.

She giggled. "One, two."

He fled to an alley across the street, to the end, and hurried past five buildings. He cut through a hotel lobby with its painted on elevator doors, fake plants, desk and wooden benches. A rusted car sat out front and he squatted behind it, keeping his bad leg forward. He searched the windows for movement.

There. Angel exited a building and crept to the next. He stood and took three shots, knowing the distance would throw off the accuracy. One hit her arm.

No squeal this time as she took off.

"One, two, three, four, five."

He shouldn't think of it as cat-and-mouse, since she could shoot back, but she was so bad at creeping up on him. Over the next ten minutes, he hit her three more times before she got in another shot.

He couldn't remember the last time he'd had this much fun. His stump started to ache, but he concentrated on the hunt, and it faded into the background. He got in a few more hits, and Angel succeeded once more.

His timer chimed as he stepped out of a building. Angel mirrored him and shot first. He turned off his timer and stalked her. She stood still, and frowned. "Um. One, two. What are you doing?"

He tore off his mask, and tackled her, twisting to land on his shoulder, then once they hit the ground, he rolled her under him. "That was fantastic." He clicked the latch on her mask and whipped it off. Maybe she started to say something. He didn't give her a chance before he kissed her.

She took him by surprise when her arms circled his neck and her tongue met his in a duel every bit as exciting as the one they just ended. He dropped kisses under her chin and nibbled her ear. She wiggled, and then startled when a loud buzzer pierced the silence.

"What was that?"

"Our time is up." He tipped his head back to see her face. "*Jasmine Thai.*"

Her eyebrows dropped down. "What?"

"That's where we're eating."

He scrambled to his feet and held out a hand and helped her to her feet.

She looked him up and down and stared down the front of her jumpsuit. "I guess we are."

"But maybe we should count to make sure." He touched

her shoulder. "One." Moved to her belly. "Two."

She grabbed his hand with one of hers and covered his mouth with the other. "I don't think it's necessary. I concede."

He kissed her fingers and she snatched her hand away.

He picked up their masks. "Let's go. I'm sure the next group is ready to rush in. And I'm starved."

Chapter 6

Angel stowed the ham and cheese sandwiches along with yogurt in an insulated bag, two cans of soda and an ice pack. She grabbed a bag of potato chips from the cupboard and dropped it on the counter, then stuffed two spoons and napkins into the side pocket of the cooler bag. From another cupboard, she took two bottles of water.

She brought all of it to the door, put on her shoes and grabbed her already packed small backpack. She flipped the lock on the door on her way out and stored all but her keys in the trunk on her motorcycle. As she turned to sit on her steps to wait, a motorcycle roared down the street and into her driveway.

It was a good-sized Harley. She wouldn't be able to handle it. On the phone the night before, Steve had told her he practiced a few times, but hadn't taken it far yet.

He turned off the bike, kept his eyes on his foot as he kicked out the kickstand, and awkwardly dismounted on the wrong side. He stripped off his helmet and set it on his seat.

She fumbled for something to say. "You look good on your bike."

He grinned. "It feels good to be on it again. Your uncle tuned it up while he had it. Purrs like a dream."

She giggled. "Hondas purr. Harleys growl."

He chuckled, wrapped his arms around her and gathered her close. "You may be right." His lips met hers.

This was their first hello kiss. She slid her hands up his chest, palmed the back of his neck and furrowed the other fingers into his hair. His growl was sexier than the Harley's.

If they hadn't had a time limit at *Urban Jungle Adventures* she wasn't sure how far they would have gone. His kisses made her forget where she was. He seemed to temper their good-bye kiss after lunch that day, and after dinner on Wednesday.

This kiss promised more to come, and she'd be sure he didn't break that promise. She leaned back, and his lips tried to follow her. She dove into his neck and dropped a kiss there, which wasn't a good idea because he did the same. A shiver coursed through her body, making her crave more.

She wiggled. "Mmm. We should get going."

He yanked his arms away and spread them wide. "Okay. I can do that."

The twinkle in his eyes made her want to curl into his arms again.

"First." He tugged a mike and receiver from his pocket. "Let's put this in your helmet."

She handed the helmet over. Those didn't come cheap, and their alone time playing paintball hadn't been cheap either.

He removed the backing from the Velcro and stuck the headset into her helmet, and held it out to her. She took it back, put it on, and got on her bike.

He donned his helmet, and his voice filled her helmet. "Ready for that ride, sexy?"

"I guess your mike works."

The lower part of the helmet covered his smile, but his eyes crinkled, giving it away.

Steve circled to the right side of his bike. It had to be hard getting on when the bike leaned away from him.

"Have you tried mounting on the proper side?"

"Not yet."

"Give it a try. I'll be your physical therapist for a

minute."

"Okay." He switched sides, and grabbed one grip and lifted his right leg.

"Wait."

He lowered his leg and straightened.

"Face forward so you don't twist your left leg. Left hand on your grip, right hand on the gas tank."

He followed her directions.

"Now lean toward the left handgrip and lift your right leg up and around."

He completed the rest on his own. "That wasn't half bad. It's certainly better than mounting on the wrong side. I'll just have to remember not to twist. Thanks. Now, good-bye therapist." He grinned and started his bike.

She started hers, and pushed backwards, giving him room to turn, then shot out of the driveway behind him. She didn't hear her own bike above the roar of his, only felt its purr under her. If she could convince him to kiss her like he had the first time, she'd be sure to purr, too.

They worked their way north, and stopped at Wilson Canyon Trail. Angel had chosen it because it was relatively flat and not long. She opened her trunk and deposited her helmet, then stuck a bottle of water into the pocket on her backpack, and shoved her arms through the straps.

Steve had locked his helmet onto his bike and was extending a shiny, black hiking stick.

"That's a good idea."

He tapped the stick on the ground. "I probably can't put a lot of weight on it, but it should help with balance if we hit rough terrain."

They started side-by-side on the red dirt path, Angel holding his right hand while his other held his stick.

"I'm signed up for classes," he said. "They start in two weeks."

"All general classes?"

"General except two psychology classes. I decided to become a social worker for vets. I had a really good conversation with one at the VA."

She squeezed his hand. "That's wonderful. I think you'll be great at it. With what you've been through, you'll be able to empathize and be willing to do your best for every vet."

They continued down the path at a slow pace, others passing them. She itched to ask him how his leg was doing, but he wouldn't like what he considered a therapist question. She didn't want him to overdo because it could cause him days of pain and set backs. She kept quiet on the subject, but checked his face for any twinge.

They arrived at the end of the trail. The choice was to turn around or climb for a view.

Steve's gaze tracked the climb. "Let's climb."

"You've been up there before. You know what the view is."

His eyes met hers. "I know. I want to see it."

She bit her lip. "It's kind of strenuous. You might hurt yourself. And it'll be harder coming down."

His brows dropped. "Don't be the therapist."

She put her hands on his shoulders. "I'm being the friend. I'm allowed to worry."

His arms surrounded her, and pulled her to his chest. Her nose, buried in his neck, filled with the delicious scent of Steve. Not able to resist, she brushed her lips across his skin.

He tightened his hold before releasing her. "You're going to make me forget where we are." He gave her a kiss that didn't last nearly long enough. "I'm making that climb."

She followed behind, and cringed as he negotiated steeper sections. Twice, he sat on a ledge, swung his legs around and got back up. At least, he was being smart about it. He attained the top and sat, facing the view.

Angel dropped beside him and leaned her head against his shoulder.

Steve plucked his phone from his pocket. "Let me get a picture." He twisted around. "Face the camera."

She smiled and he snapped a shot. Then he checked the photo and showed it to her. Their smiling faces and red rock behind them.

She leaned against him again. "You did it. I bet a month ago you would have thought it was impossible."

It took so long for him to respond, she gave up on him saying anything. "You're right. I would have. I wouldn't have thought I could ride my bike again. I wouldn't have thought I could run again, but the new prosthetic you talked me into should arrive in a week or so, and I can work my way up to running." He wrapped his arm around her shoulders. "I wouldn't have thought I could go on after Tiffany dumped me. I can do all of this because of you."

Panic struck. She didn't want him to feel dependent on her. He had to stand on his own. "I helped you through one rough spot, made you see there was more to live for. You did all the rest. You visited the psychologist. You set up your physical therapy and followed through on exercises. You signed up for classes. You moved on after Tiffany."

"But—"

She covered his mouth. "No. You're stronger than you think."

He pulled her hand down and grinned. "Okay. But I'm glad you're here with me." He kissed her.

If she wasn't careful, she could forget she shouldn't get too attached until she was sure he could stand on his own without being dependent on her.

Angel kept an eye on Steve as much as her own progress as they worked their way down the boulders. He took care, sitting several times to swing his legs to the next level.

Finally, they reached the main path.

He took her hand and trudged, maybe leaning a little more heavily on his hiking stick.

They arrived at their bikes and he unlocked his helmet. "Are we still going to Crescent Moon Park to eat lunch?"

She waved her hand. "It's a better view than this." They could have carried their lunch through the canyon and eaten while they rested, but she hadn't expected Steve would want to climb to the great view at the top. She stored her backpack and put on her helmet.

They raced to their next destination and parked on the edge of the parking lot. No picnic tables were free, so Angel grabbed the blanket and handed it to Steve. She picked up the food bag and chips and headed to a shady spot with a view of Cathedral Rock. Steve followed, using his hiking stick, so he must have a bit of pain. It was hard to clamp her lips together and not ask.

Steve spread the blanket and she set the food in the center, then dropped beside their feast and slipped off her shoes and socks, wiggling her toes. She removed food and drink from the bag, and glanced at him. "Come sit down."

He lowered himself on the opposite side.

"Take your boots off."

He raised his brows.

"Okay. Take your boot off. Take your foot off if you want. I don't mind."

He glanced around. "I don't want to make people uncomfortable."

"Okay. Just the one boot. I know you want to." She grinned, using the tactic he'd used against her about paintball.

He chuckled. "Fine." He tugged off his right boot and sock then draped the sock over the top, and wiggled his toes. "Happy?"

She handed him two sandwiches in zip-lock bags. "Yes." Maybe someday she'd get him to take off the foot in public. With pants, no one would see his stump.

He removed one half sandwich from a bag and peeled back the whole wheat bread. "What are those greenish squiggles?"

"Alfalfa sprouts."

His eyebrows dropped. "Aren't those for salads or something?"

"They're for whatever you want them for. You'll like them." Next time he could make lunch. It would probably be something unhealthy like potato chips and cheese wiz on white bread. She gave the bag of chips a guilty stare. At least she had lean ham and Swiss cheese on the sandwich.

Steve took a huge bite, and chewed. He nodded. "It adds a bit of crunch. Flavor's not bad."

They finished lunch and continued their ride, stopping every once in a while to take in the view.

Near dusk, they roared into Angel's driveway, turned off their bikes, got off, and removed their helmets.

Steve snuggled her into his arms. "That was the best hike I've had in over a year. Best ride. Best date. Three months ago, I thought I'd never ride again. You proved me wrong. On a lot of things."

He kissed her and her world exploded with color like the sunset they'd watched on their last stop. She pushed onto her toes, and tightened her arms around his neck. He groaned and deepened the kiss. It had been forever since a kiss had made her crave more.

The last few guys she'd dated, kisses had been sort of warm and fuzzy, like cuddling with a kitten. Steve's kisses made her tingle in all the right places, made her crave his touch on all those places.

He nibbled kisses along her jaw and a whisper in her ear

made her shiver. "I better go."

She tipped back her head. "What? You're not coming in?" His body's response told her he wanted to go further.

His forehead met hers, and he pulled in a long breath. He threaded his hands through her hair, resting his thumbs in front of her ears. "I would love to"—her heart skipped a beat—"but we haven't known each other long, and I want to make sure there's more than sex between us before making love."

She stared at him, not hiding her surprise. Earlier in the day, she'd wanted to keep some distance between them, and now Steve was the one drawing away. She understood he wouldn't want a relationship similar to the one he'd had with Tiffany. Maybe he wasn't the one she had to worry about becoming dependent.

He put his arm around her and nudged. "I'll walk you to your door."

At her door, he gave her one more long kiss. "I really have to go. I'll call you."

He stepped back and she unlocked the door and stepped inside. She stared into his eyes, not able to shut the door in his face. He chuckled and pulled it closed.

Chapter 7

Angel had never been so nervous discharging a patient before. Her last patient had cancelled, leaving her with too much time to think. Steve would arrive any minute, and likely, it would be their last session. He'd done better than she could have hoped. Not many patients had worked as hard as him.

She drew in a deep breath and headed from her office to the reception desk. "Hey, Megan."

"Angel, Steve Halloran is here."

"Thanks." Angel tapped her tablet screen as if nothing was unusual. There was a possibility of never seeing him again. He might decide he didn't need her at all once he was finished with physical therapy. That would prove his independence and strong mind, but she hoped he felt more for her.

She swung the door open. "Hi, Steve."

He smiled and strode across the floor, with a barely perceived hitch in his step, a leather bag in his hand. "Morning, Angel."

He followed her to a work room, and removed his sweat pants, leaving him in workout shorts. "Do you want me to put on my running foot?"

"Yes, and keep your shoe on. I want to watch you run on the treadmill and then our track." She checked his stump before he switched prosthetics, then put him through his runs. She made a couple of slight corrections and they were done.

Angel typed in some notations. "It was amazing how

hard you worked. You finished your therapy so much faster than I expected."

Steve stuffed his running prosthetic into its bag and took her hand. "I had incentive to keep up with my girlfriend."

She hadn't thought of herself as his girlfriend. She cared a great deal for him, but was still concerned it was so soon after being dumped by his ex.

He took her hands. "School starts next week, so between classes and homework, I don't know how much time I'll have for dates. But I'll need my Angel fix, so I'll make sure to find the time."

"I want to keep seeing you, too." She didn't want to be referred to as a fix. It made her think he was too dependent on her, that his life could spiral out of control again if she wasn't in it. Maybe as they spent more time together, she'd see him settle into his new life, and she'd become sure he was stable.

He gave her a quick kiss. "See you Saturday."

~~~

This was the third time Steve ran the track at the college before class. The first two times, his stump needed a three-day recovery before running again. In a couple weeks, he figured he could run three days a week. Not like nearly daily when he'd been in the army, but this was wonderful, considering he thought he'd never walk without a cane, let alone run. He felt almost like his old self as he raced the track.

The carbon fiber running blade had taken some getting used to, and he still took extra care at the curves. After he got more comfortable running on it, he could run on the less even streets in his neighborhood. It would save time to head out his door instead of going to the school first.

The first two runs had been uncomfortable when he noticed the stares of other runners or walkers. Today, most had already become accustomed to seeing him. He'd overcome his disability, and it no longer mattered what others thought.

A guy fell in beside Steve. "I'm Brad."

"Steve."

"You're in my sociology class. I had no idea you had a prosthetic. I think it's great you didn't give up on running."

"Thanks. I had a good physical therapist who convinced me I could do it."

"How'd it happen?" Usually children were the ones who were this direct.

"IED in Afghanistan."

"Sorry, man. Glad you made it back."

"Me, too. I've got a new girl I wouldn't have wanted to miss out on."

Brad chuckled. "Yeah. Can't miss that. See you in class." He increased his speed and soon, half the track separated them.

This was the first time he'd mentioned to anyone that Angel was his girlfriend and he liked saying it. She'd been invaluable as he learned to use the new prosthetic, helping him adjust his stride and balance. It had been wonderful spending time with her, even though she worked him hard.

Thoughts of Tiffany didn't hurt anymore. It was like a healed injury that twinged occasionally. Comparing his feelings for Angel to what he'd had with Tiffany was like winning a marathon instead of dropping out halfway through. He loved Angel.

Examining his relationship with Tiffany, he could admit it was all about the sex. They'd started dating as seniors in high school at a time when he thought explosive sex meant love. She'd done them both a favor by breaking up with him.

That left him open for real love.

His stump began to ache, but half the track was left to finish his two miles. Easy. The pain had started earlier on previous runs.

Angel was special in so many ways. His whipsaw change in attitude from suicidal to happy, and from thinking he was in love with Tiffany to falling in love with Angel must have made a record. She touched other lives as well, going the extra distance to make them work harder for themselves.

His Angel was an angel. He checked the time as he approached his car. It was still before her first appointment. He leaned against the door and removed the cell phone from the band on his arm. A smile touched his lips at the picture beside her name, a wide grin lighting her face. A close second favorite would be a picture of her with fire in her eyes as she saved his life.

"Angel Carrera."

The sound of her voice filled him with warmth. "I love how your name describes you. When you were born, your parents must have known how special you would be."

"Steve. I wasn't expecting your call."

"I couldn't help it. I haven't seen you in three days and I miss you."

Was that a pause? "I missed you, too."

"Want to have dinner tonight? Just dinner since I have to get back to homework. I can bring pizza."

"Okay. Six-thirty. You know what I like."

He knew she liked kisses. And he wanted to find out all the places she liked them. "Yeah, I do. See you tonight." He also knew what she liked on pizza.

~~~

The doorbell rang, and Angel checked the table one last time. Place settings and napkins. She grabbed two glasses from the freezer half full of ice, and two bottles of soda, and set them on the table, then raced to the door, and threw it open.

Steve stood in front of her with a large pizza box in his hands. "Pizza delivery. Do I get a tip?" One corner of his mouth rose.

She hiked her eyebrows up. "What do you want for a tip?"

"A kiss?"

She grabbed the box near his hands, and leaned over it. "That I can do." She kissed him. It had only been three days since she'd last seen him, but her life away from work had become boring without Steve. The box between them, with its aroma of sauce and pepperoni, reminded her she was hungry.

She straightened, and tugged until he released the box. "Let's eat."

Back in the kitchen, Angel set the pizza on the table and opened the box. Not only did he get her toppings correct—pepperoni, sausage and peppers—he remembered her favorite pizza shop.

They sat and each grabbed a slice. Without setting it down she bit off the point, and closed her eyes as the flavors exploded in her mouth. "Mmm. It's so good. I haven't had pizza since I had it with you."

He chuckled. "Like all of two weeks ago." He wiped the corner of her mouth with his napkin. "Maybe the company makes the food taste better."

She couldn't deny that. She was falling for him, but didn't know where he stood. Maybe she should break off things with him before her heart was more involved.

His eyes squinted. "What? What's going through your

head?" His voice had risen. He must have recognized something in her face.

She stared at her food and took another bite. He seemed emotionally stronger than the first few times she was with him. Chances were he wouldn't try again to kill himself.

He grabbed her hand. "Angel, talk to me."

She bit her lip and gazed at him. Concern and worry brightened his eyes and tensed his mouth. He probably thought she was turning this into something like his last dinner with Tiffany. And in a way, she was. She didn't want to.

She tried to pull away, but he wouldn't let her. "I'm afraid I'm a rebound for you. You're spending all this time with me so you don't have to think about her."

He ran a hand through his hair, smudging a bit of grease on his forehead. "With Doc's help, I did a lot of thinking about Tiffany. Do you know the first thing we always did when I got home on leave?"

She shook her head.

"We tore our clothes off and had sex."

She glanced away, heat flowing up her chest and into her face. She and Steve hadn't had sex yet. Maybe he didn't think it would be as good as with his ex.

"Look at me." His low voice pleaded.

She swung her gaze back to him, and bit her lip.

"That was the way we got our connection back. Because there wasn't anything else. When I was away, we very rarely emailed or talked, and it was always about her work or my field duties. It was never about our future, or what we wanted to do together when I came home on leave."

It wasn't the type of relationship she wanted to have. He seemed to understand.

He ran a finger along her jaw. "Angel, you're special. I knew the first time I saw you. I want to build something special between us that's more than sex." He grinned. "And I do want that, too, but sex doesn't hold a relationship together."

They were the right words. Probably talking with the psychologist had gotten him to work through his emotional issues faster, made him see it more clearly.

She grabbed his hand. "But if she hadn't broken up with you, you'd still be together."

He shrugged. "Maybe. But it wouldn't have lasted. Especially since she's pregnant."

Her breath rasped. "What?"

He waved his hands. "It's not mine."

"Oh." Of course, he wouldn't abandon his own child. What kind of woman got pregnant while she was still engaged to another man who was serving his country?

He pushed their plates aside and took her hands in his. "I can think of one way to prove you're not a rebound."

She tipped her head and squinted. "How?"

"We won't see each other for two weeks. No phone calls. Nothing."

"How does that prove it?"

He waved a hand between them. "If this is just a passing fancy, I'll be over it by then. If it's still real, we'll go out."

It made sense. He'd gotten over his fiancée in a few weeks after they'd been together for years. He probably would get over her, too, if it wasn't real. She hoped it was real for him because it sure was for her. "Okay."

He frowned. "You agreed awfully quickly."

Maybe he hadn't wanted her to go along with it. "If you still want to see me in two weeks, then I'll know you're serious about me."

He let out a long breath. "I am serious. Keep two weeks from tonight open because I'll call you. Now, let's finish our pizza, so I can go do my homework."

Staring at two weeks—or forever—of not seeing him brought the love that had been building, front and center. If she was important to him, she'd see him again. If not, breaking her heart in two weeks would be easier on her than after she fell more in love with him. Maybe. This had better not be a colossal mistake on her part.

Chapter 8

Steve ran a comb through his wet hair. It had been a mistake. Only a week and he was ready to jump on his bike and race over to Angel's house. How many times had he taken his phone out and scrolled through his contacts before realizing what he was doing? He ended up slapping a sticky note to the face saying, *Don't call her.*

That night had been a ghostly reminder of the night Tiffany had broken up with him, including him bringing dinner to her place. He'd had no control over that evening with Tiffany. He hoped the way he'd handled Angel's doubts would make them stronger together and not drive her away from him.

Whoever said, *absence makes the heart grow fonder* wasn't kidding. If he suspected before he loved Angel, he knew now with every fiber of his being he did. His life would be perfect if she felt it, too, and wasn't working on getting over him. Or maybe she didn't have to work at it.

This was another sign he hadn't loved Tiffany. In the army, he couldn't call her, but it hadn't bothered him. At times he'd gone days without thinking of her.

An hour couldn't go by without Angel coming to mind. A discussion they'd had, how hot she looked on her bike, how determined she'd been running around with the marker, the sweet sounds she made when he kissed her.

Dr. Ferrell had been a godsend in his last visit. She'd pointed out how strong he'd been to suggest the temporary separation to ease Angel's concerns. It showed he trusted his love as well as hers, but it didn't help him miss Angel less.

He stalked to his dresser and dug out underwear, socks and a t-shirt, and put them on. In his closet, he grabbed a pair of new jeans off a shelf, ones that fit over his fake foot, and slipped into them. Now he conformed to college campus wear.

He wanted to hear Angel's laugh.

"Uh." He rubbed his hand down his face. To make the time go faster, if that were possible, he'd done all his homework. He had two projects that weren't due for a couple more weeks, but he'd completed them already. He'd read ahead in his psychology and history books. By the time his self-allotted time was done, he'd have some free time to spend with Angel.

Back at the dresser, he opened the small velvet box sitting beside his wallet. The diamonds twinkled, a big one with a smaller one on each side. He'd made sure they didn't stick up too high, not wanting the ring to interfere with Angel's work. He didn't want her to remove the ring for work because he wanted everybody to know she was claimed. He'd purchased it three days after their pizza dinner since he wanted to spend the rest of his life with her. He'd taken Tiffany's ring with him and gotten credit towards Angel's ring, not that it was anywhere near what he'd paid for it, but it saved him figuring out what to do with it.

One week down and one to go. He could do this. There was nothing he wanted more than being with Angel, and spending every night with her.

~~~

Angel wished she hadn't agreed to this two week abstinence. No smiles from Steve. No seeing his determination to do what he didn't think he could do. No long talks over the phone or in person, discussing nothing and everything. No kisses. She touched her lips and glared at the clock on her desk. Five minutes to her first appointment.

If it had been a matter of Steve having to go away and not being able to contact her and knowing he would be back, she would have missed him, but it wouldn't have bothered her to this extent. Waiting though was hard because she didn't know if she'd see him again at the end of the two weeks. Either way, he'd call, either to tell her she was right and it was a rebound relationship, or to ask her out.

She hoped and prayed he'd ask her on that date, and they could resume where they'd left off. Maybe not quite. Over their time apart, she realized how much she loved him, and it would hurt so much more if he broke it off. If he asked her on a date, the first thing she'd tell him when they were face-to-face was she loved him.

She made it through four appointments and no call from Steve. Two patients asked if she was okay. Of course she said she was, but each passing minute, her shoulders tensed more, her stomach twisted. She might not be able to eat her lunch. Maybe she could get lost in a book instead of eating. Not a romance.

Back in her office, she glanced at the clock. Twelve-o-five. She rummaged in a drawer, sure she had a sci-fi book someone had given her.

The phone rang. She let it ring twice before snatching it from the cradle. Fear and hope warred in her heart. "Angel Carrera."

"I've missed your voice, my angel."

She flopped against the chair back. "Steve." Missing her had to be a good sign.

"Wear your prettiest dress. I'm picking you up at six-thirty."

Her heart soared. "We're back to dating?"

"I hope we are." Doubt tinged his voice.

"Yes."

"Good. I'm running to a class, so I'll see you later, sweetheart." The phone silenced.

"Steve?" She pulled in a long breath and her shoulders relaxed as she released it. Must be whatever he had to say he wanted to say in person.

Angel grinned as she stood, suddenly feeling hungry. She gobbled down her lunch in their small break room, and put so much energy into her appointments that the afternoon flew by.

She still had a chance with Steve and she was going to make every effort to show him how much he meant to her.

~~~

Angel slipped on her white strappy sandals and paced near her front door. She hoped their date didn't include a long walk because her feet wouldn't be able to handle the heels.

She scanned the front of herself. There'd been no time to buy a new dress, but the one she dug out of her closet hadn't often seen daylight. The soft lemony cotton hugged her body and flared at her hips, swirling out when she changed directions. She'd never worn a dress for Steve, so she hoped he'd liked it on her. And maybe it would induce him to hold her tight and kiss her.

The doorbell rang, and a shiver ran through her. She sucked in a breath and opened the door. Steve stood in front of her in a made-for-him black suit and white shirt. His wide shoulders and perfect chest would have every woman's eyes following him everywhere.

His gaze traveled down her body and his eyes widened. "You're gorgeous."

He held out his hands and she placed hers in them.

Now was the perfect time. "I love you."

He said it, too, as if they'd rehearsed saying it together. Her heart soared.

He grinned, gathered her in his arms and spun, lurching and bumping his shoulder into the door frame. "Oops. I totally forgot about the foot."

His lips touched hers, but left too quickly. His gaze met hers, then he reclaimed her mouth. This kiss, so much energy and love flowed through it. The loneliness and heartache of the last two weeks seeped out, replaced by a glowing warmth.

He stepped back and took her hand, his breathing as unsteady as hers. "Let's go. I don't want to be late for our reservation."

"You made reservations? Where?" She loved his thoughtfulness to go to that trouble, and hoped she was dressed up enough for the place he'd chosen.

"You'll see." He tugged her out the door. At his truck, he helped her into the seat, and ran his hand down her thigh as he tucked her dress in beside her. He leaned in and kissed her. "I can't stop touching you."

He closed her door and came around to the other side, barely giving her a chance to notice his truck gleamed, the cleanest she'd ever seen it. The inside of the vehicle hadn't been littered before, but now the dash was polished, and no sand covered the floor.

She had so much to catch up on. "How's school?"

"Good. I'm really enjoying it. I didn't go to college before joining up, so I'd forgotten the immaturity of kids fresh out of high school."

She rested her hand on his thigh. "You've had a lot of experiences since then."

He turned into the parking lot for *Prime Steakhouse*.

Her breath caught. "This is where we're eating? A friend and I stopped here once and they said they were booking reservations into the next week."

He found a parking space and turned off the truck. "I booked it the day after I last saw you."

She took his hand. "You were pretty sure, huh? It was just me worrying."

"I was very sure about me. I wanted you to be sure, too." He grinned. "And I could have canceled."

Steve jumped out of the truck, and she waited for him to open her door. It was a little high and she didn't want to stumble in her heels or show off too much thigh. The door swung open and his hands settled on her waist. He lifted her and set her feet on the pavement. Then his arms surrounded her in a tight hug. "I missed you."

Her stomach growled, probably because of the wonderful aromas coming from the restaurant's vents.

He chuckled. "You just miss eating."

She kissed his neck. "I missed you, too. Now feed me."

He took her hand and led her inside, to the hostess desk. "I have a reservation for six-forty-five. Halloran."

The pretty blonde woman made a checkmark on her paper and picked up two large, leather menus. "This way Mr. Halloran."

Angel scanned the room as she followed the hostess. Nearly every woman's eyes were trained on Steve. She glanced behind and he smiled, his gaze on her. She mouthed the words, "I love you," and his smile widened.

She faced forward as the hostess stopped at a table in a corner. Steve seated her and then himself kitty-corner from her. They were handed menus, and from the center of the table the woman lifted a pitcher containing water, ice and a couple lemon wedges, and filled the two goblets next to their plates. "I'll give you a few minutes and send over Stacey."

Angel opened the menu and ran her gaze down the prices. There were no appetizers under fifteen dollars. Offerings for the main course listed nothing under twenty-five.

Steve tipped her menu. "Hey, don't do that."

She frowned. "Don't do what?"

"Don't check the prices. Pick out what you want."

She straightened her back. "How did you know I was doing it?"

"I watched your eyes run down the page. No way were you reading the food items."

She tipped her head. "Aren't you a starving student?"

He snorted. "Hardly. My school is paid for, I'm getting a small disability payment and spent very little when I was in the army. I'm getting the sixteen ounce ribeye."

He wasn't going for economy here. She studied the menu. Since it was a steakhouse and Steve was ordering steak, she might as well, too. And she hardly ever had a good one. "Okay. I'll have the smallest fillet."

A woman with dark hair pulled into a ponytail arrived at their table with a small iPad in her hand. She wore black pants and shirt with a white collar. "Good evening. I'm Stacey. Would you like to order drinks?"

Steve glanced at Angel and lifted his brows. "Red wine?"

She shrugged. "Sure." She didn't drink often, but seeing Steve again deserved a celebration.

"Two glasses of the house red wine, and we're ready to order."

Stacey swiped her pad as they told her their choices.

After she left, Steve took Angel's hand. "How have you been?"

"It's been pretty average without my hardest working, favorite patient."

He smiled. "I was your favorite patient?"

"You're the only patient I ever dated."

The server stopped at their table. "The house red wine. Enjoy." She set the wine glasses down, and strode away.

He lifted his glass. "A toast?"

She held her glass up.

"To spending time with the one you love."

She clinked her glass on his. "Yes."

They each sipped.

He set down his glass. "I've been getting ahead on my reading and assignments so I could spend more time with you. Are you busy this Saturday?"

"I'm hiking with my brother."

"Mind if I tag along so I can meet him?"

"He'd probably like to meet the man I'll be spending so much time with."

Their food arrived and while they ate, he told her about his classes and the other students.

With their meal finished, Stacey returned. "Would you like dessert?"

"We'll have the sweetheart cake."

She smiled. "Oh, yes. I'll get that right out." She picked up their plates and left.

"I didn't see that on the menu."

He took her hand. "It's a very special dessert."

Stacey returned with a plate and set it in front of Angel. Then she retreated.

It held a heart-shaped cake big enough for two with chocolate frosting, and cream colored lettering, flowers and a couple swirls. *Will You Marry Me?*

She gasped and stared at Steve as he set a small open box beside the cake. She hadn't expected this so soon. Her mouth hung open and she snapped it shut. She loved him, even more so after not seeing him for two weeks. Apparently, he was sure, too.

He raised his eyebrows, and took her hand. "I love you, Angel. You don't know how hard it was to not call you or stop by your place, but I wanted to give you the time you needed to make sure of me."

She squeezed his hand. "Oh, I think I do. There were a number of times I almost called you, but reminded myself you were doing this to reassure me."

He kissed her fingers. "Angel, will you marry me?"

She grinned. "That's what I wanted to hear. I know, the question was already out there, but this is the only time I'm going to be asked, so I wanted to hear your voice." She lifted their joined hands to her mouth and kissed his. "Yes. I'll marry you."

He slid off his chair and knelt beside her. He took the ring from its box and held her left hand, sliding the ring onto her finger, then kissed it.

His eyes melted her. "You've made me the happiest man in the world."

She leaned forward and nibbled his ear, whispering into it. "After we have cake, can we go back to my place and make love?"

"We could take it with us and eat it later."

"Uh-uh. It could get smooshed on the way home. I want to eat it when it's perfect."

He stood more gracefully than he would have a month ago and took his seat. She drew a few lines with her fork then turned the cake around.

He smiled. "Ah. She says 'yes'." He picked up his own fork.

"Wait." Angel yanked the cake back and spun it around. She fished her phone from her purse and snapped a picture of the cake and texted it to Carole. She wouldn't believe a guy could be so romantic otherwise.

Angel centered the cake between them, took a bite and closed her eyes. "Mmm. I love chocolate."

"Don't do that to me."

She paused with the fork halfway to her mouth. "Do what?"

He leaned forward and whispered. "Act like the cake is sex. How am I going to get through this and get you all the way home?"

Her face heated. "Steve, I didn't mean it like that."

He swiveled her hand around and took her cake. "It is good." He cut off a chunk and offered it to her.

Before she took it, Stacey dropped the bill on the table. "Looks like you got the answer you wanted."

Steve set the fork down. "I sure did." He drew his wallet from his pocket and handed her a stack of bills. "That's all set. Could you bring a box for the cake?"

A Styrofoam container arrived and they ate a few more bites.

Steve picked up a knife. "You ready to stick this in the box?" His fingers rested on the edge of the plate and the knife hovered.

"Okay. I'm good." She'd be too full if she ate more anyway, but she'd had to have some of the cake with the perfect question.

He slid the cake into the box and closed the lid, then stood. She came to her feet and he wrapped an arm around her waist and kissed her. "First kiss as my fiancée. I requested the corner so I could do this. And get down on my knee without too many people noticing."

So far, the evening had been perfect. Now, they needed to get back to her place and have longer kisses and finally make love.

As they passed the hostess, she said, "Have a great evening."

Angel realized Stacey had probably told the hostess they were newly engaged, and knew exactly what the rest of their evening would be. At least her back was to the hostess when the blush crept into her face.

Steve stopped once they got through the door, and ran a finger down her cheek. "Hey, what's this?"

"The hostess said, 'Have a great evening.'"

His eyebrows dropped down. "They generally do."

"But we just got engaged, so…"

He chuckled and kissed her. "I love you."

The drive home seemed to take longer than the drive to the restaurant.

Angel dragged him through her front door, paused to unbuckle her shoes and kick them off at the closet and dropped her purse beside them, then dragged Steve to her bedroom.

Steve's voice held amusement when he spoke. "I get the feeling you're in a hurry."

Beside her bed, she faced him. Now it was time to actually make love, she couldn't just get naked and do it. Her face flamed again. So much for her sophisticated woman act.

~~~

Once they entered Angel's bedroom, she froze. Steve wrapped an arm around her waist and drew her close. He would do everything he could to make this good for her. With his other hand, he caressed her face and tunneled his fingers into her hair. "I love you. I want this to be special for you. So, foot on or foot off?"

She giggled. That broke some of the tension. "I've seen you without your foot. And since you're spending the night…"—he nodded, not telling her he had a packed bag in his truck—"you might as well take it off. And I've got crutches in my closet you can use."

A dam broke inside him, and his heart swelled with more love for this beautiful woman. He knew it didn't matter to her he'd lost his foot, but he'd had this one tiny fear about making love to her without it. "Thank you." This would be his first time since losing his foot, and he hoped the lack didn't cause problems.

Tears shimmered in her eyes, and he kissed beside each one. His fingers found the zipper at the top of her dress and slid it down. Her eyes widened and her breath quickened. He nibbled her earlobe and breathed in the fragrance of her hair, something flowery that would always remind him of Angel.

She loosened his tie and worked her way down his shirt buttons, tugging it from his pants to get the last couple. Steve yanked the tie off over his head and tossed it on the floor, then shrugged off the jacket and shirt.

The front of her dress gaped, and he slipped his hands under the edges, pushing the dress off her shoulders, and letting it pool at her feet. She was beautiful. He ran his fingertips along the edge of her lace edged bra, while the other hand unhooked the back. She wiggled her shoulders and the garment slid off her arms.

He cupped her breast. "Perfect." This woman was the most important person in the world, and he would do whatever it took to make her happy, starting with discovering how she liked to be pleasured.

Her pursed lips drew him in and he couldn't resist another kiss. He slid his hand over her smooth back, catching one side of her panties, then the other, nudging them off her hips. With the backs of her legs at the bed, Steve lifted a knee onto the mattress and leaned, lowering her. His lips didn't leave hers until he'd scooted her up to rest her head on a pillow. He straightened, his gaze traveling over her athletic body, and back to her face. She ogled him and he liked it.

He grabbed a few condoms from his pocket and dropped them on the nightstand. Angel's eyes widened and he grinned. Yeah. He was optimistic, considering she had work and he had school the next day.

His eyes never wavered from her face as he unbuckled his belt and opened his pants, shoving them down. He sat on the edge of the bed, still half facing her as he finished removing his shoes, clothes and prosthetic.

He swung his legs around and slipped underneath the covers beside her. This was exactly where he should be.

She lifted her upper body and draped herself over him. "I love you."

"I love you, too. My life is so much better with you in it." He'd had many fantasies about their first time, and he was going to show her every one of them.

He kissed her, then kissed a trail to her ear. "I'm going to taste you everywhere." And he did, and so much more.

~~~

Guardian Darrah gave a happy sigh as she stared down at Steve and Angel as they slept with their arms around each other. Angel's new ring caught the early morning light sneaking through the gap in the drapes.

With no prior experience bringing couples together, she'd panicked when Steve and Angel had agreed on a short separation. Guide Rayah told her to let them be, that Steve was strong enough if it didn't work between them, but they were supposed to be together and Darrah had to do something. She may have given them reminders of each other a bit too often, but it had worked out perfectly.

Now, another wounded warrior gave a silent plea for help. She had work to do.

THE END

Wounded Warrior Hearts: Amy

Deborah Wallace

Deborah Wallace

Chapter 1

Guardian Darrah walked along the amethyst wall and stopped in Eva's doorway, still not confident after her one success of preventing a veteran's suicide. "Goddess, I have an Intervention." She swept her blonde curls behind her ear, and ran her hands down the front of her pale yellow gown.

Eva glanced up from her glass desk and smiled. Every blonde hair was tucked into a twist on the back of her head, and her flowing forest green robe matched the green of her eyes. "Ah, Guardian Darrah. You did very well on your first Intervention."

"Thank you, Goddess." Darrah had a rough couple weeks with her first Intervention when the couple had split up, but with gentle reminders they had ended up together again.

Goddess held out her hand. "Who is it this time?"

Darrah handed her a two inch, flat, black onyx square with the information. "Captain Amy Stuart. An army nurse."

"How long has she been back?"

"Two-and-a-half months."

Goddess squeezed her hand around the square and closed her eyes. "She thinks the world is stacked against her and can't find her way out. What's your plan to prevent her from taking her life?" She opened her eyes and handed the square to Darrah.

"Get her a job so she feels useful." She didn't tell Goddess she'd chosen men who could become a love interest. The captain's life was more important to Goddess than the woman's heart. To Darrah, both were equally important.

Goddess held out a hand again. "Who have you chosen to help her?"

Darrah handed over four pale peach squares.

Goddess took them and spread them in a row across her desk. The flat of her hand hovered a few seconds above each square. She plucked the second one. "Blake Lloyd." She held the square in her palm.

Darrah took it, images from the man's life floating through her head. He'd been her favorite, but she hadn't trusted her ability to choose accurately.

"Have them meet after the eleventh rejection."

"Yes, Goddess." Darrah let the possible scenes flow through her. This veteran would be more difficult to reach than the last, and she wasn't sure if she was up to it.

She slipped the two squares into her pocket, and gathered the rejected squares from the desk.

"Darrah, remember, Guide Rayah can assist if you need it."

"Thank you, Goddess." She bowed her head and left. This soldier nurse's life depended on a guardian with only one successful assignment completed, and Darrah was worried she would fail. Amy Stuart had so much to give, if only someone could see it before it was too late.

~~~

Amy Stuart clenched her hands in her lap, hiding her left hand. She didn't want to give the interviewer more ammunition by letting him see the missing fingertips on her little and ring fingers. A hospital administrator should be more understanding of injuries.

Tom Thompson—what kind of name was that—held the

folder as if it were a shield. The head of human resources shifted in his seat and wouldn't meet her eyes. "I'm sure you can understand the scarring on your face might scare the children in pediatrics. They're already sick, we don't need to add to their stress."

She clenched her hands tighter, refusing to touch the scars on her left cheek and neck. She had applied makeup, like she always did before leaving the house, but it only covered the discoloration, not the rough surface.

"As far as I know, I haven't scared any kids yet. They seem more curious than anything." They stared until their parents stopped them. Some, with sympathy in their eyes, asked if it hurt.

Amy tried to meet his eyes, but he wouldn't make contact. "What about other departments? Surely, I won't scare adults."

Tom closed the folder. "We don't have any other openings. I'm sorry."

Never in her life had she received such a less sincere apology. So much for a shortage of nurses. Just bring in good old, scarred Amy Stuart and the shortage magically disappeared. This was her tenth rejection. The others told her she wasn't a good fit for the position. This was the first time the interviewer was so bold as to tell her it was due to her scars.

Three years of trauma experience in combat zones and glowing references should have earned her a choice of offers.

With dignity, she got to her feet, not wanting him to see her run and hide. "Thank you for talking to me." Head held high, she strode out of the office, and kept on going until she made it to her car. She dropped into the driver's seat, hunched over and let out a shuddering breath. She wouldn't cry. That man's callousness wouldn't drive her to tears.

Now, her appearance was keeping her from getting a job.

Every interview brought her closer to despair. All the interviewers had similar responses as Tom Thompson, but had been less rude at rejecting her. She had one more chance, a job interview the next day at another hospital.

Maybe she should have found a way to stay in the army. At least there she was appreciated and needed for her skills as a nurse. No one minded she was scarred. Most of her patients had scars of their own. But every day she passed the guards to enter a military hospital, the harder she had to push down the fear. Each time she reached for that door, she had to wipe her mind of the images of exploding walls and flying chemicals. The acrid odor filled her lungs, bringing back painful memories. She'd had to bury it all to help heal the injured soldiers, only to have nightmares dredge it up again.

Amy shook her head. No. She couldn't have reenlisted. Civilian hospitals held no fear. The nightmares weren't over, but without the daily terror she'd submerged, they didn't assault her every night.

She had another chance tomorrow to convince a hospital administrator she was more than a scarred face and injured hand. Surely, someone would see the dedicated nurse with skills honed by battle.

Chapter 2

Amy climbed out of her car and stared at the hospital building. This one was at least a dozen stories taller than the others she'd interviewed at, and took up the whole block with parking across the street. She'd applied for a position on the maternity floor, but would take any placement that was available.

She resisted the urge to touch her cheek, not wanting to smear the make-up. She leaned back into the car, flipped down the visor and gave a quick check in the mirror. Her face looked fine. At least, as much as it could with the slightly rough scars on her left cheek and upper neck. Her hair was in a braided bun at the back of her head, and her navy blue suit was spotless. She snatched up her over-sized handbag and dragged in a deep breath. She could do this.

Confident strides took her to the entrance doors and the elevator. She ignored the stares, and stood in a corner of the elevator, her head averted, so as to shield her scars. As she gave a quick glance to the floor indicator when the doors opened, no one was staring at her. They must have already had their fill. On the seventh floor, she was the last remaining occupant.

A long breath settled her nerves as she walked down the hall and into room seven-fourteen. A woman with short blonde hair studiously stared at a paper and typed on her keyboard.

"Hi. I have an appointment with Darlene Smith."

The woman's head snapped up and her gaze darted to

Amy's scar, then down to the screen. "You must be Amy Stuart. Have a seat."

Amy chose a chair that allowed the woman—Trisha Allan, according to the name plate on the desk—to only see Amy's good cheek. Ten minutes ticked by as Amy flipped through a magazine, staring at pictures since she was too keyed up to read. She'd been five minutes early, so it wasn't unexpected she'd have to wait.

The inner office door opened and a man wearing a dark suit and carrying a carrier bag walked out. He stopped at Trisha's desk. "She wants me to set up another appointment for next Tuesday."

The woman smiled at him. "Congrats on the second interview." She glanced down at her screen. "Two o'clock?"

The man grinned. "Thanks. Two is good. See you next week."

Amy hoped that didn't mean she was out of luck before she even entered.

"Miss Stuart? You can go in now."

"Thank you." Amy stood, ran her hands down her skirt to smooth out the wrinkles and entered the next room.

The woman behind the desk stood and held out her hand. "Amy Stuart?"

Amy shook. "Yes. Good morning, Ms. Smith."

"You can call me Darlene."

Amy took the left seat in front of the desk in hopes it would give fewer glimpses of her face.

Darlene picked up Amy's resume from her desk. "You have an impressive skill set. You've dealt with patients with gunshot wounds, broken bones and burns." Her gaze flicked to Amy's face. It wasn't hard to tell Amy's scars were caused by burns.

"Yes. I've worked triage with the wounded pouring in, to the day-to-day issues of healing."

Darlene lifted a brow. "But nothing related to maternity."

Amy forced a grin. "Our soldiers don't tend to be pregnant, but I spent one rotation on a maternity floor and enjoyed being a part of helping women bring their babies into the world."

"And you could go from trauma to drama?"

"Bringing life into the world is much better than seeing death walk in the door nearly every hour."

"There are deaths in maternity, too. It's heart-rending when a mother loses her baby or a husband loses his wife."

Through her three years in the army, Amy had gotten used to death, almost immune to it. Until the explosion where she'd lost three co-workers and twenty-eight patients, and been injured herself. She twisted her hands in her lap. "I can handle it."

Darlene's gaze dropped to Amy's hands. Amy pulled them apart and flattened them on her thighs.

Darlene shook her head. "I'm sorry. I don't think this is going to work out. You've got wonderful experience for an ER."

"I was hoping for something less stressful than an ER."

Darlene stood. "You've got a great background, and I'm sure you'll do a wonderful job in the right position, but unfortunately, I don't think this is it." She patted the resume. "I'll keep you in mind if I find a suitable position."

It was the nicest brush off Amy had ever gotten, but it still meant she didn't get the job. Amy got to her feet. "Thank you for speaking with me."

"I really appreciate your service to our soldiers."

Amy nodded and walked out the door. She held back the tears until the elevator doors opened in the lobby. Fortunately, the exit doors were the brightest area. She didn't have to see too clearly to head to the light. And maybe she should find that other light to head to, and then she wouldn't have to put up with rejection after rejection with nobody at her side to help her through it.

~~~

Dr. Blake Lloyd wasn't late, but had an urge to check his watch as he strode through the hospital doors. A small body barreled into him and his chin was struck by a head. "Oof!" His arms automatically surrounded the body to prevent a fall and he discovered it was a woman.

"Sorry." The voice sounded older than he expected. He'd thought she must have been a careless teenager.

She twisted to go around him, but he saw the tears streak her face and couldn't let her go outside like that. If she could blindly run into him, she might step in front of a moving car.

He squeezed her shoulder. "Hey, wait, wait. Let's get you calmed down before you go out there."

She scrabbled through her big bag and found a tissue as he led her to a marble bench near the door. She wiped her cheeks, removing some of the heavy make-up covering them. A burn scar marred her left cheek near her ear and traveled onto her neck. It was a bit bumpy, but not as raised as some scars he'd seen.

"I'm Blake."

"Amy."

"Amy, can I do anything to help?"

She drew in a long breath, but kept her head turned away from him. "Probably not. I had a job interview today. It was my eleventh. Every one of them rejected me for one reason or another, but I know it's because of this." She waved to her face. "And this." She held her left hand up. The tips of two fingers from the first knuckle were gone. "They don't affect how I can care for people."

"Do you have a copy of your resume with you? Could I see it?" He didn't know why he asked. He likely wouldn't be able to help her.

She fished a folder from her purse, and handed him a sheet of paper.

Her name was Amy Stuart, a nurse. He scanned down and the air froze in his lungs, the sensation flowing to his head. "You were in the bombing at the Qatari hospital?"

Her head swung around to him and her eyes widened. "You've heard of it?"

He nodded. "My brother. He was injured and recovered there. At the time of the explosion, I thought he was still there. It took days to find out he'd been discharged the week before."

She grabbed his hand. "Wh-what's his name?"

"David Lloyd."

Amy fell back against the wall and closed her eyes. "He was so excited he'd get to go back out there and fight. He was incredibly lucky. There were men who were supposed to be discharged the next day who died in the explosion."

And she had survived that same blast. Blake read through the resume again. She had impressive nursing experience, way above the level he needed in his office. And David had said all the nurses had really cared. "You're hired, pending a background check."

Her eyes popped open. "What?"

"I'm an orthopedic surgeon. One of the nurses in my office is leaving in two weeks. Her husband's been transferred. You can take her place."

"But you don't know me."

He chuckled. "I didn't know the other three nurses I interviewed for the position." He hefted her resume. "This is all true, isn't it?"

"Of course."

He stood. He wished he had time to talk to her for a while. "I've got to make rounds." He fished in his pocket and handed her a business card. "Here's our address. Come on Tuesday and Hannah can show you the ropes." He folded her resume and slipped it into his shirt pocket.

"Thank you. You don't know how much this means to me. I'll see you next week."

Amy leaned her head back and closed her eyes. Blake studied her for a moment more. He couldn't imagine how difficult it would be for a beautiful woman to learn to live with her scars. He'd do his best to make it easier for her.

~~~

The tension left Amy's shoulders, and she tried to let go of the pain of all those rejections, but each one had made her think of Jeff, her most painful rejection.

Today, she'd lost all hope of finding a job. A lack of meaningful employment had nearly ended her life. Not the work so much as lack of anyone needing her. If not for the fateful blinding tears, she wouldn't have slammed into her new employer. She would have gone home and ended the pain.

Amy stumbled to her feet with hopes this new lease would allow her to nurture others the way she craved. And maybe help mend her heart.

Chapter 3

Amy closed her car door and stared at the two-story building, her new home for eight hours a day. It sat between two identical structures. She'd scoped it out the day before, driving the same time of day she would for work so she'd know how long it took with traffic. Then she'd found Dr. Lloyd's office, but didn't go in.

The only job she'd had outside of the army was when she was in high school. She'd been hired at a fast food restaurant with two other students and they learned the procedures together. In the army, there'd been thirty nurses getting up to speed on hospital procedures. One-on-one would be a new experience and she wasn't sure how she'd like it.

She wasn't sure how she'd relate to the patients. In the hospital, she saw each patient several times a day for days or weeks, and got to know them. In an office, she might see a patient a couple of times, weeks apart. She dragged in a breath and blew it out. This was the job she found and she would do her best. Dr. Lloyd deserved it for hiring her.

She glanced at her dress pants and button down shirt. Her plain navy blue scrubs were in her bag. Maybe the nurses didn't wear scrubs, or maybe they wore cute ones. She'd find out soon enough.

She strode into the building, and took the stairs to the second floor. She yanked the door open and nearly ran into a man with his hand stretched to the door.

"Sorry," they said in unison.

His gaze landed on her scar and bounced away.

She turned her cheek away and stepped back to hold the door wider. "Go on through."

"Thanks." He passed her and galloped down the stairs.

Maybe this wasn't such a good idea. All day, every day, she'd be subjected to stares from stranger after stranger. But she'd already committed to this and she'd have to see it through. Hopefully, it would get easier.

The corridor was empty. Three office doors lined each side of it. She turned left. Dr. Lloyd's office occupied the corner space on her right.

She drew in a deep breath, pushed the door open and marched to the reception window. "Hi. I'm Dr. Lloyd's new nurse, Amy Stuart."

The woman frowned. "I thought he was still interviewing."

Amy bit her lip. "He didn't tell you?" Maybe he'd lied. Maybe it had slipped his mind.

A woman bustled up behind the receptionist with a folder in her hand. "Amy?"

Amy nodded.

The woman handed the folder to the receptionist. "Miranda, Blake told me yesterday when the background check came in that he'd hired Amy. Here's her new hire packet to fill out."

Miranda's eyebrows rose, and she glanced at the folder. "Oh. I guess I better cancel the rest of the interviews." She squinted at Amy. "I don't remember seeing you come in."

Amy shook her head. "I'm sorry he didn't tell you." She hoped they didn't think this was a pity hire. She'd prove she could do the job.

Miranda stood. "Come on in. You can fill out the paperwork in Hannah's office." The door to the right of the window opened and Miranda stood on the other side. She wore a dark green skirt and an off-white light-weight sweater.

The other woman wore solid medium blue scrubs. She held out her hand. "I'm Hannah. You're my replacement. When you're finished with the paperwork, I'll show you the ropes."

Amy shook her hand. "Hi, Hannah. I wasn't sure how to dress. I guess navy blue is okay."

"That's perfect. I'll see you in a bit."

Amy followed Miranda to the first door and they stepped inside. "Have a seat. Bring the forms back to me when you're done."

"Thanks."

The small room held a medium sized desk, two chairs, and a filing cabinet. The desk faced the window wall. Amy sat and opened the folder. On the top was her resume with creases from being folded twice. She set it face down on the other side of the folder and lifted the first form. The last time she'd filled out this many forms was when she graduated nursing school and enlisted in the army.

Whispered voices in the hallway caught her attention. "How did he end up hiring her?"

"She was leaving a job interview at the hospital when he got there to do rounds. He said he practically bowled her over when he checked his watch. They talked and he asked for her resume."

"I can't believe he hired someone off the street."

"You'll have to look at her resume. She's got more varied experience—"

The voices moved away and Amy couldn't hear anymore. It sounded like Blake hadn't mentioned she'd been crying. That relieved her. Neither woman had made more than a passing glance at her scars. Maybe she could have camaraderie like she'd had at the base hospitals. She buckled down and filled out line after line on the papers.

Amy found Miranda back at the reception desk, and waited while she scheduled a patient appointment over the phone. Amy ignored the call while studying the seated patients as they waited for their turn. One patient was an elderly woman with her arm in a cast. A younger woman sat beside her, maybe her granddaughter.

Another was a muscular man who reminded her of the soldiers she'd treated. Their eyes met and he looked away. She'd never been beautiful, but had considered herself pretty, and used to get appreciative stares from men. Who wouldn't when working in a hospital that catered to mostly men and almost no women around? Now, they couldn't stand the sight of her for more than a few seconds.

That wasn't totally true. The injured men at the bases were more understanding than most. Soon enough, they got past her scars and treated her kindly, but none of them flirted with her anymore. A line she hadn't heard since the explosion was, "When I get out of here, do you want to…" Even when they did, she'd always turned them down because of Jeff, but it was nice to have that ego boost. No more. She hadn't been on a date in almost a year.

Miranda dropped the phone in the cradle, and glanced up at Amy. "All done?"

"Yes. Should I go find Hannah?"

"She'll be back in a couple minutes." Miranda waved her hand at the seat next to her. "Why don't you sit and wait." She pulled a stack of papers out of the bottom tray of an organizer and sorted through them, coming out with a small booklet. "Here. You might as well read this. It's our office procedures and practices. Boring reading, but you'll have to get through it eventually."

She accepted the booklet and settled back in the chair. The military was filled with procedures, stacks more than this thin book. It was easy to read, with no military legalese, straightforward and some of it intentionally funny.

"Amy?"

She glanced up at Hannah. "You ready for me to shadow you?" She set the booklet, half read, on the desk, and stood.

"Let's start with a little tour." At the first door, she stopped. "We'll share my office until I leave and then it's yours."

As they passed the door, Amy spotted her bag. "My lunch. Do you have a refrigerator to store it?"

"Yes. I'll show you the break room."

Amy retrieved her bag and followed Hannah.

"These are the exam rooms." She waved to both sides of the narrow hall. "Miranda will indicate which room to take them to. You'll see it on your tablet." She pointed to a corner of a patient screen on her electronic tablet. "See? Right here." She continued up the hall. "There's the bathroom. Patient and staff."

She pointed to an office, larger than the one she'd been in, with windows the full length of one wall. "That's Harry's office. He's with a patient right now. I'll introduce you between patients."

The gold nameplate on the wall beside the door read, *Harry Talbot MD*.

"Oh. Blake has a partner."

"Yes. They went to school together." She turned left, down a side hall. "There's Blake's office."

The light was off. He was probably still doing rounds.

"And here at the end is the break room." The corner room had windows on two sides, the left wall overlooking the building beside it, and the other, a green lawn and woods beyond it.

Amy dropped her lunch beside the other paper sack and a splashy psychedelic fabric one in the refrigerator. A microwave sat on the counter, and a single-cup coffee maker next to it with its accompanying boxes of coffee choices. A wooden table and six chairs sat in the middle of the room, and three cushioned chairs next to the windows.

"I don't know why we have so much seating," said Hannah. "We normally have no more than two people at a time in here. Even when we have our every-other-month meeting, there's still room at the table."

It would be a cozy place to have lunch.

"Okay. Why don't you change, then we'll get the next patient." Hannah headed to the front of the office.

Amy changed her clothes in the bathroom and, folding the ones she'd removed, slipping them into her bag. She withdrew her stethoscope and placed it around her neck then set the bag inside Hannah's office before joining her and Miranda.

Amy had only ever been a hospital nurse, so the routine of an office was new to her. Weighing patients, taking blood pressure and temperature were normal for her, but patient histories were already taken and logged as the patient was admitted. And most military patients' records were already in the system.

Mid-morning, Dr. Talbot came out of an exam room, staring at an electronic tablet in his hand.

Hannah grabbed his arm. "Harry, I want you to meet our new nurse. This is Amy Stuart."

Harry's gaze strayed to Amy's scar for a millisecond before meeting her eyes. "Hi, Amy. Blake was impressed with your resume. Welcome aboard."

"Thank you. It's good to be here."

He glanced at his tablet. "I'm behind. I'll see you later." He disappeared into the room Amy and Hannah had just left.

The rest of the morning flew by as Amy learned the intricacies of procedures. They finished checking in a patient.

Hannah checked her watch. "Let's have lunch. We've got about forty minutes before the next appointment."

Amy rubbed her stomach. "Okay. I've been hungry for a while. At the hospitals I worked, I was used to scheduled breaks."

Hannah gave a head shake. "It rarely happens here. Lunch is supposed to start at noon, but if the doctors are running behind, we start late and it shortens our break. Especially on Fridays when neither doctor has hospital rounds or surgery."

Amy followed her down the hall and nearly ran into her when she stopped.

Hannah rested her hand on a doorframe. "Hey, Blake. You're back."

Amy stepped around her and peered into Blake's office.

Blake set down a Styrofoam cup that was halfway to his lips. She'd barely noticed him the last time. She should have remembered running into that hard chest. And she'd been too wrapped up in despair to notice those beautiful, kind brown eyes, and the smile that could melt ice cream. A wrapped sandwich sat in front of him. "Nice to see you, Amy. What do you think?"

"It's quite different from a hospital, but so far, I like it. Thank you for hiring me."

He waved his hand. "You were the best candidate."

But she hadn't been a candidate. She hadn't considered applying to private practice, and some weird coincidence brought her resume to his attention. However it happened, she was grateful.

Hannah collected the fabric bag from the refrigerator, and Amy retrieved out her plain paper one. They sat across from each other at the table.

Amy eyed Hannah's bag. "You could find that with your eyes closed."

Hannah laughed. "The last place I worked was a huge office. I hated sorting through all the same brown bags to find mine. I used to write my name on it with a red marker, but it still wasn't easy to find. My husband got me a bunch of these."

"That was thoughtful." Jeff had never done anything for her she would consider thoughtful. He did buy her flowers occasionally, but that could be a gift for any woman.

Hannah's eyes widened. "Blake!"

He sat down beside Amy. "I thought I'd join you two ladies for lunch." He opened the wrapper on his sandwich and took a bite. "Hannah, did you find a house yet?"

"Yes, thank God. We're going to be crammed into a hotel room for almost two weeks after we get there, but we found the perfect house."

He took a sip of coffee. "How's your job hunt?"

Hannah shook her head. "I'm not even looking until after I get the house settled. So, it'll probably be a month before I start my search."

"You'll get a glowing recommendation from me. I'm sure you'll have a new job in no time."

They talked about various topics until it was time to return to work. Amy enjoyed getting to know both Hannah and Blake.

As Amy and Hannah approached the door to the waiting room, she grabbed Amy's arm and whispered. "I can't believe he did that!"

Amy frowned. "Who did what?"

"Blake ate in the break room. He's never done that before."

"Oh. He probably realized you'd be gone soon."

Hannah chuckled. "No. I think he wants to spend time with you."

Amy clenched her hand, so she wouldn't touch her scar.

"I don't think so."

Hannah raised her eyebrows. "I guess you'll know if he still eats lunch with you after I'm gone." She checked her tablet, and opened the door to the waiting room to call the next patient. "Mary Saucier?"

Chapter 4

It was Friday. Amy checked her tablet and opened the door to the waiting room to call the last patient. "Julian Foster."

The eighty-three-year-old man shoved on the arm rests and stood. He shuffled toward her. He'd had hip replacement surgery six weeks before.

She frowned. "Mr. Foster, why don't you have a walker?"

Up until he'd gotten close to her, she'd kept her face slightly turned, so he only now got a view of her scar.

He squinted. "Hey, pretty lady. You're new. What happened to Hannah?"

Pretty? The man's eyesight had to be failing.

"She's in her office packing up. This is her last day. I'm Amy. Now, why don't you have a walker?"

He patted her arm. "I'm a bachelor. What self-respecting woman is going to go out with a man and his walker? I worked extra hard on all those exercises the physical therapist gave me to do."

"Good for you. Come on back and we'll see what Dr. Talbot thinks."

Amy took him into an exam room and started checking his vitals.

"Since I'm your last appointment, you want to go get dinner when we're done?"

She used to get this all the time from the soldiers before the accident. Now, the only one interested was a man old enough to be her grandfather. "Sorry, Mr. Foster. We're having a going away party for Hannah after work."

He grinned. "I could go as your date."

Harry entered the room. "I heard that, old man. Leave our new nurse alone."

Amy tapped in the final numbers in her tablet. "He's all yours."

Back in the office she shared with Hannah, she turned off the tablet and stuck it in the tray on the desk.

Hannah picked up a beautiful picture of herself in her wedding dress, standing beside a gorgeous man, and set it on top of a box with books and knickknacks.

Amy had thought she was coming home to that. Jeff hadn't proposed, but he'd hinted at it, talking of their future together. With one look at her scarred face, he'd torn her life apart. She was no longer good enough to be the wife of a man who wanted to partner in a law firm. It was probably for the best that she found out how shallow he was before they married.

She glanced around the room. Before, it had been inviting with all the little touches Hannah had added. Now, all those items were stored in her box and the room was a sterile, impersonal office.

Hannah picked up her box. "See you at Vincenzo's at seven."

~~~

Amy stared at her reflection in her cracked bathroom mirror. She wore a forest green dress that fit perfectly and was Jeff's favorite. She shook her head. Like it mattered anymore what he thought. This was the first time she'd worn a dress since the explosion.

She brushed her hair. She'd leave it down since it

partially covered her scar, or if she tipped her head forward, it covered all of it. She knew most of the people who would be at the dinner. Hannah was bringing her husband and Miranda her fiancé, but the women had probably told the men she was scarred, so they wouldn't be surprised. She could do this.

She locked up and slipped into her car, then stared at the small two-bedroom house she'd inherited from her grandmother. If this job worked out, she could do some remodeling on the worn out house, but she still wanted it to feel like her grandmother's house.

The drive to the restaurant was short. She hadn't eaten there before and was looking forward to trying the food, but more so, this would be the first time going out since coming home. And she'd get to talk to Blake in a setting outside of work. She'd known him for two weeks and he was always kind. But he was that way with everybody.

Amy parked in the second row of the large parking lot. She hadn't expected Vincenzo's to be this busy. She'd have to pass a lot of people before getting to the private room. She got out of the car, closed her eyes and took a deep breath. She could do this. These were strangers and she wouldn't let it matter what they thought. She marched to the door and presented herself to the hostess.

"I'm here for a private party."

The woman smiled. "Dr. Lloyd's party?"

"Yes."

The hostess pointed. "Do you see that door there?"

"Yes."

"That's where you'll find them."

"Thank you." Amy made her way past the seated patrons, keeping her eyes on the door at the back of the room. With her hand on the door handle, she breathed a sigh of relief. She made it. And now she had to face the strangers mingling with the people she'd come to know.

She opened the door, stepped inside, and let the door close behind her. A long table sat at the back of the room, silverware wrapped in burgundy cloth napkins and water glasses marked each place. A table at the side of the room held appetizers and bottles of wine. In the center of the room, a small group of people stood in a circle, their voices mingling into a buzz until one man's laugh rang out above them.

Amy stepped forward and all eyes focused on her.

Blake broke out of the group and came over to her. "Now that you're here, we'll toast Hannah." He led her to the appetizer table and poured a glass of champagne, then lifted the bottle to the group. "Anyone need to be topped off?"

A man resembling Harry approached her, waving his glass around. His gaze rested on Amy's scar before meeting her eyes. "I'm Jarrod, Harry's brother. His wife couldn't come, so he invited me. You must be Hannah's replacement."

"Yes. I'm Amy." He made her slightly uncomfortable, so she was glad when they joined the group.

Blake pointed to the man standing beside Hannah. Amy recognized him from the wedding picture. "This is Hannah's husband, Antoine, the man who's taking her away from us." Blake grinned. "And beside him is Zach, Miranda's fiancé. You've already met Jarrod. You'll meet Harry's wife, Ellen, another time." He rested his hand on Amy's shoulder for a second. "Everybody, this is Amy, our new nurse."

Blake lifted his glass. "Now, a toast. To Hannah, who's been with us from the beginning. Our office wouldn't have been as successful without you. The way you helped us plan the layout, organized our office procedures, and kept us all in line. You will be missed. We wish you the best in your new state, your new home and in whatever nursing position you choose."

Glasses lifted and agreement sounded. Amy took a sip. She didn't care for champagne, and set the glass down as soon as she could.

Amy joined the woman-of-the-hour and was surprised when Hannah gave her a hug.

Hannah stepped back and grinned. "I'm glad we got to know each other. It's too bad we're going to be states apart."

Amy couldn't tell her she'd been her only friend since leaving the army. While dating Jeff, she'd lost track of her friends, and hadn't reconnected. Maybe she should give it a try.

The hostess stepped into the room, and headed to Blake. They conversed and she left.

Blake called out, "Hey, everybody. Take a seat. The server will be back in a few minutes to get our orders."

They gravitated to the table. Amy was nervous about where she'd sit, not wanting to sit next to a stranger. Hannah grabbed her arm at the table and they sat next to each other. Blake sat on her other side.

A cream colored half-sheet of paper in front of each person was an abbreviated menu with four meat choices, and a selection of salads and vegetables. Amy decided on the chicken Kiev best with rice pilaf.

After the server took their orders, Jarrod retrieved three bottles of wine from the appetizer table, and filled everybody's glasses, then sat down across from her.

During the meal, Amy had pleasant conversations with the people at the table. She didn't contribute much personal information, but it was nice finding out more about the people she worked with. It made her wish even more Hannah would still live nearby.

Amy had cheesecake for dessert, then excused herself to use the restroom. When she returned, Jarrod was pouring another glass of wine at the appetizer table. He stopped her half-way back to her seat. "Do you like it so far at my brother's office?"

"Yes. They're nice people. And the patients are great, too. It's a different atmosphere than I'm used to."

"Where were you before?"

"I was on army bases outside of the country." In the two weeks she'd been in Blake's office, no one had asked her that. Maybe they'd all read her resume.

"You were in the army? How did that happen?"

"I took my nurse's training through the ROTC. A condition to have my schooling paid was to join the army."

"Got to see the world a little, huh?"

She shook her head. "Not really. Most places, it was too dangerous for women to leave the base."

Jarrod's eyebrows dropped. "Where were you?"

"Mostly the Middle East."

He ran a finger down her scar. "Is that where you got this?"

She backed up a step "I was in an explosion." His question didn't bother her as much as the fact he'd touched her. Would he have been so forward with another woman so soon after meeting?

He took a half-step closer. "I bet you haven't been with anyone since it happened."

Her breath stopped in her throat. He implied no one would want to be with someone who looked like her. She didn't know how Harry could have a brother who was so insensitive.

He took another half-step closer. "Come home with me and I can give you what you've been missing."

Anger warred with despair. He figured he could take advantage of her because of her disfigurement, and she should accept him as doing her a favor. Maybe that's all there ever would be. No man able to tolerate her face, but willing to have her body. She didn't want a life like that—fending off sexual advances, but never meeting anyone wanting to get to know her, despite her scars.

Blake rammed his palm into Jarrod's chest, shoving him several feet. "You ass. Apologize and get the hell out of here."

Jarrod's eyes widened, then narrowed. He glanced at Amy. "I'm sorry, Amy. I didn't mean to cause you any distress."

Blake shoved him. "Now leave, and don't expect another invitation."

Jarrod glared. His eyes swept the room then he stalked out the door.

Her hands shook, so she clenched them into fists.

Blake placed a hand on her shoulder. He could probably feel her shake. His voice softened. "Amy, are you all right?"

She stared at a button on his shirt. "I think I should go home."

"Everything will be fine now that he's gone."

"No. I think I should go." She couldn't pretend nothing had happened. Jarrod thought it would be easy to use her with no thought of her feelings. Before her accident, Jeff had used her, too. Only, she hadn't seen it until he dumped her when she really needed his support.

He let out a long breath. "Okay. I'll drive you."

"No—"

"I'm driving. You're obviously upset. I don't want to worry about you making it home all right."

"But my car is here." Sure, she was upset, but it didn't mean she couldn't drive.

"I'll help you pick it up tomorrow."

He wouldn't change his mind, so there was no sense fighting him, and it didn't really matter anyway. Maybe everybody would have been better off if she hadn't survived the blast.

Chapter 5

Blake took shallow breaths, the weight on his chest not allowing anything deeper. If he didn't know better, he'd think he was having a panic attack. He hadn't been able to get Amy to talk to him on the ride home and he didn't know how to help her. She'd mumbled thanks at her door before going inside. Ever since, the weight had worsened the farther he got from her house.

He pushed harder on the accelerator. At least, he thought he did, but his speed didn't increase.

"Screw it." He checked the mirror and made a u-turn, heading back to Amy. Something wasn't right. He sucked in a deep breath. The weight in his chest had disappeared, only to be replaced with a twisting fear. He drove well above the speed limit.

After dropping her off on her doorstep twenty minutes ago, he was back again. He rang the doorbell. A minute dragged by, and a fist grabbed his heart. She couldn't be asleep already. He rang the doorbell and pounded on the door. "Amy, it's Blake." He waited a few seconds and pounded again. "Amy, open up!"

Another half-minute passed before the door swung open, with his fist still in the air. "Thank God."

Her eyelids drooped. Maybe he had wakened her. Her pupils were pinpoints. Not again.

Blake grabbed the tops of her arms. "Amy! What have you done?"

Her head rolled back and her knees gave out. He eased

her to the floor, turned her on her side, and checked her pulse. Slow and weak. He pulled his phone out and dialed.

"Nine-one-one. What's your emergency?"

"This is Dr. Blake Lloyd. I have a possible drug overdose. Female. Twenty-six." He panicked for a moment, not knowing the house number. Amy had pointed out the house when he dropped her off. He stepped onto the porch and found it over the door, then gave it to dispatch with the street. He raced through the house, scanning the kitchen, and peeking into the bedroom. He paused at the bathroom doorway. There. Two prescription bottles sat open on the counter. He snatched them up. Both were empty, with no way to know how much she'd taken. "Positive on the overdose. Ambien and Norco. Hurry!"

He rushed back to Amy, and set the bottles beside her. He checked her pulse and noted the slow, shallow rise of her chest.

Blake hustled to his car and grabbed his medical bag. As he hurried back inside, he found the Naloxone injector to counter the Norco. He squatted beside Amy and jabbed it into her thigh. That was the best he could do until the EMTs arrived. He hoped it was enough to keep her alive until she got to the hospital.

He cupped her cheek. "Stay with me, Amy. You survived a bomb. Don't let an idiot take that away from you. You need to live."

He caught the distant wail of sirens. They'd never sounded so sweet.

"Amy. Hear that? They're coming for you. Hold on. Don't give up. You're not alone."

Red rotating lights bounced off the walls of the room and the sirens silenced. Blake jumped up from the floor and at the doorway, waved his arms over his head. "She's right here."

Two men grabbed equipment and a gurney and ran to the door. Blake stepped aside to let them in. He pointed at the bottles. "She took Ambien and Norco. I don't know how many." He handed over the injector. "I gave her Naloxone a couple of minutes ago."

The nearest paramedic's eyebrows rose.

"I'm a doctor."

"She seemed to know what she was doing. One or the other would have been a whole lot easier to treat than both."

Blake sighed. "She's a nurse. Army nurse."

The man's gaze landed on her scar.

Blake nodded. "Yeah. Bombing at her base hospital." Tonight was the first he'd seen the scar without makeup covering it. His only concern when he'd arrived was saving her life. Now that she was in the paramedics' hands, he studied her face. It was surprising she'd removed the makeup before taking the drugs. He'd almost expect her to want to look her best when her body was found. He shivered at the thought he could have found her body in the morning when he arrived to take her to her car.

The other man fitted Amy with an oxygen mask. He cut the front of her dress open and slapped electrodes on her chest. A slow heart rhythm blipped on the monitor.

It was reassuring to hear Amy's heartbeat, but it was too slow.

The second man picked up a clipboard. "Her name?"

"Amy Stuart. Age twenty-six."

"And you are?"

"Dr. Blake Lloyd."

"Relationship?"

"Employer."

"Emergency contact?"

"None listed on her employment app." At the end of Amy's first day, her paperwork had been filed, but he'd found it and read through it. He'd been saddened that she had no one.

The first paramedic wrapped an elastic around Amy's arm above her elbow and tapped the vein. He pushed an IV needle into place, taped it down and removed the band.

"Ready on three." The men positioned themselves to lift Amy. "One. Two. Three." They effortlessly shifted her to the gurney. "Let's go."

One man wheeled the gurney and the other picked up the equipment.

Blake stood in the doorway. "I'll meet her at the hospital." He needed to find her purse so she could get back in after he locked up. It sat on the coffee table with the keys beside it. He snatched up the keys and his medical bag, heading out the door.

~~~

Blake easily found a space in the sparsely populated parking lot near the emergency entrance. He jogged through the doors and hurried to the triage nurse. "Amy Stuart came in by ambulance. Where is she?"

"Dr. Lloyd? I don't think we called you."

He was in the rotation schedule for emergency orthopedic surgeries. "Amy's a nurse in my office. She doesn't have family."

"But you're not family."

He leaned over the desk. "She just tried to kill herself. Do you think she should have no one with her?"

The nurse bit her lip and stared at him for a few seconds. "She's in exam room three."

He could have walked back there when he arrived, but hadn't known if she'd still be in emergency. He shoved the doors open and headed straight for Amy's room, and stopped in the doorway. Dr. Martina Ruiz and two nurses hovered over Amy, calling out vital signs, and checking IVs as her life blipped on a screen behind them.

Martina stepped back, stripped off her gloves and dropped them in the trash. "Monitor her closely for two hours. If there are no issues, give her a room." She strode halfway to the door and paused. "Blake, what are you doing here? We haven't had any orthopedic emergencies."

His gaze fell on Amy, pale and unmoving. "I'm here for her."

Martina frowned and came closer. "Family?"

He shook his head. "She works for me. I found her. As far as I know, she doesn't have family."

Martina took his arm. "Let's talk in the hallway." Outside the door, she stopped. "She's stable now, but she coded in the ambulance."

He sucked in a breath. She'd died. For a few seconds, or however long it was, she'd gotten her wish. And his heart broke. She'd given so much of herself to so many, it was time others gave to her and helped her heal.

He stiffened his back. "What happens after this?"

"We'll try to find her a bed on the psych floor, but it's crowded. We might have to put her in a regular room and release her in a couple days."

"You can't do that. She needs help. She's a veteran."

Martina's eyebrows rose. "She is? Then we have more options for her. Let me see what I can do."

Blake rubbed the back of his neck. "What's the best option for her?"

"Daily therapy sessions. Maybe more than once a day at first." She shook her head. "I'm not a psychiatrist."

He extracted a business card, and wrote his cell number on the back. "Call me when you've worked out something."

She slipped the card into her pocket. "I won't be able to

reach anyone 'til morning. Oh, tomorrow's Saturday. It might not be until Monday."

"All right. Can I talk to her for a minute?"

"She—" Martina patted his arm. "Sure."

Slow steps took him to the bed, his gaze never wavering from her face. Now, she appeared to be sleeping, and not…almost dead. The profile that faced him was beautiful. He circled to Amy's other side and caressed the scars on her cheek and neck. Despite the scars, he still found her attractive, although she didn't believe that. How many others had hurt her the way Jarrod had?

Blake covered Amy's hand with his and squeezed. "I'm here for you, Amy. You're not alone anymore. Do what you need to do to get better. I'm leaving now, but I'll see you in the morning."

He hoped his words had seeped deep inside to be a balm on her heart.

Chapter 6

Blake woke and stretched. Seven-thirty. He never slept that late, but with the late night at the hospital and not being able to sleep because of his worry, he'd had too few hours of quality shut-eye. A quick shower gave him more energy. He dressed in jeans and sat on the edge of the bed. In the wee hours, he'd made several decisions.

Number one. Check up on Amy. He called the main switchboard to find out if she'd been put into a room.

"Northwest Hospital. May I help you?"

He'd flaunt his doctor status to get information he might not otherwise be able to. "Yes. This is Dr. Lloyd. Is this Miriam?"

"Yes, Dr. Lloyd. How are you?" It paid to be friendly with the hospital staff. He'd never understood the doctors, usually surgeons, who acted better than everyone else.

For once, he wished he didn't have to go through the small talk routine, but he did it. "I'm calling to find out if Amy Stuart has been put in a room."

"Is that S-T-E—"

"S-T-U-A-R-T."

Five seconds ticked by. "Ah. Here she is. Room four-thirteen. That's not your normal floor."

Surgical was on the floor above. And psych was on the sixth floor. They hadn't found a place for her there. "No. She's not one of my patients, but an employee. Can you put me through to the desk on that floor?"

"No problem."

"Thanks, Miriam."

He waited a few seconds. "Fourth Floor station."

"This is Dr. Blake Lloyd. I'm calling for status of Amy Stuart in four-thirteen."

"Dr. Lloyd. Let me check. She was awake on the last rounds. Her vitals are within normal range."

"Do you know if she's going to be moved?"

"Hmm. There's nothing on her chart about it."

"Okay. Thanks." He ended the call.

Number two, Hannah. He dialed her number.

"Blake? You know yesterday was my last day. Do you miss me already?"

He squeezed circles into his temples between his thumb and ring finger. "I hope you can come back for a week or so."

"What? Why? Is there something wrong with Amy?"

He'd already decided he needed to be honest with her. "Amy tried to commit suicide last night."

Hannah gasped. "Is she—"

"She was awake this morning. I'm going to see her in a little while."

"Which hospital?"

"Northwest. I called to ask if you'd stay on for a week or two."

"I wish I could, but our apartment is all packed up, and we gave our notice. The movers are going to be here any minute."

He rubbed his neck. She hadn't said no. "You can stay with me. You have your pick of three guest rooms."

"Antoine and I are supposed to drive our cars down there together. I don't want to drive all that way on my own."

Blake sighed, and closed his eyes, tipping his head back. There had to be a way. "How about this? When it's time for you to leave, I'll pay to transport your car to your new home and you can fly. I'll even drive you to the airport."

"Well…The first two weeks, I'm going to be stuck in a hotel room. Let me call you back in a few minutes, after I talk to Antoine."

"Thanks for considering this." He lay back on the bed. One of his other goals, he had no idea how to go about.

A few minutes later, Hannah called and he rolled on his side and answered. "Please say yes."

"Yes, I'll do it."

He relaxed a bit. One hurdle taken care of. "Thank you. Now, one more thing. I think Amy would feel better about herself if she got lessons from a makeup specialist, or whatever they're called. Do you know how I can find someone?"

"That's a wonderful idea. I thought she was being too heavy-handed with her makeup, but I didn't know how to tell her. I know someone who does makeup for weddings. I'll ask if she can do it or knows someone who can."

"That sounds great."

"How are you going to convince her?"

He puffed out a breath. "I thought I'd route it through her psychiatrist. See if we could make it part of her healing experience."

"That should work. I'm glad you're trying so hard to help her. Amy deserves it."

"She does. Thanks again, Hannah."

Number three. Harry. He glanced at the clock as he dialed. A little after eight. Harry should be awake.

"I hope you have a good reason to call so early on a Saturday." He didn't sound sleepy, but they were both used to snapping awake for emergency calls.

"Did I wake you?"

"No, but—never mind. What do you want?"

"First off, Hannah is going to stick around for a week or

two while Amy recovers."

"Recovers from what?"

Blake hated for so many people to know about this. "A suicide attempt."

"What? Maybe we should run through those resumes again."

"No! She's going to be fine. And this wouldn't have happened without your jerk brother."

"Surely, Jarrod didn't do this."

Blake sighed. "I can't believe you didn't hear him. He basically told her that with her scars he'd be the only one willing to have sex with her and she should go home with him."

Harry swore. He almost never did. "You're right. My brother's a jerk. Where is she now?"

"At Northwest, waiting for a bed on the psych floor. I'm going over there shortly to make sure she gets what she needs."

"Sounds like you have everything under control."

Blake let out a breath. "One more thing. Jarrod is no longer welcome at any of our staff get-togethers."

"Agreed. I'll let him know. After I chew him out."

"Good."

"Keep me updated."

"Will do. See you Monday."

~~~

Blake stepped out of the elevator on the fourth floor of Northwest Hospital. He hoped to slip past the nurses station without being noticed.

"Dr. Blake?"

He rested his arms on the counter. "Jenny, what are you doing here?" He was used to seeing her on the surgical floor.

"I pick up extra hours on the other floors on weekends. What are you doing here?"

"I'm visiting a patient. One of my employees."

"Which one?"

"Amy Stuart in room four-thirteen."

Her eyes widened, and she leaned closer, whispering. "She's on suicide watch."

"I know. I called it in. She's going to be okay. She's got people in her corner now."

Blake strolled down the hall. The layout was the same from floor to floor, so he knew about where the room would be. He paused beside the open door when two female voices reached him.

Hannah. "You were there one minute and gone the next. I didn't realize anything had happened."

"I'm sorry I ruined your evening. It's just that Jarrod…"

A chair squeaked. "You didn't ruin it. What about Jarrod. He tends to drink too much, but I've never known him to step over the line."

Amy sighed. "That's because you're pretty and have a nice husband."

Blake suppressed the guilt of listening to their private conversation, hoping he might learn something more about why Jarrod's twisted advance had affected Amy so badly.

"You're pretty, too."

He could imagine Amy covering her cheek.

"Maybe once, but not anymore."

"You are. What did Jarrod say to you?"

The silence lengthened to the point she probably wouldn't answer. "He suggested I hadn't had sex since my injuries, and he could make up for it if I went home with him."

Clothing rustled and Blake wondered if Hannah gave Amy a hug. It would be just like her.

"He's an idiot. You shouldn't have listened to him."

A sob escape from Amy. "But it's true. My boyfriend. We always talked about the future. He didn't propose to me, but he made it clear that once I finished my enlistment, we'd be together. I got back, and he took one look at my face and told me a man in his position couldn't have a wife who looked like me."

Blake seethed. This man, whoever he was, had Jarrod beat by a long shot in the callus department. No wonder Amy's appearance bothered her so much. She thought she'd come home to a man who would gather her up and care for her. Instead, he tore her heart out.

He waited a couple of minutes as the two women whispered to each other. He assumed Hannah was consoling Amy. Then he knocked on the doorframe, and took a step into the room.

"Hey, you two. I didn't expect to see you here, Hannah. I figured you'd be overseeing the loading of your furniture."

"Antoine can handle that. I wanted to make sure Amy was okay."

He gazed at Hannah. "You told her you're covering next week?"

Amy grasped Hannah's hand. "She told me. And thank you, both of you. Hannah, I'm sorry I messed up your plans."

Hannah waved a hand. "Hey, Antoine will be working. I'd have to laze beside the pool and be bored within hours." She grinned. "And this extra week of unexpected pay will buy the patio furniture Antoine said I couldn't get. So, it's a win."

Blake chuckled. Hannah was good at finding the right thing to say.

Hannah leaned over Amy and gave her a hug. "I've got to get back to make sure the movers load everything. I'll come see you in a couple days." She wagged a finger at

Amy. "And don't forget. There are people who care about you."

Amy grabbed her hand. "Thanks for coming."

Hannah gripped Blake's shoulder. "See you later, Blake."

He had a feeling she read deep into his soul. Now he was alone with Amy, self-consciousness kicked in. He patted her arm. "How are you feeling?"

She stared down at her twisting hands. "Foolish." Her gaze snapped up and met his eyes. "You saved my life. How did you even know?"

He sat down so he wouldn't tower over her. "I don't know. Gut instinct? I felt better the moment I turned around and went back for you."

She bit her lip. "I talked to a psychologist during breakfast. She suggested I didn't really want to die because I answered the door when you knocked."

He held back a chuckle. "You probably answered in self-defense. If you hadn't answered, I would have broken it down. I wasn't leaving without making sure you were all right." He wrapped his hand around hers, the damaged one. "I was sure you needed help."

Amy stared at their joined hands. "I thought I was totally alone. Then Jarrod reinforced what my ex said...about how ugly I am."

He tightened his fingers around hers, anger rising up over the pain these men had inflicted on a woman already suffering. "You are not ugly. You're still beautiful."

She sighed. "You just don't want me to...hurt myself again."

He sat on the edge of the bed and cupped her unscarred cheek. "It's true I don't want you to harm yourself, but you're beautiful inside and out."

He took her hand again. "I like seeing your face,

searching for that rare sparkle in your eyes when you're enjoying yourself. I'm going to make sure I see more of it."

She gazed over his shoulder. "It's hard to feel sparkly when I'm tired most of the time. I'm afraid to fall asleep because I don't want the...nightmares to come. The sleeping pills help keep them away, or drug me enough I don't remember I've had them."

He wasn't surprised there was more to her suffering. "What are your nightmares?"

Amy closed her eyes. "I'm trapped in the rubble after the explosion, but in the dream, they don't find me. My face hurts." She lifted her hand with the missing fingertips. "My hand hurts. My throat is sore from screaming for help." Tears track down her cheeks. "The pain gets worse as the days go by...until I don't exist anymore."

"They found you. You do exist. You were meant to live. Don't throw that away." He couldn't imagine the physical and mental pain she'd gone through, but he wanted to help her get strong again.

She blinked and he held the tissue box from the rolling table out to her. She snatched one and wiped her cheeks. Her composure returned.

"I don't know if it will help, but if you ever want to talk about it, you can tell me what really happened that day." He wasn't a psychologist, but guessed if she talked through the actual events a few times, the nightmares wouldn't have as strong a hold on her. Maybe he shouldn't have asked. It would be best handled by professionals.

Amy looked anywhere, but at him. "It started like any other day. I made rounds, taking the patients' vitals. One asked for an extra blanket. I had two patients left to check, so I finished with them and went to the supply closet. That's when the bomb struck."

She closed her eyes. Blake wished he knew what

emotions ran through her at that moment. Fear. Worry.

"I think an oxygen tank was hit by shrapnel. Flame flew out and I threw my arm up to shield my face. Not well enough. Good thing the air conditioning was overworking that day since it forced me to wear a sweater or it would have been worse. Then the ceiling fell on me, putting out the fire. Yay me."

"So, the ceiling coming down was a good thing?"

She shrugged. "I guess. The burn was a whole lot more painful than the smashed fingers from a stud landing on them."

"Were you conscious the whole time?" Blake figured he would have developed a case of claustrophobia if it had happened to him.

She shook her head. "I came to, curled up on the floor with my arm still over my head, and a heavy weight on top of me. The first thing I did was yell for help."

"I can see why you have nightmares."

"I knew I couldn't constantly scream or I'd lose my voice before they got close, so I did it in short bursts. Then I found I could move one foot and I kicked out to try to make noise. Soft soled shoes aren't good at making noise, and I was afraid I'd kick out a support and more rubble would tumble down on me, so I stopped."

Blake was sorry he'd asked her about it when more tears streamed down her face. She'd been through so much, and the bombing was only half the trauma. People's reactions were the other. He snatched a tissue and dabbed her cheeks. "You got through it. You didn't lose your composure. You assessed your situation and did the best you could."

"I was in the right place. Most of the ones who survived were in a bathroom, or dove under a bed or desk. Three co-workers and twenty-eight patients weren't as lucky, including the one who asked for a blanket."

He brushed her hair behind her ear. He wanted to wrap her into his arms and take away all the bad memories. "That man saved your life. If he knows, I'm sure he's overjoyed he did one last thing to save another person."

"I never thought of it like that. My thoughts were more along the lines of 'why did I survive when all those fine people didn't?'"

"You were meant to live. You're a wonderful person and you do good things for others."

Her eyes drooped. Telling him her ordeal seemed to have sapped her strength.

Blake stood. "I'll let you get some rest. You've had a difficult time. I'll come back and see you tomorrow."

"I don't want to ruin your whole weekend."

"It's my choice what I do with my weekend, and I choose to spend some of it with you." He kissed her forehead. "Take care, Amy."

Her eyes closed.

"Have pleasant dreams today," he whispered.

Chapter 7

This place was driving her crazy. Amy whipped her head around, hoping she hadn't said that out loud. The psych floor was not the place to tell anyone she was insane. It was bad enough all the staff had been told she'd tried to kill herself.

She wore sweat pants and a sweatshirt like all the other patients. At least, they were warm and not revealing like the hospital gown she'd worn on the other floor. She wasn't confined to her room, but there wasn't much to do between sessions. Watch inane daytime TV or read. Their library was well stocked, probably from books left behind by patients, but she couldn't concentrate to read.

She'd been transferred to the floor on Monday morning and for three days had two psych sessions a day. A private session then a group session with four other vets.

Going into a group session had scared her. She didn't want to tell other people her private fears or draw even more attention to her scars. Before attending, she hadn't known that the other patients would be vets. One man's face had a scar from the middle of his eyebrow to the corner of his mouth as if he'd been slashed with a knife. Another was missing more fingers than her. And a third had a prosthetic arm with a metal grip. All, including her, had emotional injuries. She had never thought emotional troubles—being afraid to sleep because of nightmares, or the fear of entering the base hospitals, or the misery of seeing others' reactions to her scars—as injuries to be healed from. Accepting them as such gave her hope she could recover emotionally.

"Amy!" The feminine voice from across the room made her jump.

"Hannah." Amy hurried to her friend.

Hannah hugged her and stepped back. "You look more like yourself now than when I saw you last time."

Amy bit her lip. "Yeah. I was kind of out of it for a while. Come to my room." She'd made her bed when she got up, so she climbed on it and sat cross-legged. It surprised her when Hannah did the same rather than sit in the chair beside the bed. Like two teenagers about to gossip.

Amy racked her brain for something to talk about. She'd never been one for small talk. "How's Antoine?"

Hannah smiled. "He's settled into the hotel and started his job yesterday. He already complained about some things he wished he hadn't put into storage."

"I'm sorry I took you away from him."

Hannah waved a hand. "I'm keeping busy. I would have been bored silly if I'd had two weeks to sit by the pool, reading. It's not like a vacation where Antoine and I can find fun things to do." She took Amy's hand. "So, how are you, really?"

Amy drew in a long breath and let it out. "I'm good. Better than before this happened. Understanding that what I'm feeling isn't unique makes it easier to cope. Even the guy in my group is having a hard time dealing with the scars on his face, so it's not just a girl thing."

"I hardly notice it anymore." Hannah leaned forward, as if telling a secret. "Blake is back to his old ways."

Amy narrowed her eyes. "What old ways?"

Hannah grinned. "He's eating lunch in his office again."

"But he always ate lunch with us."

"No." Hannah pointed at Amy. "He always ate lunch with you. Before you started working here, he ate in his office."

"Oh." Her cheeks grew warm and she again felt like a teenager talking about crushes. "I didn't want to think of him like that because…" She touched her cheek.

Hannah rolled her eyes. "See? It doesn't bother people. It's just the initial surprise. That's all."

"Maybe."

"Not maybe. Besides, Blake took you home after that lout, Jarrod, insulted you. He could have let you leave the way you wanted to. And then he had a feeling something was really wrong and went back to check on you."

Amy tucked her lips in and blinked back tears. "I don't know how he figured it out. I can't believe he saved my life twice."

Hannah's eyes widened. "Twice?"

"The day he hired me. We ran into each other, literally. I was crying because I'd been rejected at another job interview. He calmed me down and asked to see my resume. If he'd brushed past me with an 'excuse me', I would have gone home and…" She didn't have to finish.

Hannah's mouth opened and closed a few times. "You must have a guardian angel." She slapped Amy's knee. "See? You're supposed to be here. It wasn't some fluke you survived what happened to you."

Peace settled into Amy's chest. She hadn't thought of her life like that. She'd survived when so many others hadn't, and she'd been all too willing to throw away the gift. She lunged and wrapped her arms around Hannah. "Thank you."

Hannah laughed. "You're welcome. Now I better get going." She scrambled off the bed and winked. "Blake promised to cook me dinner. The things he'll do for you."

Amy got to her feet. "How is cooking for you something Blake's doing for me?"

"It was one of the inducements to get me to stay so you had time to recover. I'm also staying in his guest room since

I'm currently homeless."

"Is that awkward?"

"Nah. After dinner, I tell Blake I'm going to my room to call Antoine, and I don't come back out until morning." She squeezed Amy's hand. "I'll see you in a couple days. They're springing you on Saturday, so I'm flying out that morning."

"How do you know I'm leaving Saturday? I don't even know."

"Blake has his ways. Take care, Amy."

"Bye, Hannah." She sat back on the bed and pulled her knees up under her chin. It was amazing how many twists and turns a life could take. Three weeks ago she'd been totally alone and as if she was buried again. Now, she had so much to live for.

~~~

Blake rushed through the office door and back to the break room, a sack lunch in hand. Surgery had taken longer than expected, then he had to visit two other surgical patients. Normally, when running late, he would have eaten in the car after picking up a sandwich in the hospital cafeteria, but he wanted to have lunch with Amy on her first day back.

He stopped in the doorway as Amy turned around with a cup of tea in one hand and a brown bag in the other. She hadn't eaten yet. He strode to the table and set his lunch down. "Hi. Is everything going okay today?"

He selected a k-cup and plopped it into the coffee machine.

"It's been good. Thank you for holding the job open for me."

He shrugged. "It was only a week. No way I could have a replacement for you so fast."

"I know, but I've only worked two weeks."

It was more awkward between them than it had ever been. Their conversations at the hospital when he'd stopped to visit for fifteen or so minutes several times the week before had been easy going and carefree. Now, an invisible barrier separated them.

Blake sat across from her.

Amy emptied her bag of a sandwich and apple. "I suppose I have you to thank for emptying my refrigerator of perishables and restocking. I expected the stench to knock me down when I opened it. I owe you so much." Tears glistened and she blinked.

He dropped his eyes to his food and unwrapped his sandwich, giving her a chance to recover. She didn't mention her car, but Hannah must have told Amy they'd collected it and taken it to her house together.

"You mean a lot to me." He gazed into her eyes. She'd recovered. Surreptitiously, he checked out her scar. It was much less noticeable. The makeup artist had done a good job teaching Amy how to use makeup to hide it, but not overwhelm her face color. He was sure that would give her confidence a boost.

He took a sip of coffee. "I—my sister tried to commit suicide when she was a teenager."

Her eyes widened. "Blake, I'm so sorry. And I brought all those memories back with my—stunt."

"It did remind me. Brandy's a year-and-a-half older than me." His lips twitched into a semi-smile. "She liked remind me of that when we were growing up. One evening, our parents were out. David and I were spending the night at different friends' houses. Brandy was home alone."

Amy stared at him with rapt attention, her hands on the table, one covering the other.

"I had an argument with my friend and ran back home. It was around nine o'clock and I was all worked up, so I figured I'd talk to Brandy."

Amy took his hand across the table. "You found her?"

He nodded. The memory of his sister lying so still on her bed was as clear as if it had happened the day before.

"I'm sorry I put you through the same nightmare."

He clasped her hand. A living, breathing Amy. "She didn't answer when I knocked on the door, so I figured I'd peek in to see if she was asleep or just not responding. She lay on her back with her arms above the blankets and her fingers laced together. Something was weird about it. Then I saw the prescription bottle beside the bed. She had taken all my Mom's sleeping pills."

Amy squeezed his hand, and he glanced up at her. Tears shimmered in her eyes, and he had to look away, being too close to tears himself. He had cried that night.

"I yelled at her, but she didn't wake up, so I grabbed the phone beside her bed and called nine-one-one. I was too afraid to touch her to see if she was still alive. I wouldn't have known what to do, anyway."

"How old were you?"

"Fourteen."

"I can't imagine going through that at fourteen."

"It was rough. I had nightmares. Turned out, she was pregnant and her boyfriend had broken up with her. She lost the baby, but she survived."

Amy gave him a small smile. "Because of you. You're good at turning up at the right moment."

He shrugged. "We're closer since that night. Now, she's happily married with two kids and she's a nurse."

She grinned. "But not your nurse."

He returned the smile. This part was so much better than remembering that horrid night. "She works in a psych ward specifically for children and teens."

"That sounds perfect."

"It is. Now, we better finish eating and get back to work."

"Yes, boss."

Chapter 8

Amy stood in the doorway of the waiting room on her fourth day back to work and glanced at her tablet. "Keith Baker?"

A blond man, age thirty, crossed the room on crutches. He moved faster than most patients on two legs and stopped in front of Amy with a grin. "Hi, there. You know my name. What's yours?"

"Amy."

He leaned closer. "Did anyone ever tell you your eyes are the color of whiskey?"

"No. I hope you don't get drunk staring at me."

He chuckled and she turned her back. "This way." In base hospitals, patients flirted with her all the time, but she never let it get too far since she had a boyfriend. This was the first time since the explosion anyone had tried it and she wasn't sure why Keith made the effort.

Amy entered an exam room. "Hop up on the table and I'll get your vitals." Keith leaned his crutches against the exam table and hefted himself up. First she lightly grasped his wrist and stared at her watch. She always folded her fingers under so people wouldn't stare at her missing fingertips. She recorded his pulse and grabbed the blood pressure cuff, wrapping it around his arm and inflating it.

He didn't take his eyes off her. "It might be a little high."

She put the stethoscope on his inside elbow. "It will be if you keep talking."

"No. I think it will be because of those whiskey eyes."

She didn't know how to respond, so didn't. She noted the numbers on her tablet, which weren't too high, and put away the cuff. "Have you had any problems since you got out of the hospital?"

"Nothing major. Pain at first, but now that's minimal." He wrapped a hand around her left one and lifted it. "What about you? Was your recovery rough?"

She hadn't expected to get the tables turned on her by a patient. "It had its moments."

The door opened and Blake glared. "Is there something I should know?"

Amy snatched her hand back, and her cheeks warmed. This was the first time Blake had entered an exam room before she'd completed her check-in and left. Now, the two men seemed to be sending each other silent messages, and she didn't want any part of it.

"He's all yours, Dr. Lloyd." As Amy stepped past Blake, his arm blocked the doorway. She tipped up her head and raised her eyebrows.

He kissed her. His lips were gone before she had a chance to register what happened. She'd be glued to the spot, except he nudged her and closed the door between them.

She touched her lips. Maybe she imagined it. Nope. She could still feel the tingle and wished the kiss had lasted longer. But not in front of a patient. She shook her head. It had been some kind of warning to Keith to stay away, as if Blake was staking a prior claim.

A deep breath calmed her and she headed to the reception area.

Miranda typed on the computer as she spoke. "We have one—" A glance at Amy must have revealed something. "Are you all right? You're not getting sick again, are you?"

Miranda had been told Amy was out sick, which she

appreciated.

"I, yeah, I'm okay."

Miranda stood and took Amy's arm. "Are you sure? You look a little shell shocked." Her eyes widened. "Sorry. Did something happen?"

Amy nodded. "Blake...kissed me. In front of a patient."

Miranda's mouth dropped open, then snapped shut. "Was it..." She glanced at her computer screen. "Keith Baker?"

"Yes. How'd you know?"

Miranda giggled. "I overheard him flirting with you. Maybe Blake did, too, and was warning him off."

Maybe it only meant Blake suspected Keith was bad news for her and it was the best way to keep him away. She'd been half-heartedly thinking of Blake as someone she'd like to date ever since Hannah had told her about him eating lunch with her, but that short kiss had launched her over the edge. She wanted to spend time outside the office with him, hold hands, feel free to hug him, have more kisses. Lots of kisses.

Miranda leaned against the wall and crossed her arms. "You know, Blake used to have this girlfriend. She could have been a model. Hannah and I hated her, and were glad when it only lasted a couple of months."

Amy frowned. "This is supposed to make me feel better?"

"Sure. This woman stopped in occasionally and she'd try to kiss Blake on the cheek in front of us, and he always squirmed out of it."

"Your point?"

Miranda grinned. "I'm pretty sure every male patient in the office could have come on to her and Blake wouldn't have reacted. But you"—she pointed at Amy—"got him to defend you in the best way. Are you upset?"

Amy shook her head. "No. Just confused."

Miranda returned to her seat. "I suggest you talk to him about it after the patients are gone. I'm meeting Zach as soon as the office clears out, so you'll have him to yourself."

Amy wasn't sure she was ready to have him to herself.

~~~

Blake dropped into his chair and rubbed his eyes. He'd avoided Amy after his show of macho, not wanting to explain in the short space of time between patients. He'd overheard Keith Baker coming onto Amy and it had angered him. Then he'd walked into the exam room and found Keith holding her hand, and he'd lost it.

In the hospital, after the man's emergency surgery, he'd flirted with every pretty woman in sight. Amy didn't deserve to be hurt by a man like that, so without thinking it through, Blake had warned Keith off by kissing Amy.

He hadn't seen her since he'd taken the liberty and wasn't sure how she'd reacted to it. Any minute, he'd have to deal with her response.

Amy waltzed through the door, leaned back against the doorframe and crossed her arms. "What was that about?"

He laced his hands on the back of his head and tipped his chair back. "What was what about?"

She straightened away from the doorway. "You know what I'm talking about. That kiss in front of a patient."

He was relieved she wasn't screaming harassment. "That man flirts with every pretty woman in sight. I was getting him off your tail."

Her eyebrows spiked up. "Seriously? You used our first kiss to warn him off?"

Blake grinned and stood, stalking her in slow, deliberate steps.

Amy stepped back and her spine hit the wall. "What are you doing?"

He waited until he was inches from her before speaking. "You said, 'our first kiss', which means there's going to be a second kiss." He demonstrated. "And a third." He kissed her again. He pulled back and studied her face. She didn't appear upset or push him away. He purposely hadn't given her enough time to respond to the kisses. "And a fourth."

His kiss this time was going to last a good long while. Her arms wrapped around his neck. He wanted her hair down so he could run his fingers through it like he'd craved to do ever since she'd had it down at the dinner. He fumbled with pins, not caring where they dropped, then tunneled his fingers into her hair with one hand while pulling her closer with the other.

This was exactly where she should be. There'd been a connection between them from the start. He wouldn't have hired her if she hadn't been qualified, but would still have convinced her to go out with him.

He drew back. Before the day started, his intent was to have a few more lunches with Amy before asking her out. And now because of that player, Keith, he'd tipped his hand by kissing her. "I want to take you out."

Her eyes widened. He wasn't ready for her to say no, so he kissed her again. Her fingertips ran up the nape of his neck, and he moaned, deepening the kiss. He feathered kisses along her jaw.

Her whisper tickled his ear. "Okay."

He leaned back to see her face and wondered if his expression was as dazed as hers. "Okay?"

"I'll go out with you."

He grinned. "Wear a pretty dress. I'll pick you up at six-fifteen tomorrow night."

Chapter 9

Amy inspected her face in her bathroom mirror. She touched up her makeup. The makeup artist her psychologist had set her up with had worked wonders. Amy had been using the wrong kind and applying it incorrectly. She still didn't have the face she used to, but her scar wouldn't be the first thing people noticed. She hoped.

Her dress hung on the back of the bathroom door. She'd picked it out after getting home the night before. More than a year ago, she'd worn it to a less than memorable party when Jeff's firm had won a big case. She did remember some appreciative ogling from the partners that Jeff preened over. She didn't care anymore. There was more to her than the surface, and that's all Jeff had seen.

She slipped the dress over her head and zipped up the back. It fit a bit looser than the last time she'd worn it. She liked the way the sapphire blue made her hair look darker and shinier. Leaving it up gave her a more sophisticated air, but she remembering how Blake had plucked out the pins when they kissed. She fished out the pins and brushed her hair to silky softness.

Amy spun and peered at her back in the mirror. The dress smoothed across her back, from the boat neck to her waist, then flared out over her hips. Except for her injuries, she looked good. She touched her neck and wondered if Blake would kiss her there.

She flipped off the light and grabbed her two inch strappy shoes and small clutch from her bed, and hurried into the living room. She hadn't been this excited about a date since forever.

Amy had gotten one shoe strapped on when the doorbell rang. She didn't want Blake to worry if she didn't answer immediately, so she hobbled to the door, the other shoe in hand. She swung the door open.

Blake's eyes widened as his gaze traveled from her head to her toes and back to her face. "Wow! You are gorgeous." He flung his hand forward, a bouquet of daisies in his fist.

She grinned and took them. "I love daisies."

"I kind of thought you did since you sometimes have artificial daises in your hair."

She dropped her shoe. "You noticed? Come on in while I put these in water." She hobbled into the kitchen and found a vase under the sink. "

Amy worked on the flowers as she talked. "Sorry, I wasn't quite ready when you rang. I didn't want to keep you waiting."

"I could have waited."

She stared him in the eye. "The last time I didn't answer quickly enough you pounded on the door."

He sucked in a breath. "I—ah—might have done it again."

She took his hand. "Thank you for caring." But she wanted him to care because he liked her and not as a way to look out for her. Would she be able to tell?

He kissed her cheek, not the scarred one. "I more than care. Now, let's go eat."

Amy buckled her shoe on and picked up her purse. They headed outside. She liked how Blake opened the car door and made sure she was all set before closing it. Jeff had never done that, but probably few men did.

Fifteen minutes later, Blake parked in front of *Crete Street Restaurant*.

"I've never been here. Is it good?" Jeff had liked taking her to expensive stuffy restaurants. He almost always found some lawyer or judge to stop and talk to for a moment.

Blake turned off the car. "It's one of my favorite restaurants."

He ushered her inside, and gave the pretty teenage hostess a hug. "Hi, Mara."

Mara squealed in his ear. "I was so excited when I saw your name on the reservation list. Let me tell Mama you're here."

Blake grabbed Mara's hand before she got too far away. "Wait. Can you show us to our table first?"

"Oh, yeah. Okay." She picked up menus and led them to a table in a corner, then dropped them on the place settings. "I'll be right back."

Blake chuckled as he held a chair for Amy.

Amy grinned. "You're not a stranger here."

"No. My best friend in high school, and college roommate, is Mara's brother. I worked weekends and a few summers here."

An older woman, her dark hair pinned up, hurried across the floor, her arms extended. A smile brightened her face. She wore a simple black dress with a white apron over it. "Blake. It's been months."

He stepped around the table and let the woman give him a bear hug. "Lena, it's good to see you."

The woman was an older version of her daughter, and still had an attractive figure. "Who have you brought to us?"

He stepped back with an arm around Lena. "Lena Danielos, this is my friend, Amy Stuart."

The woman stepped forward and leaned down, giving Amy a hug. "It's nice meeting you."

"You, too." Amy was overwhelmed with the love lavished on her just because she came in with Blake. She wondered if all his dates got this treatment.

Lena patted Amy's shoulder. "Pick out your food. Tomas will be out when he has a break."

Blake sat and picked up his menu and flipped it open.

Amy picked her menu up, but didn't open it. "Who's Tomas? Was he your roommate?"

"No. That's Tom. Tomas is his father."

She leaned closer and whispered. "I can see why you bring your dates here. It makes you look important."

He stole a kiss. "I only brought one other woman here, and it was a mistake. She was a mistake. Coming here is sort of like taking your girl to meet your parents."

Her eyes widened and she sat back. He didn't take his gaze off her as she assimilated what he'd told her. They'd known each other for all of a month, but she couldn't deny there was something between them. Something she wanted to grow.

A man about Lena's age barreled toward them. He had dark, curly hair with wisps of gray at the temples, and broad shoulders. "Blake, my son."

Blake stood. The man was nearly as tall as him. Tomas hugged him and pounded on his back.

Blake stepped away. "Tomas. It's good to see you. I want you to meet Amy." He took her hand and pulled her to her feet.

She found herself enveloped in the big man's arms. This was not at all what she expected the evening to be like, but it was nice to feel all this love from these people purely by association with Blake.

Tomas grasped her arms. "Anyone special to Blake is special to us." He glanced at Blake. "I'll make your favorite. And I'll have Trisha bring over wine." He patted Blake's shoulder. "Come see us Saturday before we open. Tom will be here for the weekend."

"I will, Tomas. Sorry it's been so long."

Amy and Blake resumed their seats. "Tom doesn't live around here?" Amy asked.

"No. He's got a family practice a couple of hours away."

A woman arrived with a bottle of wine and two glasses. "Good evening, Dr. Lloyd."

"Hi, Trisha."

Trisha expertly opened the bottle and poured wine into beautiful fluted glasses. She snatched up their menus. "I'll bring your salads now."

Blake lifted his glass. "Thank you."

Amy hadn't opened her menu and hoped she liked Blake's favorite. She picked up her glass and sipped the wine. It was among the best she'd had, considering all the expensive wines Jeff's law firm always served at their events.

Trisha returned and set mint scented salads in front of them. "Enjoy. Tomas is already putting together your meal." She hurried away.

"Maybe I should have taken you someplace anonymous," Blake said.

She stabbed her salad with her fork. "No. It's nice seeing how much these people love you. Do your parents live nearby?" The flavor of mint and whatever else was in the dressing exploded on her tongue. "This is the best salad ever!"

Blake chuckled. "It is good. My parents moved to Florida two years ago."

"Was that rough?"

He dug into his own salad. "Not really. I'm busy. They're busy. But I'm glad Brandy wasn't the one who moved away. We try to get together once a month or so. I want to watch my niece and nephew grow up. What about you?"

She shook her head. He'd probably read her new hire

forms that showed no emergency contacts. "Nobody anywhere. My dad died when I was ten, and Mom died when I was in high school." The concern on his face touched her. "My grandmother took me in, but she died just before I shipped out. If it wasn't for her, I wouldn't have been able to become a nurse. There wasn't money for college, but she set up an appointment with my high school counselor and we all discussed how I was going to get my nurse's training. That's how I ended up in ROTC."

Blake grimaced. "I'm still paying off school loans. Your grandmother sounded like a real go getter."

"She pushed me to excel more than my parents had."

Trisha appeared with two sizzling plates. "I've got your shish kebobs and pilaf."

Amy was surprised she'd eaten most of her salad. She snatched the last Greek olive with her fingers and plopped it into her mouth before moving the bowl out of the way, catching Blake's gaze lingering on her lips. Trisha set the plates in front of them and disappeared.

The aroma made Amy hungry all over again. "This smells heavenly." She'd never eaten kebobs before.

Blake picked up his fork and a skewer and pushed the peppers, onions and lamb onto his plate.

She copied him and cut a piece of meat, taking it into her mouth. "Hmm. It tastes even better than it smells."

He lifted his fork with a chunk of lamb on it. "And this is the secondary reason I come here."

The family left them alone while they ate and Amy got to learn more about Blake. Short office lunches weren't conducive to long, rambling conversations. Tonight, he'd drawn stories out of her of her happy childhood, a nice reminder of how ordinary and blessed her life was long ago.

Amy pushed her plate away. "I ate way too much. Best food I've had in a long time."

Tomas sat down across from her. "Thank you. I'm glad you enjoyed it." His gaze swung to Blake. "So, we'll see you Saturday morning?"

"Yes. I'm looking forward to it."

He glanced at her. "Bring Amy. I'm sure she'll enjoy Allie's company."

Maybe Blake had wanted to catch up with his friend alone, and now he'd been almost forced into including her. "No. I don't want to—"

Blake snagged her gaze with his and held it. "Please come. I think you'll enjoy Tom's wife, Allie."

Even with the push from Tomas, it seemed to be a heartfelt request. "That's quite the technique to get me to go on a second date."

Tomas gasped. "This is your first date? Why didn't you say something? We would have left you alone."

Blake took her hand above the table. "It doesn't feel like a first date. We've been having lunch together for weeks."

She'd agree with that. They'd been on ten mini-dates, many of them chaperoned by Hannah. "You really want me to come?"

"Yes."

It wouldn't really be a date. It was more like doing something with his family. Almost too personal. But he seemed earnest in his appeal. "Okay. I'll come."

"Good." Blake stood, dropped a handful of money on the table. "Thanks for the great dinner, Tomas."

Tomas picked the money up and held it out to Blake. "You know I can't take this."

"And I can't have my first date with Amy look like a cheap date, so keep it." He patted the older man on the shoulder as he walked past, with Amy trailing behind.

"It was nice meeting you, Tomas." Amy kept her hands at her sides so he wouldn't try to give her Blake's money.

Once she passed the older man, Blake took her hand. The left one. He didn't seem to mind touching the abbreviated fingers. "He does that every time. I have to bring cash because nobody will run my credit card."

"I think it's sweet they think of you as family."

"It's nice having the extra family."

She'd enjoyed being included. It reminded her of when she'd had both parents.

Blake drove her home and walked her to the door. "I enjoyed tonight, getting you away from the office."

She ran her hands from the sides of his neck into his hair. "I did, too."

His arms came around her and pulled her close. His lips claimed hers. She forgot everything when he kissed her.

Blake stepped back and took her hands. His breathing came in fast bursts. He kissed the corner of her mouth. "I've got to go before I do something I shouldn't. I'll see you tomorrow at the office."

He shoved his hands into his pants pockets as if that was the only way he'd keep them off her.

Amy unlocked her door and found Blake in the same position. She gave him a quick kiss.

He growled. "You're playing with fire."

She stepped inside her house and partially closed the door. "Good-night, Blake."

He grinned and sauntered back to his car.

With the door closed between them, she leaned against it. She was falling in love with Blake. Whenever he entered her thoughts, it was as if he hugged her.

The feelings she'd had for Jeff were nothing like these. Maybe she hadn't even loved him after all.

Chapter 10

After picking up Amy, Blake pulled her hand onto his leg and held it. When he needed two hands on the wheel, he patted her hand before letting go, in hopes it would encourage her to leave it there.

She lifted her hand up between them, displaying her amputated fingers. "This doesn't bother you?"

He grabbed it and kissed her fingertips. "It felt a little weird at first, but no, it doesn't bother me."

She smiled as he put their joined hands back on his leg.

Blake parked behind *Crete Street Restaurant*, got out and opened Amy's door. She stared up at him.

He squatted down. "Hey. You were kind of quiet on the way over. Are you nervous?"

"A little."

He took her hand. "You don't have to be. It's just two more people, and they're every bit as nice as the rest of the family."

"But Tom is your best friend."

He tipped one corner of his mouth up. "So?"

"He'll want to look out for your best interests and probably grill me."

"Nah. He'll be more subtle than that."

Her eyes widened.

He chuckled, kissed her and held out his hand. "Come on. Let's go in."

They entered the kitchen as everyone bustle around. It took a minute before Mara noticed him.

"Blake! No one told me you were coming back this morning." She raced across the room and hugged him. "Hi, Amy." She grabbed Blake's hand, but stared at Amy. "Do you mind if I take Blake to help me make courgette balls?"

He tugged his hand away. "Wait. I want to introduce Amy to Tom first." Blake searched until he found Tom leaning against the office doorframe, talking to someone, and led Amy over to him.

"Hi, Tom."

Tom grinned. "Hi, yourself. And who's this?"

"Amy, meet Tom."

Tom shook Amy's hand. "Nice to meet you. Girlfriend?"

Amy's gaze flew to Blake.

"I'm working on it."

Tomas chair squeaked as he stood. "This is their second date."

Tom chuckled and waved his hand around. "This is a date? Clearly, you need some pointers."

Blake patted Tom's shoulder. "Where's your wife?"

Tom waved toward the kitchen. "Out there somewhere."

"She's working while you stand around chatting?"

Tom shrugged. "I'll get there."

Blake took Amy's hand. "Let's find Allie." He spotted her sitting at a table, cutting peppers into large pieces. "Everyone pitches in so there's time to talk before they open."

"I'd like to help."

He grinned. "I knew you would." He stopped in front of the table. "Hey, Allie."

She dropped her knife and stood. "Mara said you'd arrived." She rounded the table.

Blake took her hand. "Whoa! Look at you."

Allie patted her tummy. "I was pregnant the last time I saw you, but we were keeping it a secret for a while." She'd miscarried the first time she was pregnant, so he understood. "And who's this?"

He wrapped an arm around Amy's shoulders. "Allie, this is Amy."

Allie hugged Amy. "It's nice to meet a friend of Blake's. Do you want to cut peppers with me?"

"Sure."

Allie found a knife, cutting board and more peppers and set them on the table. Amy washed her hands and sat across from Allie.

Blake leaned close. "Do you mind if I help Mara?"

"Go ahead. I'll be fine."

He washed his hands, donned vinyl gloves and joined Mara across the room. Through the years, he'd done a lot of work in this kitchen, everything from preparing food to cleaning up after.

Mara dropped the wooden spoon she'd been using to stir a gigantic bowl of courgette. "I like Amy."

He raised his brows. "How did you figure that out? You haven't exchanged a dozen words with her."

"She's cutting peppers, and she and Allie are talking like they're best friends. That's better than Janice ever did. She was a b—"

He scowled. "Watch your mouth, little girl. Let's not talk about Janice." Biggest mistake of his life. She'd thought a family who ran a restaurant was beneath her and wouldn't help the way Amy had jumped in. It was a good thing it only took a couple of months to realize Janice was a snob who didn't deserve his time.

He scooped out some of the vegetable dough and formed it into a ball, setting it on a tray covered in waxed paper.

Mara scooped her own dough. "So, where did you meet Amy?"

"She ran into me at the hospital and I hired her on the

spot."

Her eyes widened. "She works for you?"

He grinned. "That way I have her captive, so she has a chance to discover what a great guy I am."

She set down a perfectly formed ball and bumped his shoulder. "You make it sound like she's in jail and you're her jailer."

"Hey. I didn't mean it like that."

She giggled. "I'm just teasing you. Besides, I can tell you like her a lot. Otherwise, you wouldn't have brought her to meet the family. And you must be sure of her, since she didn't go screaming in the other direction."

"She needs family." He wrapped an arm around Mara's shoulders, careful to not touch anything with his hands. "And this is the best one around." He hadn't consciously chosen *Crete Street* to introduce Amy to the family, but because he loved the food and enjoyed the overall atmosphere. It was mere coincidence that here were more people who would love her.

After the dough was gone and all the courgette balls made, Blake scanned the kitchen and didn't see Amy or Allie. He wandered over to Tom and leaned his back against the wall.

Tom stirred a large pot of tomato sauce that would go over the keftethes and into the moussaka.

"Where are the ladies?"

"If you mean my wife and your girlfriend, they're in the dining room, rolling silverware in napkins. Mama wouldn't let the pregnant girl or the new girl cut onions. But I know for a fact she cut onions when she was pregnant with Mara." Blake and Tom had been in high school when Mara was born.

"Congrats on the baby. Is everything progressing all right?"

Tom grinned. "Everything's perfect." He pretended to polish his fingernails on his shirt. "It's a boy. What about you?"

Blake raised his brows. "What about me?"

"You don't want to be an old man when you have kids."

Blake poked his friend in the chest. "Don't push it. My relationship with Amy is too new for this." Although, he could imagine Amy glowing with happiness, pregnant with his child.

"So, there is a relationship even though this"—he waved around him—"is a second date. You dated you-know-who over a month before you brought her here to meet the family, but you did it on your first date with Amy. That's telling, man."

"She's special. She was an army nurse. Would you want to practice in a war zone?"

"Is that how?" Tom waved at his cheek.

"Yeah." He lifted his hand. "Her fingers, too. You remember how I thought we'd lost David in that hospital explosion?"

Tom's eyes widened. "She was in that?"

"She survived because she was in a supply closet when the bomb hit."

Lena called out from the doorway. "Hey, boys. Come eat lunch."

Fridays and Sundays were the only days the restaurant opened for lunch, so only the family and one employee gathered around the big table for the meal. Luckily, there was still an empty seat next to Amy.

He squeezed her shoulder before sitting. "How's it going?"

She smiled. "I love this family."

Blake had hoped she'd hit it off with the Danielos. He had every intention of it working out between him and Amy, but if it didn't, this family would still hang on to her and not let go.

~~~

Amy stretched out on her couch. Her second week without Hannah had gone well. It was especially nice how Blake stole short kisses whenever their paths crossed, and they crossed more than the week before. He'd catch her in her office as she wrote patient notes or as she left an exam room. Best of all, were the evenings after the last patients left. He'd take her to his office and sit in his chair with her on his lap. Those were the best kisses. Then they headed home separately, except for Wednesday night, when they had dinner out. She had a feeling he was giving her time to get used to them as a couple.

Tonight, they'd planned on going to a movie, but near the end of the day, he'd gotten called to the hospital for emergency surgery. He'd given her a kiss and an apology with a promise to do something on Saturday, then she'd gone home to be alone for the evening.

Feeling lonely, she picked up her cell phone and dialed Hannah.

"Hello, Amy?"

"Hi, Hannah. How's it going in your new home?"

"I can't believe how long it takes to unpack and figure out where everything goes. I've got boxes everywhere. I'm ready to go back to the hotel and sit by the pool."

Amy laughed. "No, you're not. I bet you love being in your own house."

"You're right. I'm figuring out color schemes and where to hang everything. I bought that furniture for my deck. It looks amazing. What about you? How are those therapy sessions going?"

"Really good. I'm only doing group sessions now and I've had three since leaving the hospital. Some of those guys have been through so much worse than me and I'm the one who gave up."

"You don't know that. Maybe some of them did, too, until the right person came along to help them."

"Yeah. We've all talked about what turned us around."

"Which brings us to Blake. Is he still having lunch with you?"

Amy giggled. "That and more."

"What more?"

Amy told her about the date and meeting the Danielos and going back on Saturday.

"That's wonderful," Hannah said. "He wouldn't have taken you there if you weren't important to him."

"Thanks. Oh. They all hugged me when we left, so I think they like me."

"Of course, they did. Oops. Antoine's yelling. He probably can't find something. I better go. Bye, Amy."

"Bye, Hannah."

Amy hadn't realized the significance of Blake taking her to *Crete Street* and meeting the Danielos. She closed her eyes and smiled. Her heart filled with more love for Blake. In so many ways, he showed her he cared. If not for him, she wouldn't be here. He'd brought her soul back to life, allowing her to love him.

Chapter 11

Blake rolled his head then his shoulders to loosen them as he pulled into Amy's driveway. Surgery the night before had gone past midnight and sleep hadn't relieved the tension.

Amy must have heard him drive in, and met him at the door in snug jeans and a t-shirt. Without a word, her arms circled his neck and she kissed him. He didn't fail to notice it was the first time she initiated one. He took full advantage and hugged her close, taking over. Her warm response made him forget about his stiff muscles.

After a minute, she relaxed against him and he lifted his head, grinning. "I like your good morning kiss."

She scanned her neighborhood. "You make me forget where I am. We're on the porch, for any of my neighbors to see." She ran a hand up his neck. "Your muscles feel tense."

He let out a long breath. "Surgery went late. A seventeen-year-old boy was thrown from a motorcycle, and shattered his shoulder. Repair took hours, but it will never be the same."

"That poor boy. I'm sure nobody could have done better than you."

"Thank you."

She backed away, took his hand and dragged him toward the kitchen. "How about a neck massage and some coffee?"

"I don't know which sounds better."

Her beautiful amber eyes peeked over her shoulder. "Well, it's a good thing you don't have to choose." Amy pointed at a kitchen chair. "Sit. I'll pour coffee."

He took a seat, not sure what to expect. Some people thought they could give a massage, but they only pinched and caused more pain. He hoped Amy knew how to do it because he didn't want to hurt her feelings by telling her to stop. He rocked his head, and hoped the massage would help.

She set the cup and a lotion bottle on the table in front of him. He gulped down a couple swallows of coffee, hoping the caffeine buzz wouldn't take long to hit. He hadn't bothered to stop on his way over, not wanting to delay seeing her.

Amy's tentatively squeezed his shoulder. "Why don't you take your shirt off so I can massage your shoulders, too?"

Without a word, he yanked the short sleeved Henley over his head and tossed it on the table. No need to ask twice.

He liked how she stared at his chest before picking up the bottle, and squirted the liquid into her hand. Warm, slippery fingers pressed into his neck, coaxing every stiff muscle into relaxing.

He groaned, and she giggled. Adding more lotion, her thumbs worked the tight muscles of his shoulders, pulling another moan from him. "I can't believe how good that feels." If he hadn't made plans that he knew she'd enjoy, he'd be tempted to talk her into staying here.

Warm fingers pushed and prodded. The lack of two fingertips made no difference in her ability to give a massage.

"When I was in nursing school, one of the other student's boyfriend was a masseuse. During one long study session he taught us how to massage each others' necks and shoulders. It was a lifesaver."

Blake tipped his head forward. "I wish I'd thought of that when I was in med school." He grasped her hands, pulling her to his side, and kissed the backs of them. "Thank you." He lifted his brows. "Maybe you could do this when I come into the office after surgeries."

She bit her lip. "If I do that, Harry will probably ask for the same thing."

He frowned. "We'll have to make sure he doesn't know." Even though Harry was married, Blake didn't want Amy's hands on the other man's body.

She bit her lip. "So it was good? I haven't done a massage since I…lost my fingers."

He shoved the chair back and pulled her into his lap. "It was wonderful. I'd let you massage any part of my body."

He held back a chuckle when she blushed and looked down at his chest and her gaze skittered away. "He only taught us necks and shoulders."

He kissed her. "I love you." His lips skimmed hers again. He hadn't meant to tell her yet, thinking she wasn't ready, but he couldn't hold back the extent of his feelings any longer. For better or worse, it was out there for her to accept or reject him.

"Y-you do?"

He framed her face between his hands. "You sound like you don't think you deserve it." He nibbled her lips. "You're kind and unbelievably gentle with our slow, elderly patients. You make me happy. And you're beautiful."

Her hand covered her cheek and he pulled it away. "You survived something traumatic nobody should have to experience." He trailed kisses from the top of her scar to the bottom, just under her jaw, then hugged her. "I thank God you're here with me."

"Blake. I can't believe you love me. I love you, but—"

His heart soared. He rose to his feet and spun with her in his arms, then kissed her. "I love you. Believe it." He wiped a tear from her cheek with his thumb, reminding him of the first time he'd seen her and knowing he couldn't let her disappear. "Now go get ready. We're leaving in five minutes."

She scampered away and he donned his shirt, then finished his coffee. She loved him. He hadn't expected her to tell him, at least not so soon. He believed her, but he'd be overjoyed when she said it to him without him saying it first, the same as with the kiss she'd gifted him with when he arrived.

At the click of the coat closet door opening, he stood and strode to the front door. Amy tied her shoes and stood. "So where are we going?"

He gave her a quick kiss. "You'll see when we get there."

On the way to their destination, Amy kept a tight hold of his hand, as if he'd take back his declaration if she let go.

"Are we going to that movie we missed?"

He grinned. If she got too close in her guesses he'd stop answering. "No."

"Are we doing something outside?"

"Yes. We're going to enjoy the sunny day."

She tapped her lips with her finger and he wished he could be touching them. "Are we going to walk?"

"That's part of it." Blake pulled into a parking lot and found a spot.

She clasped her hands. "We're playing miniature golf?"

"We are. Are you a golfer?"

"No. I bet you are."

He grinned. "Why do you say that?"

Amy pouted. "Everybody knows doctors and lawyers play golf."

He laughed. "This doctor doesn't. We're probably on par."

She slapped her forehead. "That was bad."

He opened his door. "Let's go play."

They joined a line and soon had golf clubs, a red ball and a pink one, a score sheet and a three-inch pencil.

They left the office and when Amy started to follow the group ahead of them, he tugged her the other way. She frowned.

He pointed at the group. "Do you really want to play behind a group of eight?"

She shook her head. "I guess not."

He resumed walking. "That's why we're playing on the other course."

She squinted. "You seem to know what you're doing. Should I be worried?"

He chuckled. "I played a couple of months ago with my sister and her kids. I beat the kids, but not Brandy."

"How old are the kids?"

"Ashley is ten and Cameron is eight."

The first green was empty and a group of three played a couple of greens away. He waved a hand. "After you."

She shook her head. "Uh-uh. You first. I want to see where you send your ball so I can figure out if I should do the same."

"That's an unfair advantage."

She shrugged. "You picked the activity. I pick the method."

He pecked her cheek and grinned. "You are devious." He positioned his ball, sighted it, and swung. It glanced off a bumper, but maintained enough momentum to roll up the hill and disappear on the other side. The ball dropped into the hole in two more shots and he plucked it out, holding it aloft. "See if you can top that!"

Amy whacked her ball and it rolled over the hill, bounced off the wall, and nearly dropped into the hole, stopping a foot past it. She came up beside him and gently nudged the ball, allowing it to fall into the hole. She smirked.

"Got it in two."

He recorded the scores, and led her to the next green. The players ahead were still at the third green, so Blake propped his club against the number post and wrapped Amy in his arms. "I'm so glad you could join me today." He had to remember where they were when he kissed her, not wanting to go too far in public. He nibbled her jaw on his way to her ear. "I think I better play now."

She leaned back, her eyes wide, then she blushed. "Oh. You mean golf."

He laughed. "Yes. I mean golf. There will be time later for…other types of play."

He took his turn. He hadn't planned on teasing Amy with kisses between greens, but spur of the moment pleasure was sometimes the best kind. By the time they finished the nine holes, with Amy winning by two strokes, he was more than ready for privacy. Unfortunately for him, that wasn't the next item on his itinerary. She was going to love their next stop every bit as much as the first one.

A short drive took them to Holland Farms. Lines of a half dozen people stood at each window.

Amy squealed. "I love Holland Farms ice cream. I haven't had it in a couple of years."

"I brought Brandy and the kids here after we played golf."

"So, this is more a family thing than a date?"

He glanced at her as he parked. "This is a date. My plan is to have a burger or chicken then get back in line for ice cream, but if you want to skip right to ice cream, I don't mind."

She glared at him. "Doctor, we shouldn't have ice cream for lunch, but I may have to split one with you."

He kissed her. "Do we split lunch so we can have more ice cream or split the ice cream after lunch?"

Her mouth dropped open before a slow grin spread across her face. "I love how you think. Let's split lunch."

They got out of the car and hurried to the end of a food line. Blake pointed to the sign above the window. "Burger, chicken, chicken wrap?"

He studied Amy as she gazed at the sign. He'd deliberately chosen to stand on her left side, so she'd see her scar didn't bother him, and to partially shield it from others.

She frowned. "What? Why are you staring at me?"

He couldn't help it. He loved kissing her and took advantage. "I like looking at you. What did you choose?"

"I thought we'd have to argue about it."

"There's nothing here I don't like, so whatever you want is fine with me."

"Okay. The chicken wrap."

"Perfect. And potato salad, too." The line advanced and then it was their turn. He gave their order to the teen girl. "I'll have a soda."

"I'll have iced tea," Amy said.

Blake paid and was given their drinks and a number. "Let's go sit."

Picnic tables were set end-to-end in long rows under a huge canopy. He chose a spot with more space than most, and they sat next to each other.

A boy about five stared at Amy. "What happened to your face?"

Amy tugged her hand, but he held it tighter. She didn't need to cover her scar.

"She's a nurse, and was helping soldiers when a bomb went off."

The boy's eyes went round. "You're a hero."

"N—"

"Yes, she is." It was about time she saw herself that way.

The woman beside the boy glanced at her son then Amy.

"Thank you for your service. It takes a lot of courage for a woman to go into a war zone."

"I-umm. Thanks."

The woman gave the boy a side hug. "Come on, Chad. We've got to get home."

Chad gracefully extricated himself from the table, and waved. "Bye." He ran ahead of his mother.

Blake wrapped an arm around Amy's shoulders and whispered in her ear. "You're my hero, too." The speaker called out a number. "That's our order. I'll be right back."

He collected their tray and returned, setting it half in front of Amy. He took his seat, scooped up some potato salad and held it an inch from her mouth. She wrapped her mouth around the fork and pulled off the food. And that shouldn't turn him on so much.

She closed her eyes. "Mmm. That is the best potato salad ever. Why have I only had the ice cream here?"

He chuckled. "Because you'd rather have ice cream than food?"

Her eyes sparkled. "Maybe." She picked up half of the huge sandwich. "Let me try this wrap."

~~~

Blake tooled around his kitchen the following Saturday, putting together a picnic lunch. He'd had one dinner with Amy that week and was more than ready to spend the day with her.

It was supposed to be sunny and warm, and he had a fun beach day planned. His phone buzzed and he picked it up from the counter, hoping it wasn't an emergency since he was on call.

He grinned. "David! I'm so glad it's you. I was planning on calling you tonight." He figured he'd end up leaving a message for David to get back to him when he could.

"Hey, big brother. What's going on?"

Blake propped the phone with his shoulder, and retrieved a container of potato salad from the refrigerator, and dropped it into a cooler. "First, tell me how you're doing. Are you stateside?" He added soft drinks, tea and water bottles.

"Not for a few more weeks. I'm good. Keeping my head down. You the same boring sawbones?"

Blake pulled a small box from his pocket and flipped it open. The diamond ring he'd picked out twinkled. It was going to be a big day. "I'm working real hard at not being boring. Can you get exact dates when you'll be home?"

"I can try. Why?"

Blake grinned. "I want you to be my best man." He hadn't asked Amy yet, but was pretty sure she'd say yes.

"You're getting married? I didn't know you were dating. At all."

Blake tucked the box back into his pocket. "Hey. I wasn't that bad."

"Yeah, you were. Do I know her?"

"As a matter of fact, you do. Amy Stuart."

Something clanged on the other end of the line. "The nurse?"

"Did you just fall down?"

"Not exactly. Is this the nurse from Qatar?"

Yes. And—"

"I'm so relieved. I thought she died in the bombing. How did you meet her and what happened with that boyfriend she used as an excuse whenever the guys asked her out?"

"She was in the bombing and has scars and missing fingertips to prove it. That jackass of a boyfriend took one look at her scars and told her he didn't want her anymore."

His brother swore.

157

"David, she's really sensitive about it, so don't—just be aware of that when you see her." He couldn't protect Amy from everyone, but at least family should treat her right.

"Not a problem. You found a wonderful, caring woman. I'm jealous."

Blake grinned. "You should be. Let me know ASAP when you can get here."

"Will do, bro'. And congrats."

"Thanks. Keep your eyes peeled and your head down."

As he tucked his phone in his pocket, it rang. The hospital. No. Not today when he had the most important plans of his life.

"Blake Lloyd."

Chapter 12

Amy set her beach bag by the door and slipped into flip-flops. A beach day with Blake would be heavenly. She'd get to see his sexy chest for hours. She grabbed a light jacket from the closet and jammed it into the already full bag. She wore her swimsuit under her clothes. She'd searched for days for the right one, not wanting a bikini, but had found the sexiest one-piece in a boutique she'd never visited before.

Her hair was pulled back in a ponytail that threaded through the red baseball cap on her head. She'd used a small amount of waterproof foundation over her scar, but didn't know how it would hold up in the water.

Blake had called to tell her he'd be a few minutes late. A patient at the hospital had required instructions for care. She hoped that was the only emergency he had that day.

The doorbell rang and her heart fluttered. She saw Blake nearly every day and still hummed with excitement. She flung the door open.

A sexy, smiling Blake stood in shorts and a t-shirt. He grinned. "Cute outfit."

While she was at the boutique, she'd gotten red shorts, and a short sleeved, white, gauzy shirt with ship's wheel buttons. "Thanks."

Amy rested her wrists on Blake's shoulders and leaned in for a kiss. The beak of her cap struck his forehead. "Oops. Sorry." She knocked it off and the cap tumbled down her back. Fifteen hours since she'd last seen him was way too long. She loved the way his arms wrapped around her,

159

pulling her close. It was as if love surrounded her before their lips even touched.

"I missed you," he said against her lips before devouring her. He stopped much too soon. "Gather your stuff and let's get going. I have a reservation for nine."

Amy picked up her bag and cap. "You need a reservation to go to the beach?"

"You'll see." She loved how his face lit up when surprising her with fun activities. She'd have to come up with something, too.

A half-hour drive brought them to the lake. A slight breeze ruffled the water. Sunbathers lay scattered on the beach, and children ran and splashed in the shallows. A floating rope separated the swimming area from the boating lane.

While Amy surveyed the crowd, Blake rounded the car, and opened her door. She got out with her beach bag.

He took it from her, and stuck it back in the car. "You don't need that yet."

She waved around her. "But we're at the beach."

"Right now, we're at the water." He yanked his shirt over his head, and tossed it into the car. She wanted to run her hands over his chest and into his hair, but not with all these people around. From his wallet, he pulled out a credit card. He stripped off the shorts, and stuffed his keys into the swim trunks pocket and zipped it shut. He'd removed his shoes before getting out of the car. "Your turn."

Amy unbuttoned her shirt and Blake's gaze followed every move. She tossed the shirt on top of his, and unbuttoned her shorts.

His eyes went to half-mast and his breathing quickened. "You're gorgeous, but I kind of hoped you'd wear a bikini."

"Not happening. Now, if you had a pool in your backyard, I'd wear a bikini for you."

He grabbed her hips. "There's an idea. I always swim at my gym, but getting my own pool might be worth it."

She rolled her eyes. "So not worth it." She slid out of her shorts, turned her back to him, and tossed them on the seat. Her deep red swimsuit was cut high, making her legs appear longer, with most of her back exposed.

He grasped her arms. "Whoa. I love this." He kissed the bottom of her neck and every inch or so all the way down her spine, planting one between each of the three thin strips crossing her upper back, all the way to the low dip of the bottom. "I don't know if I'm going to be able to do this."

She faced him. "Do what?"

"Watch you all day in this swimsuit. Have I told you today you're gorgeous?"

She rested her wrists on his shoulders. "Yes." Now she was glad she'd made the purchase instead of wearing her old suit.

His lips brushed hers. "Just making sure you know." He lifted her wrists from his shoulders, and slid his hand into hers. "Come on. You're going to love this."

"Wait." She put her cap on and grabbed her sunglasses from a pocket in her beach bag. "Ready."

They strolled across the sand and Blake stopped short. "I forgot my credit card."

Amy raised her brows. "You need a credit card at the beach?"

"Today we do." He scanned the area and pointed. "Why don't you wait under that tree and I'll be right back?" He gave her a quick kiss and jogged toward his car.

She sauntered to the huge tree and leaned against it. Two children caught her attention. The six-year-old girl dug in the sand and a boy a couple of years older walked up with a bucket of water. He poured it into the hole, and the girl grinned, plunging her shovel into the hole.

A muscular, tanned man blocked her view as he paused, his gaze on Amy. He grinned and changed course towards her. A foot from her, he leaned his hands against the tree, on either side of her head, making her uncomfortable. His eyes widened, then he leered. "Such a sexy swimsuit. I bet the body under it is just as sexy."

He'd caged her in. She'd have to duck and brush against him to get away. She shuddered at the thought. She'd dealt with the rare handsy soldier, she could deal with this. She tipped her chin up. "You better keep on walking."

He dropped his hands to her shoulders, and leaned closer. "Why would I want to do that? We could have some fun together. My place isn't far from here."

The air froze in her lungs, and then she dragged in a ragged breath. In one smooth motion, she brought her arms up, drove her fists into his chest, and he stumbled back a step. She sidestepped so the tree no longer blocked her, and poked him in the chest. "You are rude, demeaning, and-and pond scum."

He leaned closer. "Listen w—"

Amy jumped when an arm wrapped around her shoulders. Blake. "Is there a problem here, honey?"

She relaxed a bit. "Yeah. This jerk—"

The man held his hands up. "Was mistaken." He hurried away.

Blake folded her into his arms. "Pond scum, hmm?"

"I was so mad I couldn't think straight." She ran her hands up his chest and to the back of his neck. "I'm glad you showed up when you did."

He kissed her. "I wish I'd gotten here a few minutes sooner. But you were doing pretty well on your own. You've become a strong woman. The real Amy Stuart."

"With help from you." She nibbled his jaw.

He snuggled her closer then let go. "Let's forget about

him and get on with our day." He took her hand and led her to a small shack next to a long dock. Inside, he stepped up to a counter. "I have a reservation for two jet skis. Blake Lloyd."

Amy squealed. "Really? I've always wanted to try one."

Blake paid the rental and the man handed him two keys. "Have you used jet skis before?"

"I've used them before. I'll show her how it's done. Thanks."

Amy strode down the dock beside Blake. "This is going to be so fun."

He stopped. "Here we are. Numbers fifteen and sixteen." He stuck a key into the ignition of the closest one, explained how to mount and how the controls worked. After she mounted, he turned the key, and kicked out the front so it faced the open water, then he got on the other jet ski and started the engine.

Blake drove up beside her. "I'll stay close for a few minutes until you're comfortable. Now, give it a little gas."

Amy turned the handle and jumped forward. She released it and slowed down, then played with the control until she was able to handle it.

"Great job," Blake said. "Try some turns. Don't turn too sharply at first or you might flip yourself off."

"That's comforting." She turned away from Blake and he fell back. It was exhilarating as she swayed right then left. There were small islands in the distance. It would be fun to go around them. Adding some speed, she bee-lined to the nearest one. A glance over her shoulder found Blake not far behind, grinning.

She should let him go first since he was more familiar with the sport than she was. Nah. She was having too much fun in the lead. As she approached the island, the water became shallow. A slight turn had her running parallel to the shore, as she kept a watch below as well as ahead. Couldn't hit a sandbar and fly off the machine.

On the backside of the island another jet skier approached. She laughed when he got close enough to see it was Blake. He passed on her right and looped around and fell in beside her. "Having fun?"

She grinned. "This is a blast." She sped up and picked another island to circle. A speed boat crossed her path and she and her jet ski catapulted over the wake, dragging a scream from her. She held steady to the handlebars, hoping she didn't hit the water wrong. She stared at the front of her machine, imagining the nose going straight down into the depths or hitting on an angle and flipping on top of her. Her breath whooshed out and she grinned when it made a perfect landing, giving her the thrill of a rollercoaster. She went in search of another wake to cross.

Jeff would never have done anything like this with her. He chose activities he liked and never consulted her. It was as if he made plans for himself and added her to them to string her along. She'd been dragged to all kinds of activities she'd told him she didn't like doing. His revelation when he rejected her showed how shallow his feelings had been. She was a means to an end to secure his place at the law firm. Her scar had saved her from marrying a selfish man who didn't love her. A man who probably would have ignored her except when he wanted to show her off to his colleagues.

She and Blake crisscrossed the lake until he sidled up next to her. "Time's almost up."

"Already?"

"When we get close to the dock, slow down and I'll help you get docked."

She nodded and took off, needing to enjoy every last minute of this new experience. Near the dock, she slowed to a crawl.

Blake stopped alongside her. "Watch me and after I tie up, do the same."

"What? I have to pull up there by myself?" The whole time she was out, she avoided getting close to anything. Now, she had to bump into something, and not hurt the dock, the jet ski or herself.

"You'll be fine. If you get too nervous, I'll jump in and drive it in for you."

"Okay." Every day she spent with Blake, she loved him more. He supported her in every way, and stepped in when she need him.

The jet ski idled as Blake looped his machine and barely brushed the dock. He cut the engine, jumped off and tied the front and back, then waved her in.

She drew in a long breath, pretty sure it wasn't as easy as Blake made it seem. A long sweep later, Blake pushed his flattened hands down and she slowed, angling closer. He made a slash across his neck and Amy wasn't sure he meant for her to cut the engine or let it idle. She released the speed control and waited.

"Just a little closer, honey, and I'll grab on." He stretched and wrapped his hand around the handle. A shriek behind them startled her and she revved the engine, yanking Blake off the dock. He let go, went underwater and popped back up.

"Blake, I'm so sorry." She held her hands up, not wanting to accidentally cause more trouble.

He grabbed onto the side of the machine. "That's what the swimsuits are for. Scoot back. I'm getting on in front." She slid to the back of the seat and he hauled himself up, throwing a leg over. He twisted around and kissed her then chuckled. "I did say I could bring it in for you, but didn't plan to get into the water that way."

He steered the jet ski into its space as flawlessly as the

first one, then turned off the engine. Blake jumped to the dock, and tied the lines to the cleats.

She scrambled onto the dock and swirled around with her arms in the air. "That was so much fun." She lost her balance and Blake grabbed her and she wrapped her arms around his neck.

"Whoa, there. Be careful." He backed up a couple of steps, dragging her with him.

He rubbed his hands up her mostly bare back. "I'm glad you enjoyed it. I wasn't sure. Come on. Let's turn in the keys and find a shady picnic table for lunch." He took her hand and they strode to the shack, and handed over the keys. They turned towards the parking lot and Blake pointed to a shady area. "Why don't you go save that table and I'll get the cooler?"

"Good idea." She raced off for the table, wanting to make sure they didn't lose out since not many were empty. She climbed onto the tabletop and planted her feet on the bench seat, facing the water, and leaned back on her hands. The sun felt wonderful on her skin, warmer than when she'd been in the wind created by the jet ski.

Something thumped behind her and she jumped, then spun around. "Blake." She glanced at the cooler sitting on the bench seat. "What did you bring for lunch?"

"Come sit on this side so we both have a view of the water, and I'll show you."

She scooted across the table and sat beside him as he unpacked the cooler. Ham and cheese sandwiches, potato salad, and cold sodas. No plates, but she didn't mind sharing. "You remembered forks?"

He grabbed them from the cooler. "Here we go."

Amy removed the napkin tucked into the sandwich bag before taking out half the sandwich. "It's been forever since I had this much fun." She kissed his cheek.

"Hey, I wasn't prepared for that." He tapped a finger to his lips. "Right here."

She smiled and gave him what he wanted. "Now we better eat before…sand blows into our food."

She enjoyed watching people in the water throwing balls, chasing each other, children running in and out of the gentle waves.

She took a last bite of potato salad and stuffed the fork into the empty plastic bag. Maybe they would lie on the beach for a little while before going into the water.

Blake gathered up the remains of their meal. "You ready for dessert?"

She patted her tummy. "I don't know."

He gave her a quick kiss. "You're going to love this." He rummaged in the cooler. It seemed to take way too long to pull out whatever dessert was. He set a luscious chocolaty cupcake in front of himself. Maybe she could eat dessert after all. She sucked in a breath and held it when he set her cupcake down. A diamond ring sparkled on the top, the band buried in frosting.

Blake took her hand. "I love everything about you. I want to spend my life with you. Please say you'll marry me."

Tears sprung to her eyes. "Blake." Sitting side-by-side on the bench seat was awkward for kissing him the way she wanted to. She swung her legs to the bench, and shimmied into his lap. "I love you. Yes, I'll marry you." She wrapped her arms around the back of his neck and kissed him.

"Let's make this official." He plucked the ring from the cupcake, licked off the frosting, and slid the ring onto her finger, sealing it with a kiss. "We should get a picture."

The three-stone ring sparkled in the sunlight. Her two shortened fingers detracted from the gorgeous sight, but Blake didn't seem to mind.

Blake took a burgundy linen napkin from the cooler, and

spread it on the table. Then he unzipped his pocket and pulled out his cell phone, protected by a Ziploc bag.

"Wow. You were prepared."

He grinned, and tapped his phone. "Of course. Put your hand on the cloth." With care, he slipped his thumb under her hand, and arranged his fingers over hers, covering the amputated fingers. He snapped three pictures, shifting his phone for each one. He moved his hand away. "Now, you put your other hand like I did."

She copied him and he took more pictures. He tapped the screen, and turned it so she could see. "What do you think?"

Instead of looking at the screen, she kissed him. "I think you're wonderful. You always know what to do to make me feel special." She pulled his hand closer. "Now, let me see how they turned out."

He flipped through the pictures. She liked them. In the outdoor light, the ring practically glowed. Their joined hands were a symbol of their love. She liked those pictures better than the ones with only her hands.

"Which one do you like best? I want to send it to my family."

Amy chose the second picture he'd snapped. "Send it to Hannah, too. She'll be excited. She knew before I did you were making a move on me."

"She's perceptive." He typed a message and sent it out. "Now, do you want to play in the water?"

~~~

Amy clung to Blake's arm as they walked up to *Cristo's Restaurant*. She'd gone with Jeff a number of times, but only for his firm's events. He must not have thought she was worth the price. The chances of running into him on a Tuesday night were remote, but telling herself still didn't calm her nerves.

Blake stopped and turned her into his arms, then brushed the hair back from the unmarred side of her face. "I can feel tension radiating through you. Do you hate this place? Should we go somewhere else?" He lifted her hand with his ring on it and kissed her fingers. "Or are you regretting having to claim me for your fiancé?"

She kissed him. "Never. I love you. It's just that this is the restaurant Jeff's law firm has their celebration dinners."

"We can go somewhere else. Or, if he's here—"

"You wouldn't punch him, would you?"

He lifted his hands, and spoke in mock indignation. "No. These are the hands of a surgeon." He grinned. "I've got a better way to punch him in the gut. We can stop in front of him and I'll give you a kiss that knocks your socks off."

She lifted a foot. "I'm not wearing socks. But a kiss that makes me swoon would work just as well."

Blake wrapped her in his arms. "We should practice."

She wound her arms around his neck. All but his shortest kisses made her swoon. No practice needed, but she wouldn't pass up a chance to be in his arms. All too soon he ended the kiss and backed away.

He shook his head. "We're standing right outside the door and we're going to be late for our reservation."

She blew out a breath. "That's a perfectly good reason to be late."

"Amy?"

She swung around and faced a man in his fifties. "Mr. Bremen! It's so nice to see you. And you, too, Mrs. Bremen."

He shook her hand. "I miss you at these dinners, my dear. That new woman Jeff brings…she's just not you."

Amy suppressed a laugh. The light wasn't the greatest outside, but Mr. Bremen didn't seem concerned about her scar. That he enjoyed her company better than Jeff's other choice boosted her confidence.

"I miss our conversations, too." She dragged Blake up next to her. "I'd like you to meet my fiancé, Dr. Blake Lloyd. Blake, this is Peter Bremen, senior partner in Bremen-Reilly Law firm, and his wife, Marion."

Blake shook the man's hand. "Nice to meet you, sir. Ma'am."

"You've got yourself a special woman, Blake."

Blake wrapped an arm around her waist. "Yes, she is. Does Jeff happen to be in there?"

She snapped her head up to him. "You're not really going to—"

"Yes, we are."

"I thought it was just empty talk so you could kiss me."

He snuggled her closer. "Empty and kissing do not belong in the same sentence."

Peter chuckled. "I don't know what you have planned, but Jeff should be here already. Amy, I'm sure there are a few people who wouldn't mind if you stopped to say hello."

Blake nodded. "Thank you, Peter."

Blake kept his arm around her as they entered the restaurant behind Mr. Bremen and Marion. He took a few seconds to tell the hostess they had arrived, but were going to talk to friends before being seated.

She hadn't seen the people from the law firm in nine months and was excited to talk to them. None of them had been close enough friends to go out other than these company sponsored dinners. She hoped they wouldn't reject her the way Jeff had.

They stepped into the private room and Mr. Bremen waved them over, introducing Blake to the others.

Carly Reilly gave her a hug. "I've missed you." She whispered in Amy's ear. "These dinners are boring without you." Anyone looking at Carly and Mr. Reilly would think she was his daughter or trophy wife, but a closer examination found the two inseparable. Amy had previously been envious of their relationship, but now was ecstatic to have a similar one.

"Sorry."

"Call me and let's get together next week." She leaned close. "And congrats on that yummy fiancé. You deserve someone who looks at you like he does." She squeezed Amy's arm and rolled her eyes. "I've got to mingle."

Amy talked to a few more people, surprised how quickly most recovered from seeing her scar and continued as if it wasn't there.

She turned and there was Jeff with an arm slung over a blonde woman's shoulders. She was beautiful except for her overuse of eye makeup.

Amy stiffened. Blake must have felt it since he pulled her closer and gave her his full attention. "You okay?"

She darted her gaze to Jeff and back to Blake. Jeff was one of the causes of her self-destruction. Between Blake and therapy, Amy had grown stronger, but she didn't feel ready to face Jeff again. At least she wasn't facing him alone like before.

"That's him, huh?"

"Yes."

Blake kept his arm around her and took the remaining few steps to the couple. "Jeff. We heard you were here. I wanted to thank you for giving Amy up." He kissed her cheek. "If not for you, I wouldn't have met the love of my life."

Jeff's girlfriend elbowed him in the ribs and whispered too loud. "You broke up with her over that? You made it sound like it was her whole face." She stalked away.

Amy's gaze followed her retreat. The woman didn't think Amy looked bad and seemed to be disgusted with Jeff.

She smirked at the trouble in paradise she'd inadvertently caused.

Blake took Amy's hand, his gaze on Jeff. "Don't expect an invitation to the wedding."

Blake turned her to face him, smooth cheek toward Jeff. "I love you." He gave her a quick kiss, nothing like he said he would, but still perfect.

One person applauded and Amy jerked her head around to find Mr. Bremen smiling and clapping. Others joined him. Blake grinned and waved as they left the room. Apparently, a few people in the firm didn't like Jeff. She wondered how he would redeem himself to his girlfriend.

Blake found the hostess and they followed her to their seats. He took Amy's hands. "Are you all right? I was satisfied with that. How about you?"

She grinned. "I can't believe we did that." She kissed him. "I think you just slayed my dragon."

"Any time you need a knight, I'm here for you."

"And after we eat, you can take me away on your white charger."

"Gladly."

~~~

Darrah smiled down at the happy couple. Their first meeting had gone exactly as planned, and she'd expected everything to go smoothly after that. Fortunately, she'd peeked in during the farewell dinner and sensed how distressed Amy had become. Darrah had used a tremendous amount of power to convince Blake to return to Amy's house, and it had almost been too late.

Goddess Eva had chosen wisely when she picked Blake. Once he realized Amy's mental state, he took all the appropriate steps to help her heal, and in doing so, they'd fallen in love. It was perfect.

A tug pulled at her heart. Another wounded warrior needed her help.

THE END

Wounded Warrior Hearts: Russ

Deborah Wallace

Chapter 1

Guardian Darrah leaned against the amethyst wall beside Goddess Eva's office, her hands twisting into her pale yellow gown. If she'd followed in her mother's footsteps, she wouldn't be stressed about taking on a new assignment and worrying about a failure leading to someone's death. Of course, all her mother's charges died, and that's why Darrah had chosen a different path. She wanted to save people's lives. Calming dying children, and keeping them from getting scared was important, as well as welcoming them into their new home upon death. But Darrah wanted to prolong people's lives on Earth, especially one's who had served others.

Darrah peeked into the room. Eva studied a paper in her hand, with rare sunlight giving her neatly coiffed blonde hair almost a halo. A huge potted fern under the window seemed to glow in the rays. She wished she could stare out at the Earth below, rather than bring this mission to Goddess.

She had two successful saves, but distress squeezed her heart, sure that this request would be rejected. She pulled in a breath and stepped through the doorway. "Goddess, I have an Intervention."

Eva dropped the paper to her glass desk. The color of her eyes matched her forest green robe. "Guardian Darrah. Who have you brought this time to save?"

Darrah swallowed a lump and approached the woman. She'd already presented one warrior who had been back less than the minimum time. Now, she had another who didn't meet the most important criteria.

Eva lifted a brow. "How long has this one been

stateside?"

"About six months."

Goddess laced her fingers on the desktop. "Is there a particular event that causes this Veteran to take his life?"

Darrah bit her lip, her blue gaze on Goddess' hands. "He doesn't actually try to commit suicide."

Eva frowned. "Then he doesn't need our help." She picked up the paper she'd been reading.

Darrah's soft, blonde curls swung forward when she placed both palms on the desk. "Please. He does need help. He's an adrenaline junky. He seeks out risky activities to feel the rush he used to get in battle. It's his addiction and if we don't intervene, he's going to die by accident that's not really an accident."

Eva pursed her lips. "This type of emotional state isn't what we're used to dealing with. I'm sorry, Darrah, but I don't think we can help him."

Darrah stood tall and clenched her trembling hands into fists. It would be a senseless death like others she'd witnessed, often leaving those who loved them in emotional pain. A valuable life lost. "I think he can fight this addiction by helping someone who is in danger."

"And you know of such a person?"

"Yes. It's someone he's acquainted with."

Goddess sighed and held out her hand. "Give me his information."

Darrah pulled the two inch, flat, black onyx square from her pocket and handed it over.

Goddess folded her hand around it and closed her eyes. "Corporal Russ Dresher." After several seconds, she opened her eyes and handed the disk back. "All right. I'll let you handle the details. Given the likely outcome without Intervention, you can't make it worse." She lifted her paper again. "Report back with your results."

"Thank you, Goddess." Darrah had the complimentary disk in her other pocket in case Goddess had asked for details on Darrah's choice. She was both worried and triumphant that the woman had let Darrah's decision stand.

She hurried away, considering and discarding ideas. Both her rescues would have been suicides, but maybe the mindset of an adrenaline junky was so different she wouldn't be able to influence him. And since she was out of her jurisdiction to intervene with the woman, they both might be lost.

~~~

Russ dusted chalk onto his fingers and reached for the next handhold, tucking his foot deeper into a crevice, then pushed his body up the side of the cliff. He tipped his head back. Halfway up, but with his face inches from the rock, he couldn't see the top. Sometimes he looked down, enjoying the thrill of knowing all that kept him from plummeting to the rocks below were the strength of his fingers and finding good toeholds. He climbed like a spider from ledge to crevice.

Russ craned his neck, searching for his next hold. There. It was a long stretch, but it was the only one, so he'd take it. A thrust with his lowest foot propelled him the extra inch he needed. As his fingertips gripped the crimp, his foot slid from its perch, yanking the other hand from its hold. His heart pounded, and adrenaline pumped through his system as his body swung away from the rock. He tipped his head forward to counterbalance as his hand found purchase.

Three holds. He was good. His face against the sun-warmed wall, he slowed his breathing, commanding his heart to return to normal. He scrabbled the free foot until it secured a place to rest. A quick glance confirmed he'd found an inch wide ledge.

"Yes!" Although the loss of his holds hadn't been intentional, he loved the rush of knowing his life was on the line and he'd pulled it off. Survived. Again. Free solo climbing wasn't for wimps. It took skill, determination, strength, luck, and a little crazy.

Maybe more than a little.

Sometimes, the rush of hitting the limit and coming through was the only thing that made him feel alive. More alive than his squad, who'd been blown to bits a half-mile from him. He couldn't dwell on that. Not now. Not here. It worked best to toast his buddies when he was alone with a bottle of strong scotch.

Another twenty minutes, and Russ crawled over the top and lay on his stomach on the bald rock, catching his breath. After a short rest, he pushed up, staring over the familiar trees and sparkling lake. He tugged off his climbing shoes and set them beside him, then took a long swig from his water bottle. He stretched his sore muscles, and massaged his neck and feet, then shook out his hands. He pulled a banana from his small pack, peeled it, and took a huge bite.

A sound behind him drew his attention. A teenage boy popped up from a trail, turned back and held his hand out. Another hand took it, and the boy hauled a girl up beside him. They walked to the edge and stopped beside Russ. Both were out of breath.

"Which path did you come up?" the boy asked. "We took the steepest, figuring we'd get up here faster, but man it was tough."

Russ pointed down the cliff. "That way."

The girl's eyes widened. "You climbed up? Where's your gear?"

Russ chuckled. "I free soloed."

The boy leaned over the edge. "No gear? Man—"

The girl whacked the boys arm. "Don't even think about it."

He took her hand. "I couldn't do that." He gave Russ a quick glance, maybe wondering if Russ thought the boy was a wuss.

Even teenagers thought he was crazy. That was why he'd never told his brother about the kind of climbing he did.

The boy peeked over the edge again. "Are you going back down the same way?"

Russ shook his head. "No. I'll take the trail you came up."

The couple continued across the cliff edge and disappeared into a trail on the other side.

Russ finished his banana and lay back on the smooth rock to rest his weary legs and arms, enjoying the sun warming his tense muscles. After ten minutes, he'd recovered enough for the descent. He'd climbed the cliff in various places, so had used this trail many times. He pulled tennis shoes from his small pack and put them on, then tucked in his climbing shoes, sprang to his feet and raced across the smooth rock to the trail. He leaped boulders, bent down and used an arm to vault downed trees, and raced headlong to the next jumble of fallen rocks. He reached the bottom in a third of the time of the average hiker.

~~~

On the way home, Russ had an intense craving for a perfectly grilled steak, with a baked potato and grilled onions. He could almost smell and taste it. Instead of taking the turn to go home, he continued on to the grocery store. He parked the SUV, got out, and scanned the parking lot and rooftop. He hated that he couldn't be like everybody else, but had to watch for any sign of danger. The store wasn't as crowded as an Afghan market, but the thought of so many places to hide put him on edge, ready to react to the least provocation. A black car sat at the end of the building, a hundred feet from the door.

A movement at the door snapped his attention in that direction. Vivian, the cashier he always checked out with, strolled out of the building with a grocery bag dangling from one hand. He enjoyed chatting with her. She'd started speculating on what meals he might be planning with his purchases. That was nice, since he'd gotten some great ideas from it. He especially liked telling her of funny incidents from work so he could hear her laugh.

Usually her light brown hair was in a braid down her back. Now, it fell in waves past her shoulders, and the sun had turned it golden. This was the first time he'd seen her away from her register and he liked her long, lean frame. He'd thought about asking her out, but she'd been no friendlier to him than other customers.

"Hi, Vivian."

She paused at the edge of the sidewalk, her eyebrows lowered above her blue eyes for a second. She smiled, probably figuring out where she knew him from. He'd never told her his name, but he knew her first name from the brass tag pinned below the store logo on her shirt. He could rectify that now and ask her out for coffee.

The car at the end of the building revved. He glanced at it, never having considered that she might have a boyfriend and that was him picking her up. "That your ride?"

She shook her head. "No. My car's in employee parking."

The hair on his neck prickled up. He was probably overreacting. He rolled his tense shoulders. He was home. This wasn't an Afghan market where a suicide bomber might waltz into the open. Hot then cold flooded his system, the worst he'd experienced since he got home.

"Would you like to go for coffee?" Jeez. He hadn't even told her his name.

She had taken a step away, but paused, studying him. "Maybe another time?"

Yeah. He wouldn't be sure about him right now either. She turned and angled to the right across the open space.

A squeal of tires drew his attention to the same dark car. It barreled down the strip in front of the store, straight for Vivian. She froze, a deer in the headlights reaction.

Instinct took over as he ran for her. He propelled himself, hitting her just above the waist, and pulled her head against his chest. He twisted, hitting the ground on his side, knocking the wind from his lungs, and rolled with her in his arms. Luck was with them, as he spun them under an oversized pickup truck. The rush was as great as having a close call on the cliff face.

The roar of the engine reverberated through his body as the car sped past.

He struggled to draw in his first breath since the impact. At last, he wrenched in a lungful of sweet air—and his ribs screamed. He took a few slower breaths, and the pain lessened. Vivian's ragged breaths warmed his skin through his shirt. Her body trembled, and he wanted nothing more than to pull her closer. He loosened his grip and rolled to view the main thoroughfare. The car was gone.

He dropped his head to the pavement and thanked God he'd had that intense craving. Otherwise, Vivian would be a crumpled, lifeless body. His breath shuddered out as he pulled her close again. He barely knew her, but the near loss squeezed his heart. "Are you okay?"

Her cheek rubbed his chest as she nodded.

He dragged in a shaky breath. "Let's get into the store."

He climbed to his feet. She stretched a trembling hand

out, and he grasped it, lifting her slight weight from under the truck.

"My groceries." She bent to pick up a can, the closest of the scattered food items.

"We can't stay out here." He wrapped an arm around her waist to protect her, in case the car returned, and ran with her into the building. He pulled his phone from his pocket. The screen was cracked, but lit. "Damn!" He tucked it back into his pocket. It would be best to place the police call from the store phone.

He marched them to the service desk and stepped beside a woman talking to the clerk. "Call nine-one-one. Someone just tried to run down Vivian."

The clerk stared, open-mouthed. "What?" Her eyes widened when they lit on Vivian's pale face. "Vivian, are you all right?"

"I…Uh."

He slammed his hand on the counter. "Call nine-one-one, now."

She snatched up the phone. "All right. All right."

Vivian trembled and Russ wasn't sure how much longer she'd be able to stand.

"Do you have somewhere she can sit back there?"

The woman reached under the desk. "Oh, yeah. Let me buzz you in."

Russ led Vivian to the door beside the counter, opened it and took her inside. He pulled a chair from a desk and she sat, then he squatted in front of her. "Vivian, did you recognize that car?"

She shook her head, and bit her lip.

"Did you see who was in the car?"

"Sort of. Two men. I didn't get a clear look, but I don't think I knew them."

"Who would want to hurt you?"

"I don't know." She glanced at him, then over his shoulder. "My ex-husband was…well, not really abusive, but…anyway, I don't think he'd bother to try to find me."

He patted her hand. "Make sure you tell the police about him." Some women didn't want to admit even to themselves how they'd been abused. The fact that she'd run told him she needed to keep away from her ex.

She nodded. "I don't even know your name."

"Russ Dresher. Sorry. I should have introduced myself while we were under that truck."

She smiled then caught her lip between her teeth. "Vivian Lirette. Thank you for saving my life."

He waved his hand. "I'm glad I was there to do it."

She grabbed it. "Your hand! You're hurt."

He stared at the scrapes on the backs of his hands, some acquired in his climb. "This is nothing. I'll clean it up later." What hurt were his ribs, but he knew from experience they weren't broken.

The door opened behind him and he stood, shielding Vivian from the intruder. Two uniformed police officers strode in. It couldn't have been more than ten minutes since the call.

The taller man spoke. "We're here about the incident in front of the store."

Russ fisted his hand. As if attempted murder was an incident. "Someone tried to run Vivian down."

The officer pulled out a small notebook. "I'm Officer Kent, and my partner is Officer Truman. And you are?" He stared at Russ.

"Russell Dresher."

"Ma'am?"

"Vivian Lirette. I'm a cashier here."

Truman glanced over his shoulder. "Will, take Mr. Dresher into the other room and interview him."

Russ rested his hand on her shoulder. "You okay?"

She nodded. "Thanks."

"Sure thing." The man strode to the room and after Russ entered, he closed the door. He pointed to a chair in front of a desk. "Have a seat."

Russ sat and Will leaned against the desk, pulling out his own notebook. "Give me your contact info and then tell me what happened."

Russ described the car he'd seen and everything that had transpired, wishing for the first time he'd gotten the license plate number. Protecting Vivian as the car bore down on them had been his only thought. After a few questions, they were done.

The officer cracked the door open and Vivian's voice drifted through. He closed it. "We'll wait a bit." He must not want Russ to hear Vivian's version of the story.

A few minutes later, a voice came through the door. "Will, we're done."

Will pulled the door open and preceded Russ into the other room. Vivian stood beside Officer Kent, more than a head shorter than him. Her pale face and trembling lips told him that she realized she'd almost died. Sure, she'd thanked him for saving her life, but the full impact must have hit her as she was questioned.

Russ stepped up beside her and barely stopped himself from wrapping an arm around her waist. He wanted to protect her and show her he cared, but they'd formally met minutes ago. Bantering for months at the checkout register might not count for her.

Kent tucked his notebook into his shirt pocket. "Ma'am, if you think of anything else, let us know. We'll call if we have any more questions." The officers exchanged a glance and left.

Vivian sagged into the chair. "I can't believe this is

happening. I doubt they'll catch those guys."

Unless they try again. Russ was pretty sure Vivian hadn't seen the last of them. "When you're ready, I'll walk you to your car. I can follow you back to your place to make sure no one's waiting there for you."

Her eyes widened, and her hand balled into a fist over her heart. "Waiting for me…Why?"

"Because I want to make sure you get home and inside safely."

"No. I mean, why would someone be waiting for me?"

He squeezed her shoulder. "That car waited specifically for you. They know where you work. Why wouldn't they know where you live?"

She trembled under his hand. He hated causing her fear, but she needed to be cautious. "Come on. Let's get you home."

They left the room, and the woman at the service desk called out. "Vivian." She held out a bag. "One of the guys picked up your groceries."

Vivian took the bag. "Thanks, Jackie. Thank him for me, please."

Russ escorted Vivian to her car, his gaze scanning the lot for any cars with occupants. "Now, wait inside until I bring my car over."

He pushed his hand against his sore ribs and jogged to his SUV, not wanting his eyes off her for long, then drove to where she'd parked. He stayed close behind her on the way to her apartment, alert for anyone following. As they turned into the drive for a two family with parking on each side, he spotted a dark car down the street that he thought might be the same one that nearly ran down Vivian.

They exited their cars, and he followed her up the stairs. She slid her key in the lock.

He touched her hand. "When we step inside, I want you

to stay near the door while I check the place out."

He didn't know if the guys remained in their car or, if they'd come inside to wait for her. Once the door was open, he nudged her against the wall.

She caught her lip between her teeth and nodded.

Russ wished he had his gun, but he didn't like leaving it in his car in a remote parking lot when he climbed. He had other means of protection if need be. The kitchen was easy. No place to hide. In the bathroom, he pulled back the shower curtain, finding a gleaming tub, and peeked in a closet that had no room to hide with the shelves filling the space. In the small living room, he checked behind a worn overstuffed chair set angled in a corner. Not a likely hiding place, but he didn't want to take any chances.

He popped into a bedroom which held a desk and nothing else. The closet was empty. In the next bedroom, a double bed was pushed into the corner of the small room. He looked under it. Not even dust bunnies. He couldn't say the same for his bed. The closet held a modest number of clothes and three pairs of shoes in a neat row. A silky teal robe hung on a hanger over a hook on the inside of the door. He wondered if she wore anything under it.

Back in the kitchen, he approached Vivian. "Everything looks fine, but I saw a car up the block that may be the one from the parking lot. Lock the door while I go check it out."

She sucked in a breath, the fear returning to her eyes. He stepped out and waited until the lock engaged before running down the stairs. He followed a seven-foot hedge that bordered the driveway, to the sidewalk. He peeked around the edge, seeing the car where it had been before. He couldn't walk right up to it without being seen.

With his hand on his side, Russ jogged to the back and stifled a groan when his injured ribs bumped the neighbor's fence post. He squeezed through a space behind the hedge into the next yard. The stealth reminded him of missions, pumping him with adrenaline, making him hyper-aware.

He crept across the back and vaulted over the four-foot stockade fence into another yard, stifling a groan when the landing jarred his ribs. Grateful a dog didn't attack him, he crept, bent over, along the fence to the front corner of the yard. About halfway across, he dropped to his knees, so he could straighten and ease the pain in his ribs.

He peeked over the top. He'd come up even with the front passenger door. It was the same car, and two men sat staring up the street. He wondered if they'd seen him follow Vivian into her driveway and waited for him to leave. He snuck his phone out and snapped a picture. Maybe with a closer look, Vivian might recognize them, or the police might find them in their database. With pressure on his side, he crouched and worked his way to the end of the yard. A quick look found a tree blocking his view of the license plate.

If he were the only one involved, he'd go up, and throw the car door open. He'd yank the closest guy out, and pound on him until he got the information he needed. But there was no way to know if someone else was sneaking up to Vivian's door right now.

Russ tamped down the urge and hurried back to Vivian's the way he'd come. He knocked on her door, and the curtain pushed aside, revealing half her face before she let him in.

"Is it them?"

"Yes. Pack a bag. Do you have someone you can stay with?"

"No. I've only been in town four months, and I'm not that close to anyone yet."

"Then you'll stay with me."

She crossed her arms. "I don't even know you. Maybe I'm not safe with you either."

Frustration made him want to yell, except she'd be more

afraid. "I want to keep you safe." He fished in his pocket and extracted his cell phone, remembering the cracked screen when he saw it. "Did Officer Kent give you a phone number?"

"Yes." She dug into her purse and pulled out a card.

He handed his phone over. "Dial it." Once she did, he hit speaker.

"Officer Kent."

"Officer. This is Russ Dresher from the grocery store. I followed Vivian home, and the car that nearly ran her down is parked down the street. Can you send a car to take them in?"

"I'll do it personally."

Russ kept his gaze on Vivian. "You might want another car to block the other direction."

"I'll take that under advisement."

He shrugged. "Also, I'm taking Vivian to my place until it's safe to return."

"Excellent idea. Let's hope we get this resolved tonight."

Russ pocketed his phone. "There. The police know where you'll be. I couldn't possibly hurt you without getting into trouble."

Her shoulders relaxed. "All right. I'll pack."

She left the room, and he went to the side of the living room window. Only the front half of the suspicious car was visible, the back being blocked by trees. He was tempted to drive away with Vivian hiding in the backseat, park a couple blocks away and hike back, leaving the guys to think she was still in her apartment. He'd enjoy catching them breaking in. Again, that would leave Vivian exposed, and he couldn't risk it.

A police car pulled up behind the dark car, and before a cop could exit, the suspects raced off with a squeal of tires. No second police car blocked the street. Kent should have taken his advice. The case probably wasn't high enough priority to pull out all the stops. The siren wailed as the police gave chase.

Vivian came into the room with the strap of her bag over her shoulder. "Was that a siren?"

"The police came and took off after them. Let's hope they catch them." He took her bag. "We'll get out of here while they're occupied."

Chapter 2

Vivian propped her fists on her hips. "How am I supposed to get to work if I can't take my car?" She'd already agreed to go home with a near stranger, and now he wanted her trapped without her own transportation.

Russ jiggled the keys in his hand. "I'll take you and pick you up after. You shouldn't be alone when you're out."

She glanced behind him at his almost new SUV. "How about your work? I can't expect you to take time off to chauffer me."

He shrugged. "My brother's my boss. He'll understand."

She didn't want to be forced into depending on someone again. That part of her life ended when she moved. But those guys could come back and it wasn't safe to stay here alone. It made sense that they'd know her car. "If they watch the store for a few days, they'll figure out you're driving me and follow us to your house." He shouldn't risk himself for her.

"I'll make sure to lose any tail before I get home." He scanned the street, jiggling his keys again. All was quiet now that the sirens had faded. "It's still clear. We really need to get going."

She huffed. "Fine." At the moment, she didn't have a choice. She wished she had a friend here to stay with, but her only friends were back with the mess she'd run from.

He held the door open and took her bag before she climbed in, tossing it into the back, then got into the driver's seat. Fifteen minutes later, he turned into the driveway of a ranch style house, touched a button and the garage door lifted. He drove in and closed the door.

In the months she'd been in town, she'd only become familiar with the main roads. She'd gotten lost after the second turn. "How far is this really from my place?"

He pointed. "Your house is about three blocks that way, and—" He turned his hand ninety-degrees. "—two blocks that way."

"I could have walked faster than you drove it."

He opened the driver's door. "I wanted to make sure we weren't followed."

She hadn't thought about that, which was all the more reason for her to stay with him. She hopped out of the car and waited for him to come around. "Have you had experience in this kind of thing?"

He grabbed her bag from in back. "Not specifically for evading on the streets, but I was a Marine for twelve years, so I've had a lot of practice observing my surroundings."

A Marine. That would explain all his muscles. Her shoulders relaxed. Danger wasn't new to him, and he'd saved her life because that's what Marines did. And he'd continue to protect her until she was safe. She followed him into the house. They passed through a neat mudroom with a washer and dryer, and entered the kitchen.

It was spotless, not a dirty dish anywhere in sight. Amazing for a bachelor, but probably due to his Marine training. The kitchen wasn't large, but bigger than hers, with twice the counter space, and probably thirty years newer. Two people could comfortably work together in this kitchen.

Russ continued to the stairs. "I'll show you to your room and then I'll see what I can put together for dinner."

She stayed on his heels.

He pointed to the first door on the left. "That's my office. The opposite one is my bedroom. I've got my own bathroom, so the hall one is all yours."

He stepped inside the second door on the left and dropped her bag on the bed. "Here you go."

"Thanks." She followed him back to the kitchen.

Russ opened the refrigerator. "Let me make dinner. I don't have much, which is why I was at the store."

Vivian peeked over his shoulder. There was more empty space than food. "How old is that chicken?"

"I cooked it yesterday."

Her eyes widened. "You cooked a chicken?"

He thrust back his shoulders. "Hey, I can cook. I stuck it in a crock pot in the morning."

"Okay. Do you have rice?" There had been some vegetables in the crisper drawer, visible through the empty shelf covering it. She could make dinner as a thank-you for saving her.

"I think so." He opened a lower kitchen cabinet, and grabbed a plastic canister and set it on the counter.

Vivian removed the chicken from the refrigerator, and snagged a bottle of soy sauce from the door. "Do you have a wok?"

"No, but I have a big frying pan."

She needed something to do, and the thought of watching this man putter in his kitchen wasn't good for her equilibrium. She'd moved for a reason. "Why don't you get it out and let me do the cooking?"

He retrieved a pan from the drawer under the oven and set it on the stovetop. "You're my guest. I should cook for you."

She nudged him without thinking, and held her breath, waiting for the anger to build. Nothing showed on his face. She let out a slow breath. "You saved my life and you're putting me up in your home. This is a way I can thank you."

His gaze tracked from her to the stove, as if he thought she'd burn the house down. "Fine. I'll go check some things.

You know where my office is, if you need anything."

She waited for him to leave before starting the meal prep. Her head told her that Russ could watch every step she took in the kitchen and not complain. But honed instinct forced her to be alone while cooking. Bob often told her his mother cooked better than her, but during meal prep, he'd pick apart every step, and she'd finish a wreck.

She put rice on to cook and chopped vegetables. It had been six blessed months of cooking only for herself. She hoped Russ's reaction to the meal would be better than the last one she'd had from Bob.

Being in Russ's house couldn't last more than a couple of days. It was already crazy that she was there. Fortunately for her, he'd gone shopping when he did or she'd be dead. But to open his home to a stranger meant he was also opening himself up to the same danger she apparently was in.

Vivian set the table and placed the hot dishes in the center, giving it one last appraisal before going in search of Russ. He was pecking away at a laptop and looked up at her when she stepped inside the door. "Dinner's ready."

"Great. Thanks." He typed a few more strokes, closed the lid, and followed her to the kitchen.

"Wow. That's smells good." He stood beside a chair and waited for her to sit before seating himself.

She wondered if that had been drilled into him in the Marines or if he'd learned it in childhood. She uncovered the dishes. "Go ahead."

He nodded at the food. "No. You first." He smiled. "I want to make sure you get as much as you want before I gobble it all up."

She scooped some rice onto her plate, and hoped he'd like the food as much as he'd alluded to. She added the chicken-vegetable-gravy mix on top of it.

Russ loaded his plate and took a bite. "Mmm. I love this.

I couldn't figure out what it was when I smelled it, but I think there's ginger in this. I didn't know I had any."

She swallowed a savory mouthful. "There was a small piece under the carrots. I had to peel away the wrinkled part." She didn't know what to talk to him about. This was so different than the checkout line, although there was food between them, as usual. "So, are you going to make a Chinese dish out of this?"

His forehead wrinkled as he stared at her, then his expression cleared. "No. I think a beautiful woman is going to make that for me. She's a really good cook."

If he'd told her in the checkout line that she was beautiful, she would have thought he was flirting and dismissed it. Now, she wasn't sure how to take it. "Uh, thanks."

She ducked her head and continued eating. With Bob, she'd gotten to the point where she never started a conversation. He'd belittle her for talking about something inconsequential, or berate her for her opinion on anything he disagreed with. It had been better to let him talk, and appear to agree with him.

Being alone with Russ made her a bit uncomfortable, so she fell back on the same conversation pattern. It didn't work as well since he asked personal questions and she wasn't ready to talk about herself. She rushed through the meal and fled to her room, leaving Russ to clean up.

~~~

Although his priority was to keep Vivian safe, Russ thought they'd have a chance to learn more about each other while she was under his roof, but after three days she was proving resistant. Perhaps he made her nervous, and the only way to change that was if she got to know him, which wasn't

195

happening so far.

The police didn't know anything more than on the day the incident happened, so there was no telling when Vivian could safely return to her apartment. It gave him time to reach her, but it would also make her antsy to go home.

He backed out of his garage. "We're taking a drive by your place before I drop you at work, just to check it out."

"Why? Do you think something's wrong?"

"No. I went by yesterday, and everything looked fine. I just want to make sure."

"Oh. Okay."

He took a circuitous route, slowed as they passed, and scanned the area. Damn. That wasn't good.

She grabbed the door handle. "My door's open. Stop!"

"I see that, but I'm taking you to work. I'll come back after and check it out." He hadn't expected problems with her place or he would have checked after dropping her, like before.

"No. I should see. You won't know if anything's missing."

He kept driving, and she turned to stare over her shoulder.

"Let me check first. If I think you need to see it, I'll bring you later."

She settled back in her seat and crossed her arms. "Fine."

Yeah. Not so fine, but she was safer not going in, and he'd find an excuse later to keep her out.

"Why don't you give me your keys, and I can make sure it gets locked up?"

She fished into her purse then held out the keys. He took them and dropped them into the cup holder.

A couple more turns to lose a tail they may have picked up at her place, and he pulled into the store parking lot. He scanned cars for occupants and checked for any cars parked in conspicuous places. Everything appeared normal.

She opened the door and he stopped her with a hand on her arm. She stiffened and gasped.

Damn. He wished he'd remembered not to startle her that way. "Remember, call me if—"

"Yeah. Yeah. I know. If anything seems suspicious."

He sighed.

She bit her lip and stared at her lap. "I'm sorry. It's just that—when you grabbed my arm, it put me in a defensive mode, and I was rushing to appease him—I mean you." She peeked at him and back at her lap.

"No. I'm sorry. I didn't think."

Wide eyes stared at him. Maybe she wasn't used to someone apologizing to her.

He grinned "Well, now that we're both sorry, maybe you better get into work."

He scanned the parking lot again just before she stepped out, and walked into the store. She turned once inside and waved, seeming recovered from how he'd scared her. He gave a nod, and wondered what to do to make her more comfortable with him. Show her that he wasn't like her ex.

He headed back to Vivian's place, not worrying about being followed since they already knew where she lived and worked. He pulled into the driveway behind her car, noting that her door was now closed. Someone was inside when they passed earlier, or else a kind neighbor closed the door.

Russ grabbed his gun from the glove box. As always, he had another in his nightstand. A scan of the neighborhood before leaving the car found nothing suspicious. He checked the street once more as he reached the apartment door. He turned the unlocked knob. Adrenaline kicked in, giving him a pleasant surge, and upping his awareness. He crouched, threw the door open and swept the room with his gun.

Empty.

A glass, with an inch of brown liquid, sat on the coffee table. It hadn't been there when he'd brought Vivian home to pack. In the kitchen, the sink held dirty forks and a plate. He smelled old food and checked the kitchen trash as he passed. Food and empty bottles sat in the bag. Vivian had taken the trash out when they'd left before. Someone had moved in.

Gun at the ready, his senses tingling, he crept down the hall, peeking into the office, and halted at Vivian's bedroom. She had left the bed neatly made, but now it was in disarray. Someone had slept here.

In the bathroom, a razor and shaving cream sat on the sink. The wet shower curtain was pulled back and a damp towel hung over the towel bar. He'd been dropped into the Goldilocks story. He breathed a sigh of relief that Vivian had stayed with him, not wanting to think about what would have happened to her if she'd walked into her home with this intruder present.

Maybe it was a new tactic. The killer planned on waiting for her to return. He went back to the bedroom and checked the closet. An open suitcase sat on the floor. He rifled through the contents, but didn't find anything to identify the owner. He lifted out a pair of pants and held them to his waist. About three inches shorter than his own. He folded them up and dropped them on the rest of the clothes.

He was already late for work. There was only so much time he was comfortable taking off, even if his brother was his boss. On his way out, he locked the door. Make the intruder have to pick it again. He leaned against his car and found a number on his phone.

"Officer Kent."

"Hi, Officer. This is Russ Dresher."

"What can I do for you?"

Russ stared at Vivian's apartment. "We drove by

Vivian's this morning, and the door was open. I came back after dropping her at work. A man is living there."

"Who is he?"

"No idea. There's food and dirty dishes, a suitcase of clothes. Maybe it's just someone taking advantage of an empty place, but I don't think so." It hadn't been empty long enough.

"You're right. I'll take some drive-bys and stop if it looks like someone's there. Don't go back. You don't need to confront him."

Russ would love to confront this potential murderer, but for now, he'd leave it to the cops. He'd never forgive himself if he spent time staking out Vivian's apartment while one of the guys went after her. "Yes, sir."

~~~

Russ stopped the car short of the sliding glass doors for the grocery store and studied the area. Maybe the killer had noticed Russ was picking up Vivian and would come up with a different plan.

Vivian paused beside the automatic doors and he pulled forward, driving onto the sidewalk to give her less exposure. He leaned over and pushed the door open, so she could jump in. He longed to give her a kiss hello, but they weren't there yet.

She buckled her seat belt. "Okay. Let's go to my apartment."

He drove away from the building. "No."

"But you said—"

"I said, if I thought you needed to see it. Nobody robbed it."

She glared. "You wouldn't know if anything was missing."

Russ huffed out a breath. "Viv, nothing's missing. If anything, there's too much there."

She threw her arms up. "What does that mean?"

"There are dirty dishes in the sink, a can of shaving cream in the bathroom, and the bed's unmade."

Her eyes widened and her mouth opened and closed before she spoke. "I didn't leave it like that."

"I know. I was there when you packed. A man has moved in. He's probably waiting for you to come back. You're not going near the place until the police arrest him for trespassing and whatever else they can think of."

Her hands shook and she clenched them in her lap. "A stranger moved into my apartment?"

"Don't worry. We'll figure it out."

Russ turned into an Applebee's parking lot and pulled into a space marked for order pick-up. He could have gotten food before picking up Vivian, but wanted it to stay hot.

"What are we doing here?"

"You've cooked all our meals. I thought I'd give you a break." He could have gone home early and cooked for Vivian before picking her up, but he thought this would be more special.

A few minutes later, a woman came out of the building with a bag. She handed it to him through the car window and extended a clipboard. "Please sign this and take the bottom copy."

He wasn't sure how this evening would go with Vivian's apartment break-in hanging over them, but he would do his best. As usual, he took the long route home, continually checking for cars.

The street was clear and he drove into the garage. They hustled into the kitchen, and Vivian hurried to set the table as Russ pulled the cartons out of the bag. Since he hadn't given her a menu to choose from, he'd selected two different meals.

He went back to his car and retrieved the bottle of wine he'd purchased before picking her up.

Upon returning, he found she had unbraided her hair and it rested in waves around her shoulders. She plated their meals while he poured the wine. They sat across from each other.

Russ itched to touch Vivian's hair. It looked soft, and he wanted to run his fingers up into her scalp and massage her head. "You have beautiful hair."

She lifted a lock and stared at it. "It's just mousy brown."

"No, it's not. The sunlight catches it and it looks like strands of gold."

She stared at the strands, and gave him a quick glance, then tossed her hair over her shoulder.

Russ waved at the plates. "Which do you want?"

Vivian's eyebrows rose. "I figured you'd want the steak."

"I like both. Either is fine with me. It's your choice."

Her gaze darted between the two plates, but rested longer on the steak. Her eyes met his. "It doesn't matter."

Russ pulled the chicken plate in front of him and ate a piece of broccoli.

She hesitated a moment before taking the other dish.

He wanted this dinner to be different from the others, more than stilted conversation about nothing. Maybe talking about himself might help her to reveal a little, too. "I've lived here all my life, except when I was in the Marines. What about you?"

"I moved here four months ago. After my…" She took a bite of her roll.

"After your what?"

She glanced away, then down at her plate. "Divorce." She was embarrassed about it.

He already knew about the divorce, so he wasn't sure why she hesitated to repeat it. "Hey. Lots of people divorce. I'm sure you had good reasons."

Vivian grimaced. "Yeah. Tell that to my dad. He really liked Bob and tried to get me to go back to him. Of course, Bob was always on his best behavior in front of Dad."

"Is that why you moved?"

"Partly." She stared at him. "I didn't have friends anymore. Bob separated me from them and I was having trouble reconnecting after the divorce. And Bob made sure we ran into each other a couple times a week." She shivered.

He leaned forward. "Did he hurt you?"

"No. Not really. He never hit me. It was more verbal abuse. But sometimes when he yelled at me, he—" she wrapped a hand around her upper arm "—grabbed me. Sometimes it left bruises."

He touched her fingers, not wanting to take her hand in case it reminded her of her ex. "I'm glad you moved here. I know you told the police you don't think your ex is responsible for trying to run you down, but he seemed awfully controlling." He raised his brows. "Maybe it's a case of, if he can't have you, nobody can."

She bit her lip and tipped her head. "I don't think so. If I'm gone, he'd never get me back. His style would be to chip away at me until I changed my mind."

He gave a curt nod. "All right. I'll take your word on that. But the question is—who wants you dead?"

She shook her head. "I've thought and thought about it, but I can't come up with anyone."

Russ picked up his fork. "Okay. Let's not let this spoil our dinner." He wasn't going to discuss her apartment with her. Someone wanted her to show up. It could be the would-be killers, her ex or someone else.

She pushed the food around on her plate. "What about

you? After you'd been in the Marines so long, I'd think you'd want to make a life of it. Why did you leave?"

He stared at the chicken on his fork. "I lost seven buddies in an hour and I didn't have a scratch. I was through."

She took him by surprise when she clasped his hand. "I'm so sorry. That must have been rough."

He rubbed his thumb along the back of her hand, drawing from her strength. "Three of them were married. Two of those had children. I would have traded places so one of them could have gone home to his family. It just wasn't worth it anymore." He closed down the memories. Plenty of other times to relive those, like in his nightmares.

"And then you came home and worked for your brother. What's his name? What do you do?"

The change in subject surprised him. He thought she would ask more about what happened, but she seemed to understand he couldn't talk more about his loss. "Aaron. He owns a machine shop. We fabricate metal parts and repair machines and motors."

"That sounds…interesting."

He raised a brow. "Sometimes. When I get to design something." It couldn't beat the adrenaline rush of going into battle, but he didn't want to tell her about that. "Do you enjoy being a cashier?" She always seemed happy.

She shrugged. "I like talking to the customers, but it's not what I should be doing."

"And what's that?"

She hesitated and he wondered if she'd answer.

"I'm a paralegal. My plan was to move to a bigger city than this, but when I drove through here, I liked the looks of it." She shrugged. "Now I'm stuck with no lawyers hiring."

"Hopefully, something turns up soon." He didn't want her to leave town for another job, but he understood the need to do something you're interested in.

They'd made it through dinner, and Russ cleared away the dishes. He brought out the dessert he'd ordered with the meal. Two pieces of cake, one chocolate and one carrot.

She grinned. "Ooh. I can't decide."

He pushed them toward her. "Do you want both?"

She giggled. "Are you crazy? I'll split them with you."

He liked that idea, especially when she took a bite of each cake without dividing them. He moved to the seat closest to her and shoved his fork into a corner of the carrot cake, scooping a piece into his mouth. "Mmm. Delicious. They have the best desserts."

She watched him take another bite. "Thanks for this. I can't afford to eat out, so I haven't had a chance to try any restaurants."

He felt bad that Vivian's ex and father had driven her away from the home and job she loved, and now she had to scrimp to get by. He was glad he could supply her with this simple pleasure. They finished the cake, and he took the plates to the sink, but quickly returned, hoping to catch her before she went to her room for the night.

"Let's watch a movie."

She studied him for several seconds. Surely, by now she trusted him. "Okay. What should we watch?"

He settled on one end of the couch, and let her sit where she was comfortable. He was surprised that she sat on the far side of the middle cushion and not on the opposite end of the couch. He turned on Netflix. "I picked out a few I thought you might like."

Her eyes widened. "You want me to pick?"

He grinned. "Well, I did make the initial selection, but I hope you like one of them. If not, we'll find a few more."

She narrowed her eyes as if she had trouble believing him, and picked out the rom-com. Maybe it was a test to see if he'd protest. He didn't mind. The comedy might help her to relax.

The movie was funnier than he expected it to be. One time when Vivian laughed, she put her hand on his leg. He wrapped his hand around hers for a moment. It was progress that she'd touched him without thinking.

During a scene where the two characters kissed, he slanted his eyes toward her and found her blushing. It was a pretty intense kiss, but Vivian had been married, not a virginal young girl. Maybe she'd been thinking about him. He hoped.

The credits rolled and he turned off the television. "I enjoyed tonight."

Vivian gave him a small smile. "I did, too."

He vowed to plan a date for after the murder attempt was resolved.

She stood and he did also. Happiness still filled her eyes. "Tonight was really nice. Thank you." She kissed his cheek, her vanilla scent wafting through his system, and she hurried away.

"Goodnight, Viv." He would call that a successful evening. He hoped it meant her walls were starting to crumble.

Chapter 3

Russ turned off the machine he'd been milling a replacement gear on when his phone vibrated in his pocket. If it was Vivian, he didn't want to keep her waiting. He checked the screen. Officer Kent. He hit *talk*, glanced at the others working, and headed outside for quiet.

"This is Russ Dresher."

"Russ, I thought you should know. We were cruising past Miss Lirette's apartment and saw movement inside, so we stopped. Unfortunately, the perp escaped and went over the fence."

Russ wished he'd been there with them. He would have made sure the guy didn't get away. "Did you get a look at him?"

Kent huffed out a breath. "No. He had a hood up. Athletic build. He scaled the fence with no problem."

If they'd gotten him, the danger for Vivian might have been over. "What now?"

"We keep watching."

"Okay. Thanks for letting me know." He tucked his phone away and returned to his machine, his thoughts on the mystery man.

Three hours later, Russ finished the part and headed to the door. He stopped at his brother's office. "I finished the Thurston order. I'm going out for lunch. I might be a while since I'm stopping by Vivian's apartment."

Trent's eyebrows dropped. "Be careful. Taking your gun?" Russ had told him about the squatter.

"I've got it." He jangled his keys and strolled out the door.

After a short drive, he parked on the street in front of Vivian's. No car, except hers was parked in the driveway and the street was clear. Russ retrieved his gun from the glove box, and got out of the car.

He skipped the creaking step, pulled out the key he hadn't returned and opened the door a crack. He paused, his heart pounding and his senses heightened as he strained for any sound inside. Nothing. He ventured in, gun at the ready. Dirty dishes covered the coffee table worse than before. Same in the kitchen. Russ crept down the hall and stepped into the bedroom. The bed was still a mess, and glasses and bottles littered the nightstand, but the suitcase was gone. He checked the bathroom, and all the male toiletries were also missing.

The squatter had moved on. At least, out of Vivian's place. The intruder probably came back after the police chased him off to collect his property, but likely hadn't gone far.

~~~

Vivian exited the store, glad her shift was over. It was an average day, but her thoughts had been on Russ. He leaned against his SUV, arms crossed, his gaze at the far end of the building. She paused, admiring the bulging muscles in his arms, all the way to his shoulders. His chin had a hint of shadow, and she imagined kissing it and along his jaw to his neck. Maybe she'd nibble on his earlobe. His eyes turned to her, and he grinned, opening the car door. She tried not to blush.

Once they were safely inside, he checked over his shoulder and put the car in gear. "We're going to your place.

The intruder seems to be gone, so I figured we could clean up. Are you hungry?"

"Famished."

He took her to a fast food burger place. She figured they'd take the food to her apartment, but they ate inside.

Maybe the guys who'd tried to run her down had given up. If that was the case, she could move back. Somehow, that didn't appeal to her as much as she thought it would. She liked having her own space, but enjoyed spending evenings with Russ. She hoped he'd still want to see her after she was back in her apartment.

Russ backed into Vivian's driveway, rear-to-rear with her car. She wasn't sure if it was so he could make a fast getaway or to place her closer to the house door.

He touched her arm. "Wait until I come around."

He unlocked the glove box and took out his gun. She would have thought the sight of a gun would scare her, but one in Russ's hands gave her comfort. Maybe he didn't think it was over. As always, his head swiveled all around as he skirted the front of the SUV and came to her door. She still didn't keep as aware of her surroundings as he did.

"Let's make it quick."

Brisk steps brought them to the front door, and Russ held her key. He positioned her beside him as he unlocked and pushed the door open. She loved how he protected her. No one had ever looked out for her before.

They stepped in together. He closed the door and nudged her to the side, standing in front of her as he swept the room with his gun. "Stay here until I check all the rooms. He set off, gun raised.

The living room was in shambles. Besides bottles and glasses on the tables, crumpled chip bags and pizza boxes were strewn on the floor. Her throw pillows had been tossed into a corner, and the lap blanket she left folded at the end of the couch dangled precariously. No wonder they ate before coming.

Russ joined her, tucking his gun in the back of his pants. "It's all clear. Why don't I collect trash, and you can wash dishes."

"Thank you." She stacked plates in the living room and grabbed four glasses, taking them to the kitchen. After filling the sink with hot, sudsy water, she loaded the dishes. She appreciated Russ's help. After they were assured everything was over, he could have dropped her at her door to deal with cleaning up, but here he was, making it easier for her.

Bottles and cans clinked behind her as Russ dropped them into the trash can that dangled from one hand.

Vivian grabbed glasses and plates from the kitchen counter and stuck them into the soapy water, then washed and rinsed them.

Russ returned with the trash can and four glasses, setting them beside the sink. She glanced into the container. Seeing the beer cans and whiskey bottles, the brands her ex-husband drank, she froze.

He touched her arm. "What's wrong?"

She stared into his concerned face. "Those are my ex's brands. He was here."

"A lot of people drink those brands."

"Both brands? And someone who would break into my apartment?"

Russ set the can down and took her hands, ignoring they were wet. "Are you afraid of him?"

She caught her lip between her teeth. "Maybe a little."

"I know you said he never hit you, but do you think he might now?"

"No, but I can't face him." Bob was so good at wheedling her into doing what he wanted. She was more determined where he was concerned, but she didn't want to test it.

Russ wrapped an arm around her shoulders. "He's not getting near you. Why don't you grab more clothes before we leave?"

She frowned. "But he's gone. I could move back here."

He lifted her chin with a finger. "We don't know if he left town. He picked the lock to get in the first time. What if he does it while you're asleep?"

She shivered. No way would she want to wake up with Bob pawing her. "Okay. You convinced me." She propped her hands on her hips. "I wonder why he's here." She'd tried enough times to make him understand they were through. When she left town, it should have been as clear as a big banner.

Vivian returned to the sink. "I don't want to stay here any longer than I have to."

"I'll change your sheets. Do you have another set in your bedroom closet?"

"Yes. Top shelf." She wouldn't have to smell Bob in her bedroom. Once, she'd slept better with her nose pressed against his arm. Now, the thought of it curdled her stomach.

If this was another bid for her to come back to him, why would Bob stay hidden?

~~~

By the time they left Vivian's apartment, it was dusk. Russ had her wait inside until he checked the street and scrutinized the yard, gun by his side, then went back to escort her to the car. She probably thought he was being too careful, but she didn't complain.

He extended the bag to her. "Here. You carry it and stay right beside me."

He held his gun, ready to whip it up in any direction. A

shot rang out, and he tackled Vivian to the ground. She grunted and he hoped he hadn't hurt her. He pointed his gun toward the hedge near the sidewalk, but couldn't see movement. Adrenaline pumped up his senses. How had he missed this? "Are you hit?"

"No, but I felt it pass me." Her voice quavered.

If it were just him, he'd roll or crawl until he reached safety, then circle the house, coming up behind the shooter. Out in the open like this, he needed to stay with her. He couldn't roll with Vivian or she'd be exposed half the time.

He whispered in her ear. "I'm going to shift to the side. Leave your duffle bag. I want you to crouch and make a bee line between the cars." He hoped the shooter didn't change position because he didn't want to expose Vivian any more than he had to.

She wiggled the bag's strap off her shoulder, scrambled to her feet, keeping bent over as she darted toward the cars. Russ chanced a look behind as a bullet hit the ground a few inches in front of him, spewing up dirt. Vivian gasped and increased her speed.

They reached the edge of the driveway, and Russ spun and took several shots toward the end of the hedge. "Get on the other side of my car."

She scurried between the vehicles. A shot was returned. Russ fired a couple more shots as he dropped down beside his car.

Vivian sat with the tire at her back, eyes closed, chest heaving.

"Are you all right?"

"No. Yes. I mean, I'm not hurt, but I've never been so scared in my life."

He tugged his phone out and gave it a quick glance to select a number.

"Officer Kent."

"It's Dresher. We've got a shooter in front of Vivian's apartment."

"Are you inside?" He almost sounded like a concerned friend.

"No. We're hiding behind my car."

"On my way. And I'll call backup."

"Come in with sirens." Russ shoved his phone into his shirt pocket. He squeezed Vivian's shoulder. "The police should be here soon."

Russ didn't take his eyes from the spot the shots had come from. Nothing moved. Sirens in the distance assured him they were close. At least, he hoped those sirens were for them. The shrubbery rustled, and he stiffened, pointing his gun at them.

A police car screeched to a stop in front of the house, and a second blocked the street. The siren silenced, but the flashing light remained. Officer Truman sprang from the vehicle and took off toward the hedge. He must have seen someone when they pulled up.

Kent got out and swept his gun across the yard. "Dresher, where are you?"

"We're behind the cars." He stood.

Kent made his way over to them and glared at Russ's gun. "Do you have a permit for that?"

"Yes. It probably saved our lives. Do you want to see it?"

Kent waved. "Never mind. This has escalated."

"How so? Attempted murder by car to attempted murder by gun. That doesn't seem like an escalation to me, just a different means." He stared at Vivian, who had remained on the ground, her arms wrapped around her drawn up legs. He needed to get her home where she'd be safe and could calm down.

Truman jogged up the sidewalk and leaned against

Russ's SUV. He took gasping breaths. "They got away."

Russ sucked in a breath. "Two of them? Like in the car?"

"Yeah. Two." He huffed. "And they weren't as athletic as the other guy I chased."

There were three guys. *Could they have different reasons for going after Vivian?* "We went into Vivian's apartment and cleaned up."

"Was that a good idea?" Kent asked.

"With what happened afterward, apparently not. But all the guy's stuff was gone, except for his trash."

Vivian met his gaze and bit her lip.

"From the brands of beer and scotch, Vivian thinks the squatter was her ex-husband."

Kent squinted. "You think these incidents are unrelated? That's quite the coincidence."

Russ shrugged. "Why would her ex come here if he hired someone to kill her? He's got a better alibi if he stays home. That tells me he's here for a different reason."

"That makes sense. We'll pull up pictures of the ex and distribute them to the department. Maybe we can talk to him."

Russ held his hand out to Vivian. "Come on. Let's get home." Home. He liked how that sounded.

She grasped his hand and he pulled her up into his arms, then studied Kent. "Are we done here?"

Kent waved. "Yeah. You probably shouldn't come back here."

"Thanks." They walked around the car and he settled Vivian into the passenger seat then retrieved her duffle bag from the yard. He tossed it into the backseat as he slipped behind the wheel.

They didn't speak as he took a long way home, always checking his mirrors for a tail. His gaze kept straying to

Vivian. She'd tucked her hands under her armpits, and her face looked ghostly in the dim light. He pulled into the garage and breathed a sigh of relief. Vivian was safe.

He grabbed her bag, and they entered the kitchen. "What do you want to do?"

She rubbed her forehead with a shaky hand. Maybe she had a headache. "No one followed us, right?"

"No. You're safe here." He hoped she believed that.

She pushed her shoulders back and took a deep breath. "I think I'll unpack my bag and read."

"All right. I'll run it upstairs for you."

"No. I can do it."

He handed it over. "Let me know if you need anything."

"Thanks. For everything." She kissed his cheek.

Russ liked the small sign of affection or thanks. Whatever it was, it showed she was more comfortable with him.

He prowled around the dark living room, stopping at the window to peek through a crack in the drapes. Nothing. Nothing moved, just like at Vivian's apartment where he'd missed the guys behind the bushes. Only luck or divine intervention had saved them.

A cry from Vivian and a soft thump had him racing for the stairs, his heart pounding and gun in his hand. He took the steps two at a time. He hadn't thought to clear the rooms when they got home, and now Vivian might pay the price for his incompetence. He shoved open Vivian's door and swept the room with his gun.

"Where are they?" He pointed the gun at the ceiling.

Vivian stood wide-eyed in front of him, a purple shirt clutched to her chest and her bag at her feet. "No one's here."

He stuffed the gun in the back of his pants. "You cried out."

She nodded and tears glazed her eyes. "My bag. My

clothes. Have a bullet hole. It just struck me how close we came to getting shot."

He wrapped his arms around her trembling body, and she burrowed her head into the crook of his neck. Her arms snaked around him and held him like a vise.

He ran his fingers up through her hair, releasing her vanilla scent, and massaged her scalp. "But we didn't. I'll keep you safe." Warm tears dripped down his neck. "It's okay. You're fine. We're both fine." He tipped her head up. "Why don't I take the bag and give you back anything that survived? Then you don't have to see them."

She nodded, but didn't let go of him. "Don't leave yet."

He pointed at a rocker in the corner. "Okay. I'll sit there until you fall asleep."

"No. I need you to hold me for a while. Please."

He liked that he could give her comfort, but not the reason for it. His fantasies of the first time she was in his arms in a bedroom involved different emotions.

"Okay."

Russ set his gun on the nightstand, pulled back the covers and arranged the pillows so they could partially recline, then kicked his shoes off. He scooted onto the bed, and Vivian crawled under the covers and rested her head on his shoulder. He draped his arm over her and tucked the blankets around her, keeping himself uncovered.

Her body relaxed, and her chest expanded with a big breath. He could have lost her today before he got a chance to really get to know her.

Usually an adrenaline rush made him euphoric, but not today. All he felt was fear. Fear that he wouldn't be able to keep Vivian safe. Fear that she would die in his arms. Fear that he'd have to go on without her.

He kissed the top of her head, and her arm tightened across his ribs. He scooted them into a more reclined position. Her breathing evened. He should slip away, but he couldn't. Chances were, she'd have a nightmare about the shooting, and he wanted to be there to calm her. If he woke from a nightmare, afraid he'd lost her; he'd need her in his arms for reassurance.

She felt perfect and right beside him, her vanilla scent enveloping them both. He eyed his gun on the nightstand. He'd only be sleeping lightly tonight.

Chapter 4

Vivian chatted with her customers as she ran their purchases over the scanner. She enjoyed talking to them and hoped some would become friends.

She still wanted a paralegal position, but her tight money situation was less stressful than living near her ex-husband.

She'd relaxed a lot after her move, not having to worry about when Bob would pop up. Now the tension was back after seeing the evidence of Bob's presence. And maybe he was the one trying to kill her. She'd heard of that. A guy killing a woman because he couldn't have her.

The customer paid with a card, and Vivian handed over the receipt. "Thanks. Have a great day."

The next customer had only a bottle of Coke and a bag of habanera flavored chips on the belt. She didn't want to think about the person she knew who liked that combination. She glanced up. "Hi. How are..." Her tongue froze. Maybe her heart did, too. But her stomach churned. "Bob, what are you doing here?"

His handsome face didn't mesmerize her the way it used to. Now she knew what was behind it.

"We need to talk."

Vivian's shoulders tensed. "I did all the talking I'm going to at those sham marriage counseling sessions."

"Oh, but there's more." He gave her a smarmy grin. *How had she ever loved that face?*

She didn't want to talk to Bob. Ever. At one time, he'd been able to wheedle her into nearly anything. Not any more.

Except, they'd become the center of attention. Shoppers behind him and in other lines stared at them. She didn't want to lose her job because her personal life had disrupted it, but he wouldn't leave until he got the answer he wanted.

"Fine. My shift ends at six." She glanced at the items on the belt. "Are you actually buying these?"

"Yes."

She scanned and bagged the items then told him the total. He paid and took his sack. "See you later, sugar."

She shivered at the endearment. The thought of never seeing him again had made her happy, and even though he'd fought the divorce, she hoped this wasn't another play to get back together.

The woman next in line brought her back to her senses. "Are you all right, hon?"

Vivian dragged in a breath. "Yes. He just surprised me."

"Maybe you should have someone here when you get off work."

Vivian grinned. "I do. And he's a lot bigger than Bob."

The woman smiled. "Good for you, hon."

Vivian enjoyed leaving work and seeing Russ waiting for her every night after her shift. And best of all, he took her home with him. At first, her new apartment had settled her nervous spirit, giving her a calm she needed after Bob's mood swings. But she'd grown weary of her lonely space. Making friends wasn't as easy as it had been when she was in school.

Vivian searched for a manager, and not finding any, sent a quick text to Russ. *Can you come inside when you pick me up?*

~~~

Russ walked through the door of the grocery store and

straight to the end of Vivian's lane. He waited for her to see him, then pointed to the side. She gave a nod. He strode to the door of the room the police had interviewed him in and leaned against the wall beside it, arms crossed.

His gaze darted between Vivian and the entrance door, wondering why she'd asked him to come in.

And there it was. A man stepped through the door and paused, his gaze settling on Vivian. He was tall, probably Russ's height, and thin. His brown hair was neatly trimmed, not too long, not too short. He wore faded jeans and a collared pullover. Russ didn't like the possessive way the guy ogled Vivian.

The man approached her lane. She spoke to him and pointed toward Russ. Narrowed eyes took Russ in. The guy stalked to Russ and sneered. "You her boyfriend? Lover?"

"I'm not her boyfriend…yet. I'm Russ."

"Bob."

"Ah. The ex-husband."

Bob glared. "It's not going to stay that way."

"Two people make that decision, and Viv already made hers."

Bob patted his pocket. "Well, I've got something that will make her change her mind."

Vivian walked towards him, covered drawer in her hands. She paused, gaze never wavering from his. "I have to count the cash drawer, then I'll be right out." The door beside them buzzed, she pushed through, and it clicked closed.

Russ wondered what this man held over Vivian that would make her go back to him. She'd left town to get away from Bob. He hoped she was strong enough to resist. "Are you the one who moved into Viv's apartment?"

"What's hers is mine."

"That's not what the divorce decree says."

Bob Glared. "She was supposed to come back so I could

talk to her. But she's shacked up with you, isn't she?"

Russ shrugged. "She's staying at my place so I can protect her."

"Riiight. That's the scam you used on her."

Leave it to a jerk to see other people's motives as the same as his own. Bob didn't seem to know about the near hit and run, or shootout. Russ wasn't going to reveal anything he didn't have to.

They stood as silent sentinels as other employees left or entered the room.

~~~

Vivian came through the door. "Let's go to the break room." She led the way through another door and sat at a table in the corner.

Bob glared down at her, arms crossed, and thrust his chin towards Russ. "I'm not talking to you with him here."

Vivian scooted her chair back. "Then we're done, because I'm not talking to you without him." Russ's hand on her shoulder gave her the courage to stand up to Bob.

Bob's gaze dropped to her shoulder. She didn't care that he didn't like another man touching her. He dropped into the chair across from her. "Fine. But he doesn't interfere."

Russ took a position beside her, and she touched his leg. He took her hand in his, giving it a squeeze. She'd never had this kind of support against Bob before.

She thrust her shoulders back. "What's this about, Bob?"

Bob leaned forward. "It's about you and me getting back together because I have something you're going to want."

"You don't have anything I want." The thought of being alone with him sent revulsion through her system.

He drew a paper from his shirt pocket. "Sure I do." He unfolded the page and flattened it on the table, writing facing

Vivian. The top of the letter had been folded and torn off.

Russ leaned closer, his warmth giving her comfort, and read it alongside her. Patricia Andrews had died leaving Vivian her assets. They'd been searching for months and weren't sure if they'd reached the proper person. The estate would revert to a distant cousin of Patty's if Vivian hadn't been found within a year. The attorney's name and contact number had been blacked out with marker.

Vivian's fingers skimmed the name of the deceased. "Aunt Pat. My mom's sister. I haven't seen her since I was eight. She and Dad had an argument after Mom died, and he took me and left." She had a memory of raised voices, but not what they were angry about. Her eyes were glazed with unshed tears. Right when she needed a mother figure, her father had taken her away. She'd lost both her mother and aunt in the space of days.

Bob pulled the sheet back. "How sad. Now you can get her money. Marry me again, and I'll give you the contact info."

Vivian glared. "I wouldn't marry you if it was a million dollars."

Bob slammed his fist on the table and Vivian jumped. "We were still married when that broad died. Even if you don't marry me, I'm owed half."

Russ rubbed her arm, giving her courage to face the man who'd made her life hell.

Vivian shook a finger at her ex. "She died after I filed for divorce. You don't get anything."

Bob glared. "I'll take you to court, and your money will be lost in attorney fees."

She leaned back and sighed. She'd survived this long without money, she could continue, as long as it meant Bob wouldn't be in her life. "Fine. I won't do anything and the cousin can have it."

Russ cleared his throat. "How about giving him a finder's fee of five-percent if there's enough money?"

"Fifty-percent or nobody gets anything."

Russ raised his brows. "Really? You'd take nothing over getting something in your pocket? If it's a hundred-thousand, you get five grand."

Bob leaned forward. "Yeah. And it's fifty-thousand if I get half."

Anger rose that Bob would get something her aunt had intended for her. Vivian shoved her chair back, and stood, placing her trembling hands flat on the table. "Stop! This is my inheritance, and it's like I'm not even here. Ten-percent or we're through here."

Bob's mouth dropped open and he slammed it shut. "Fine."

She'd never stood up to him before. She ran when she had the chance.

Bob flipped the letter over and grabbed a pen from the table and slammed it on top. "Write it down and sign it."

Vivian snatched up the pen and printed.

I, Vivian Lirette, will give Bob Doherty ten-percent of proceeds of the estate of Patricia Andrews when I receive it.

She signed her name and dated it.

Bob grabbed the paper.

"Wait! I want a copy of it." She wouldn't put it past him to try to change it. She pulled out her phone and snapped a picture, and handed the page back to Bob. "Now, how do I contact them?"

Bob stood. "I'll get the info from my car."

After he left, Russ wrapped an arm around her. "Are you all right?"

She sunk into him and nodded against his shoulder. "I haven't thought of Aunt Pat in years. I'm surprised how hard it hit me that she's gone. I should have asked my dad how to find her."

"I'm sorry. Is this thing with Bob okay?"

She shrugged. "I guess it will have to be."

She led him to the front of the store.

A bang and a scream had them racing for the door. Bob lay crumpled on the pavement, blood pooling under his head. A quick glance in both directions found the culprit speeding away. The same car that tried to run her down.

Russ pointed back at her. "Viv, stay near the door. Call 9-1-1."

A woman leaned against the back corner of the closest car, her hand over her mouth, her widened gaze on the man on the ground. "It came out of nowhere. If I'd been a few steps closer, it would have hit me, too."

Vivian dialed and explained the situation. She hoped the ambulance didn't take long. She wanted to check on Bob, but Russ's instruction to stay kept her near the door.

The woman leaned against the end car as Russ crouched beside the unconscious man and grasped his wrist. "Hold on, man. Help is on the way."

Sirens blared in the distance and Russ stood. A red and white ambulance streaked through the parking lot, slowing as it approached the front of the store, and stopped at an angle. A police car came from the other direction. Between the two vehicles, no cars could pass.

Two EMTs squatted at Bob's side. Russ joined Vivian and held his hand out. She took it, needing the warmth and comfort.

"We'll have to tell the police about your meeting with Bob."

Her eyes widened. "Do you think it's related?"

He took her other hand as well. "Viv, it was the same car that tried to run you down."

Her hands twitched. "But why go after him instead of

me?"

"They must know who he is and realized he'd tell you about the inheritance."

Officer Truman wrote in his notebook as the witness talked. Officer Kent glanced at the scene and noticed Vivian and Russ. His brows rose. He said something to Truman, then walked up to them. "You two involved in this somehow?"

Russ glanced at Vivian. "Probably." He nodded toward Bob. "He's her ex-husband."

Kent's gaze darted between the two.

Russ wrapped an arm around Vivian and she settled against his body. She might have ended up like that if Russ hadn't saved her.

Russ tightened his arm on her. "The same car that tried to run down Vivian hit Bob."

The officer frowned.

One of the EMTs had brought out the stretcher.

"There's a paper in his shirt pocket you might want to collect before they take him away," Russ said.

"Oh, is there?" Kent hurried to the stretcher and spoke to the closest man. Kent plucked a glove from his pocket, slid it on and pulled out the letter. He stepped back and waved the men on.

Russ stepped forward. "Wait. You may want to get his car keys, too."

The EMT on the far side of the stretcher pulled the keys from Bob's pants pocket and tossed them to Kent. "Can we go now?"

"Yes. Go." Kent strode back to Vivian and Russ, and touching only the corners, opened the letter. He read through it and flipped to the handwriting on the back. His gaze darted to Vivian.

"Hold on a second." Kent went to the cruiser, found a

large plastic Ziploc bag, and slid the letter inside it. He came back to them as the ambulance drove away with the siren wailing.

He stared at Vivian. "This letter came to your old address about a month ago and your ex opened it. Did he call you?"

Vivian shook her head. "I changed phones after the divorce. I didn't give him my number."

"So he tracked you down. Do you know how?"

"He didn't tell me. I didn't try to hide. I just didn't want to be in the same town as him."

Kent waved the letter. "He showed you this today?"

"Yes." Vivian explained about the meeting.

Kent glanced at Vivian's side of the page. "And you all left to get the address from his car?"

"No," Russ said. "Vivian and I talked for a minute before heading out. We heard the scream as we neared the door."

Kent jiggled the letter. "Maybe the cousin doesn't want Vivian to claim her inheritance."

Vivian crowded closer to Russ. "There can't be that much money. I don't remember her being rich."

Kent shrugged. "You were a kid. How much does a kid know about wealth? I'd suggest you contact the lawyers as soon as possible. Then, if this is the cousin trying to kill you, he won't have a reason anymore."

Russ pointed at the page. "In that case, we should get the torn off letterhead from Bob's car."

Vivian understood Russ's point. Her life would be in danger until she met with the attorneys and proved who she was.

"Do you know what your ex's car looks like?" Kent asked.

"If he still has the same car." It might be fun to key the

225

paint when she found it. She glanced back at the police officer trailing behind them. Maybe not a good time for that. Vivian marched along the line of cars in the closest lane. She scanned the cars she passed.

Russ caught up with her and took her hand. "Whoa. Slow down. You don't want to miss it."

She tugged his hand and kept up the pace. "He always parks his baby at the end." She reached the last car, scanned the vehicles, and pointed to the left. "There."

She took off again as Kent caught up with them, and stopped beside the driver's door of a blood red Camaro. He'd had it two years.

Russ patted it. "Wow. This is sweet."

He put an arm around her.

He bought a beautiful car and she got his hand-me-down. "Yeah. I think he loved it more than me."

The car beeped and Kent stopped beside them. "Here. Let me get the door."

Like always, the inside of the car was spotless. Vacuumed once a month and a touchless carwash every week.

Kent rummaged in the compartment between the seats then rounded the car and opened the passenger door. In the glove box, he pulled out a strip of paper with his gloved hand. "Here it is." He dropped it into the bag with the rest of the page.

Kent circled the car back to them.

Vivian pulled out her phone. "Can I get a picture of that?"

"Sure." Kent held the bag up and she snapped a shot.

Russ asked, "Do you need anything else from us?"

"Yes. Vivian, do you know your ex's next of kin?"

"Just his mother." She bit her lip. She did not want to see that woman. "Do you want me to call her?"

"No. The hospital will. Give me her info."

Vivian searched through her phone and recited the woman's name and number, glad she wouldn't be the one to tell her the bad news.

Russ raised his eyebrows. "You've got your ex-mother-in-law's number?"

She shrugged. "When I got my phone, I just copied my whole contact list."

He tugged her hand. "Let's get you home."

It sounded good to her. Russ's home felt more and more like her home, too.

If the men in the car were after her because of the inheritance, it should be resolved in a few days. They just had to get safely through those days.

Chapter 5

Morning came too early. Vivian hardly slept. And when she did, nightmares woke her. Although she hadn't seen it, her dreams played over and over—the black car hitting Bob, throwing him high in the air, landing on his head and tumbling into a broken heap. She shivered.

She dragged out of bed and showered, dressing in jeans and a t-shirt. It was her day off, but Russ still had to work. He asked her to come with him so he'd be reassured she was safe. He offered the comforts of the break room at his brother's shop, and she'd bring her eReader so she could read or play games. Seeing Russ do his normal work for a little while would be interesting.

The aroma of pancakes and sausage hit her when she opened the bedroom door. She hurried to the kitchen.

Russ turned from the stove, and grinned. "Will you hit me if I tell you that you look awful?"

She rubbed her eyes. "I thought the same thing when I looked in the mirror. So, no." She stepped beside him. "That smells delicious. Thanks for cooking."

Russ skimmed his fingers down her back and kissed her temple. She liked how he touched her whenever she was close, as if he couldn't help himself, but she wished the kiss would have been a little lower. Maybe.

He turned off the burners. "Why don't you pour coffee and get out the syrup?" He placed two pancakes and three sausage links on each plate and set the platter with more in the center of the table. She wouldn't be the one to polish off the rest.

Vivian added cream to her cup and set both on the table, then took her seat as Russ sat across from her. She was halfway through her meal when his phone rang.

"Good morning, Officer Kent."

Her gaze locked on Russ. It couldn't be good if Kent was calling so early. Vivian couldn't read his poker face, and he didn't say more than one word at a time.

"All right. We'll be at *Dresher Die* today if you need anything else." He set his phone down.

She pushed her plate away, her appetite gone. "What did he say?"

He took her hand. "That was about Bob."

She squeezed his hand. "What?"

"He died early this morning without regaining consciousness."

She sucked in a breath. She didn't love Bob anymore, and she hated how he'd treated her, but she hadn't wanted him to die. She blinked back tears that surprised her. Probably lack of sleep made her more emotional. "His mom is going to blame me."

He rubbed his thumb across her hand. "Why would she blame you?"

"He came here to talk to me, and now he's dead."

"You didn't ask him to come."

"Okay-okay. I'm not blaming me." The woman disliked her. Long ago, his mother had seen the bruises on Vivian's arms and asked what she'd done to get them, as if it was her fault Bob had injured her. Vivian had stopped trying to get his mother to like her after that.

"We'll make sure she doesn't see you." He quirked an eyebrow. "Would you want to go to his funeral?"

She shook her head. "Not with his mother there. If she

wasn't…probably not."

"Come on. Let's clear the table and get out of here."

Dishes in the dishwasher, Vivian grabbed her purse and eReader, and they headed into the garage.

After a half-hour drive, they reached Russ's work. "You drive this every day? How long does it take to get to the store?"

He chuckled. "It only takes ten minutes. I took a convoluted drive in case we were followed. And the store is five minutes from here."

He escorted her inside to his brother's office. "Hey, Aaron. I want you to meet Vivian."

Russ's brother smiled as he came around the desk. He had the same dark hair and blue eyes as Russ, but was a couple inches shorter and stockier. Aaron held out his hand. "Nice to meet my brother's beautiful house guest." He gave his brother a raised eyebrow, and Russ responded with a short headshake.

Vivian hoped that wasn't brotherly communication asking if they'd slept together. She shook the man's hand. "Nice meeting you. I'm looking forward to seeing your shop and what Russ does here." A stack of papers sat on Aaron's desk. She didn't want to take up more of his time. "Russ, you ready?"

"Sure." He grabbed a pair of ear covers, led her to the nearest machine, and explained its purpose. The following two machines hummed as men worked on them. They gave a quick wave before turning back to their work. Curls of shiny steel skittered to the floor. She'd expected a metal shop to be dirty, but except for the newly created steel shavings, the work area was neat and clean.

At the next machine, Vivian paused as her gaze darted to the woman operating it. She chided herself for being surprised to see a woman working in the shop. A closer look found the woman doing fine detail work. It wasn't something Vivian thought she'd be good at.

Russ strode to another machine, bigger than the others, and patted it. "And this is where I do most of my work." He unhooked a clipboard and showed her a CAD diagram. "It's a part for an old machine that's no longer manufactured. You can watch me if you want. When you get bored, go on into the break room beside Aaron's office. I'll come when it's time to call the lawyer and offer moral support."

The news of Bob's death had made her forget about calling them. She was nervous that claiming her inheritance wouldn't stop those guys from coming after her, but relieved Russ would be there for her.

She stood back as Russ set up his part and reviewed his diagram again. He adjusted some dials, handed her ear protection, and put on the ones dangling from the machine, as well as safety glasses. He turned on the machine and in moments, curls of metal spun off the workspace.

Vivian watched for a little while as the piece took shape, then wandered off to find the break room. She pulled off the ear protection and set it on the table. A dozen chairs surrounded it, and four leather or fake leather cushioned chairs surrounded a coffee table. Not surprising, the room was as clean as the other areas she'd seen. A coffeemaker held a half-full pot. She grabbed a cup from a drying rack and poured a small amount, tasted it, then filled the cup. In the refrigerator, she found cream and added a dash to her cup, then settled into a leather chair with her eReader.

"Are you ready to make that call?"

Vivian startled at Russ's voice and glanced at the clock. Nine-eleven. "Yes. Thanks."

He sat beside her. She could have done this on her own, but his support had become important. She extracted her phone from her purse, and called up the law office's number on the screen. She punched it in, and took a shallow breath as it connected.

"Bradley and Harmon, Attorneys. Ellen speaking."

She sat up straighter. "Hi, Ellen. This is Vivian Lirette. I'm Patricia Andrews' niece. I received the letter about her will."

"Wonderful. She so hoped we could find you. I just wish it would have been before she died."

"You knew her? I couldn't remember where we lived when I was little, or else I might have tried to go back there."

"She was a sweet woman. Everybody loved her. When can you come?"

She'd have to arrange time off, but not too far out since she was still at risk from the killers. "How about Friday?" That would give her three days to get the day off.

"Nine o'clock. We need you to bring identification and your birth certificate."

"Okay." She'd returned to her maiden name when she divorced, so that would make identification easier.

"I'm looking forward to meeting Patricia's niece."

Vivian ended the call and dropped the phone into her purse. "I never thought about needing documentation. As a paralegal, I should have, but the attorneys I worked for didn't write wills."

Russ took her hand. "Do you have your birth certificate?"

"I think so. I have to go through my lock box. And I have to get the time off work."

"I'm coming with you."

She frowned. "You don't have to."

He scooted to the edge of his seat. "Vivian, it's a six-hour drive. Anything can happen between here and there."

The blood left her head. If she'd been standing, her legs would have given out. "You think they might try something on the way to the attorneys? But I've spoken to them."

"You haven't proven who you are yet. These guys have one last-ditch chance to make sure you don't get there."

She hadn't considered how desperate the cousin might be. She could die on the way to the attorneys' office. And Russ with her.

~~~

Vivian loosened her seatbelt, leaned her back to the door and drew up a leg. "I wish you'd let me drive." The in-dash GPS displayed five-and-a-half hours remaining.

Russ glanced at her. "I've driven longer than six-hours before, and in the Marines, I drove a huge truck day after day. This is a picnic."

"I never asked because I thought maybe you didn't want to talk about it. Did you go to Afghanistan?"

His hands tightened on the steering wheel. "I served four tours there."

"That must have been rough."

"It was okay—until it wasn't."

Maybe that was his way of saying he couldn't talk about it. "You lost your friends in Afghanistan?"

He blew out a long breath and his gaze darted between the two mirrors and the road ahead. "Yeah. That's where it happened."

Vivian thought that was all he'd say, and she would let it go.

Several minutes passed. The turn signal came on and he exited into a rest stop. She grabbed the door handle, but he stopped her with a hand on her arm.

Russ stared out the windshield. She could barely hear him when he spoke, his voice flat.

"Sanchez and I were sent on ahead to do reconnaissance.

We'd been gone maybe fifteen minutes when there was an explosion behind us. We raced back." Several rapid breaths did nothing to calm him. She took his hand and he squeezed it.

"There was nothing left. The two vehicles were blown to bits. Body parts were everywhere. On the outskirts…we found our lieutenant's body." He blinked several times. "It was whole, along with a chunk of metal through his chest."

Vivian stifled a gasp. She leaned into him and dropped her head to his shoulder. He tipped his head back.

"I lost brothers—friends—that day. I fulfilled the rest of my contract and left."

She rubbed his arm. "I'm sorry. I can't imagine going through that."

He covered her hand. "You had a taste of it that day we were shot at on your front lawn."

She shivered. "There's no comparison. I was scared, but we turned out fine. You lost people you cared about."

He dragged in a deep breath. "I need a few minutes. Stay in the car."

He got out, hit the lock button, and closed the door. He scanned the cars and people in the lot, then took off at a run up the walk bordering the parking lot. She was almost afraid he'd keep on running into the woods, but at the end he turned back. Almost to the car, he dropped to his hands and started push-ups, his gaze on the exit from the highway.

She almost wished she hadn't asked him, not expecting it to be so bad or hard for him to tell it.

He sprang to his feet and stretched his arms over his head. He looked way too good that way—big muscles, flat stomach. He came up to the car and knocked on the window. She hit the lock button and he opened the door and dropped into the seat.

Vivian leaned close. "Thank you for telling me. I know

it was tough."

She tipped her head to kiss his cheek, but he turned and their lips met. His hand brushed her cheek and threaded through her hair. His tongue tickled her lips and she opened for him. For a moment, the emotion he poured into the kiss nearly overwhelmed her. She pushed closer and clutched the back of his neck. If she knew it could be this good, she would have tried to steal one sooner.

He pulled back. "Sorry. I shouldn't—"

She put her hand over his mouth. "Don't say it. That was the best kiss I ever had."

His eyebrows rose. "Ever?"

She almost giggled at the slurred word behind her hand, and pulled it away. "Ever."

He gave her a quick kiss. "If we had the time, I'd show you even better, but we've got to get back on the road."

The smile dropped from her lips as memory of Bob's death and her near death came flooding back. She settled into her seat and buckled her seatbelt.

They sped down the highway, and she tipped her head to the side, into the headrest and watched Russ drive. His gaze flicked from place to place, always checking everything. The only time he seemed relaxed was in his home.

She flipped on the radio. Satellite, of course. When he drove her to work and home, the radio was always off. She tuned it to an easy listening station she used to like, way back when she could afford the subscription. His gaze met hers for a moment before turning back to the road.

They made small talk, but mostly the music filled the silence. She was glad she didn't have to do this drive alone. An hour to go, and it would probably feel as long as all the other hours put together.

Russ's gaze snapped to the rearview mirror. "Turn facing front and hold on."

Vivian stared out the back window. A black car that looked like the one that almost ran her down drove close behind. "It's not them, is it?"

"I think it is. It's too much of a coincidence that they're tailgating." He glanced at her. "Face forward. If they ram us, you're less likely to be injured."

She turned, dropped her feet to the floor, and tightened her seatbelt. How was this as scary as bullets flying at them? They were surrounded by a protective metal cage, but this was a last ditch effort for the cousin to make sure she didn't make it to her appointment.

~~~

Adrenaline surged through Russ, and he became hyper-aware, noting the placement of every vehicle surrounding them.

He wished he could confront the men in the other car, but he couldn't risk Vivian. "Hand me my gun from the glove box."

She opened the box and froze. "Do you want me to…"

He snatched it. Keeping the SUV on course with his knee against the steering wheel, he made a quick check of the gun, then sat it between his legs with the muzzle slightly under his thigh.

Vivian's voice quavered. "What are we going to do?"

He patted her arm. "For now, we're going to keep ahead of them. I'm going to weave through that pack of cars up ahead to put some space between us. We won't be able to lose them on the highway, and I don't want to get off on unfamiliar roads." He should have mapped alternate routes. Too late for that now.

It would have been better with heavy traffic and three lanes, but he'd make do with two. A semi-truck led the group in the right lane. He might be able to use that when he got closer.

He didn't want to make her more afraid, but she needed to know how serious the situation was. "They know we're going to the lawyers, so they know which exit we'll take."

"I'm sorry I got you involved in this."

He lifted her hand and kissed the knuckles. "I'm not. If I hadn't been in the parking lot at the right time that day, you'd be dead. That's not acceptable."

The threat should be over by lunchtime the next day. He just had to get her there.

Russ sped up and passed the last car in the pack. He darted into the right lane in front of it, passed a car, and jumped into the left again. Farther up, he switched lanes and back again, settling into the speed of traffic. The black car had caught up, but stayed behind the other cars. An opening presented in the right lane, and Russ dashed into the gap, roared ahead and back into the left lane.

Another twenty miles and he'd reach the exit. The guys were probably biding their time until they could get Vivian and Russ alone.

He needed assistance. He shoved his phone at Vivian and she nearly dropped it. "Can you dial 9-1-1 and put it on speaker?" Vivian seemed too nervous to talk coherently, and he needed it kept short and to the point.

A few seconds later a woman's voice came over the line. "911. What's your emergency?"

He tightened his hands on the wheel. "We're being followed on the highway by a car known to have run down and killed someone." He explained their situation, the exit they'd be taking, and requested backup.

"Sir, hold on while I call a car to that exit." A few moments later, the man came back on the line. "I've got two units on the way. Now, give me your plate number and car info and what info you have on the other car."

Russ gave the information. "What should I do when I see the police car?"

"Pull over. Our officers will try to get the other car to stop. Otherwise, they'll give chase."

Russ signed off and shoved the phone back in his pocket. He glanced in the mirror. "They're edging up."

Vivian gasped. He didn't want to scare her further, but taken by surprise would be worse.

If they rammed him, it could send their car into another vehicle or off the road. From behind, they could shoot out a tire, or if they pulled up beside him, they could shoot into the car.

He darted around another car, returning to the left lane. Only a handful remained ahead of them with ten miles to the exit. They might run out of cars to shield them.

Their faster lane approached the semi. Russ held his breath. He'd be cutting this one closer than the rest. He swung to the right lane, hit the gas and barely squeezed in front of the car that had been in front of him. A prolonged horn honked.

A glance at the mirror found his follower copying his move. Two cars behind. He came up beside the semi and slowed down, still going faster than the truck, but not as fast as before.

The car behind him honked. "Sorry, buddy." The second car came abreast the truck. With two cars between and no way for the killer to get closer, they were the safest they'd been since spotting the black car.

He rubbed Vivian's stiff arm. "Viv, relax. If we have an accident with you all tense like that, you'll have more serious injuries."

"Easy for you to say." She drew in a long breath and let it out slowly. Her arms and legs relaxed slightly.

Like now, he could be a coiled spring inside, but his body would do what needed to be done.

If he were alone in the SUV, he'd relish outwitting his opponent. He might have dropped back and had his gun ready in case the others showed theirs. Turn this into a cat and mouse game where he became the cat. He would have exited long ago, getting them away from innocent drivers, found woods to hide in, and taken out his opponents, one at a time. That's how he'd been trained.

With Vivian by his side, he needed to think smart and not take undue risks. She didn't deserve what she'd been put through. He couldn't misstep and lose her.

He wished he could match the truck's speed and stay beside it, but he didn't want to further anger the other drivers, not sure why he cared since it was Vivian's life in the balance.

As he cleared the truck, Russ hit the gas. It wouldn't be long before the black car caught up. Three miles until the exit. At this speed, just over two minutes. He hoped it was enough time for the police to be ready.

Chapter 6

Vivian clutched the armrest with one hand and wrapped the other around the edge of the seat as Russ veered into the right lane. She'd never been on such a crazy ride. At any moment, Russ might over steer and they'd flip, or their pursuers might get past the other cars and shoot them. Her last look at the speedometer had shown ninety, and she was afraid to check again since they had to be going faster.

A glance at the GPS screen showed a mile to the exit. She peeked over her shoulder. The black car had cleared the semi and swung into the right lane—and now was right behind them. At this speed, if it rammed them, it could send them careening down the embankment or spin them into the semi-truck.

The pickup truck at the front of the pack changed lanes and blocked the black car. Vivian's breath whooshed out. Her relief was short-lived. The black car dashed around the other vehicle, removing their shield. A man leaned out the window.

Her heart thumped, then pounded erratically. "He's got a gun!"

"Duck!"

She leaned forward, her cheek on a knee. The SUV lurched and sawed back and forth. Her gaze jumped to Russ's grim face.

"They shot out a tire. Stay down." Their speed slowed as he wrestled with the wheel, lessening the severe shaking. "Thank God we're at the exit."

They limped down the off ramp. She lifted her head to peek through the windshield as he eased to a stop at the sign, turned left and rumbled up behind a police car. A second car sat at the exit, facing in the other direction. She blew out a long breath.

Russ muttered under his breath. "That rim's ruined."

She straightened up and craned her neck to see the black car barreling down the ramp. "I'll buy you a new one and a tire with my inheritance." She owed him more than that for how many times he'd saved her life.

"It's fine. What's important is getting through this alive."

The black car made an abrupt turn to the right, over the grassy border and shot onto the street with a squeal of tires. The lights and siren came on the police car facing in that direction, and it tore off after the speeding car. The police hadn't had much luck so far catching it.

A knock on Russ's window startled a gasp from her. A police officer with black hair and gray at the temples stood at the door. Russ rolled the window down. "Thanks for helping out."

The man rested a hand on his hip, near his gun. "Why's this guy after you?"

Russ pointed at Vivian. "If she doesn't show up to collect her inheritance, another member of the family will get it. Her ex has already been killed. And this is the third attempt on her life." He pulled his phone from his pocket and scrolled. "You can call Officer Kent for details." He rattled off the number.

"Is this relative local?"

Russ shrugged. "Probably. Officer Kent tried to find out from the lawyer who the relative is, and the lawyer wouldn't tell him."

"When's your appointment?"

"Tomorrow at eleven."

The officer leaned a hand against the car. "I would suggest having a police officer with you, so they can witness the will and get the name of that relative."

Vivian leaned down to get a better view of the officer's face. "Is it possible to get a police escort in the morning rather than have him meet us there?"

Russ grinned. "That's a great idea, Viv." He turned back to the policeman. "Can you arrange it? It's Bradley and Harmon."

"I'll see what I can do." He held out a card. "Give me a call in the morning. After we've got this cleared up today, I'd like you to come into the station to file a report. It happens to be a couple of blocks from a tire shop."

Her gaze flicked to Russ and back to the officer. "Do you know where we could stay tonight where those guys won't find us?"

"Continue straight about three miles. The two tallest buildings are hotels. You should be pretty anonymous at either."

Russ shifted in his seat. "Thanks, Officer Delgado. Can you stick around while I change the tire?"

"Sure. No problem."

Vivian was relieved the officer would have Russ's back. No telling if the black car would evade the police and come back to look for them.

Russ squeezed her hand. "Why don't you stand with the officer while I replace the tire?"

"Okay."

They both slipped out of the car. She approached the officer while Russ opened the back hatch. She enjoyed the play of muscles along Russ's back as he loosened the lug nuts, raised the car with the jack, and finished removing the ruined rim. The tire was shredded, probably half of it strewn across the highway. She hoped it didn't cause damage to any vehicles.

"Are you from around here?" The officer's voice drew her attention away from Russ.

"I left when I was eight. I don't remember much about the place."

"Doesn't matter. It's changed a lot since then. A mall went in fifteen years ago. More stores and housing developments have popped up. Not the same at all." The officer grumbled. Maybe there was more crime since the town grew.

"Who are you inheriting from?"

"My mother's sister. I hadn't seen her since we moved."

"What was her name?"

"Patricia Andrews."

His eyes widened. "I knew her. She was a social worker. We ran into each other from time to time removing children from abusive homes. She was a good woman."

Vivian's eyes misted, and she glanced away. The few memories she had of her aunt were connected to her mother. And those always hurt. She'd missed having a mother like most of the kids had when she was growing up.

The clunk of the wheel rim being dropped into the back of the SUV brought her attention back to Russ. He closed the back and rubbed his hands on his jeans. "All set."

The officer stepped forward. "All right. Give the station a call in the morning, and we'll try to have someone accompany you from the hotel to the attorney's office."

Russ shook the officer's hand. "Thanks."

She and Russ opened their doors as the other police car pulled up. He joined the officer beside the car while Vivian stayed within the open door and hoped they'd speak loud enough to hear.

The new policeman joined them. "Sorry. I lost them. He

blew through a red light and caused an accident. I stayed with the vehicles until another unit came."

"You got their plate number?" the first officer asked.

The new guy grimaced. "I got it, but the plates are stolen."

The first officer clapped him on the shoulder. "That's okay. Maybe we'll track down that car through the relatives tomorrow." He waved Russ away. "I'll explain after we let this couple go."

Vivian slipped into the car with Russ.

He patted her arm. "Let's find a tire place. I don't want to drive long without a spare."

~~~

Russ flicked the keycard with a fingernail the whole way down the fourth floor corridor to their room at the Marriott, Vivian close on his heels. The lock clicked when he slid the card into the slot. He pushed the door open, then dropped his bag on the bed closest to the door and hers on the other one. "I hope you don't mind I got one room. I didn't even think to mention it before we went inside. I don't want you in a separate room where someone might come in, and I can't hear it."

She caught her lower lip between her teeth and studied him for a few seconds then shrugged. "I feel safer with you nearby."

He felt good with her saying that, but worried about her hesitation. He patted her shoulder. "I'm going to move the car."

Not wanting to take the time to wait for the elevator, Russ ran down the stairs. At the bottom, he chose to go through an outside door rather than into the lobby, making note that there was only keycard access from the outside. He checked for the black car before allowing the door to close. He drove to the back of the building, reversing into a space between two of the five parked cars.

He hurried to a door near where he parked, and used his keycard to get inside. All this cloak-and-dagger activity thrilled him, until remembering that it was to protect Vivian.

From the moment he got in her line at the grocery store, he'd wanted to spend time with her, find out more about her. She'd been strong enough to leave her ex, and start a new life in a town of strangers. And with the attempts on her life, she didn't run and hide. Sure she'd given in to his precautions, but she'd lived her life.

He ran down the corridor, past service areas, to the lobby, and slowed to a walk. Beside the elevator, he pushed open the door for the stairs and raced to the fourth floor.

They'd eaten lunch across the street from a tire store while the tire and rim were replaced. Now the afternoon needed to be filled. He knew what he wanted to do, but Vivian seemed nervous enough sharing a hotel room with him, let alone a bed.

Russ opened the stairwell door and paused. A man stood in the corridor halfway to their room. No. They couldn't have found her so easily. His heart pounding, Russ walked briskly until he got close to the man.

The guy glanced up. "Hey, can you read the room number for me? I left my glasses in the car." He held out his keycard in its envelope.

Russ's shoulders relaxed. Just a lost guest. He studied the sloppy scrawl and shrugged. "Four-thirty-six or Four-thirty. I can't tell for sure." He handed the card back.

"Thanks. I thought it was just me. If I go to the wrong door, I hope nobody thinks I'm trying to break in." He continued up the hall, past Vivian's door and inserted the card in the door slot, and pushed the door open. He grinned, gave a thumbs up, and disappeared into the room.

Russ knocked twice at his own door before inserting the keycard and letting himself in. Vivian sat on the farthest bed, pillows behind her back and her eBook in her hands. He'd never asked her what types of books she enjoyed reading.

Russ perched on the bed inches from her bare toes. She lowered the tablet, not saying a word. She'd probably be happy to read all afternoon, but he wanted to spend quality time with her.

"How about we go for a swim?"

Her eyebrows popped up. "I didn't bring a swimsuit."

He grinned. "I always toss one in my bag when I'm staying overnight somewhere. I should have thought to mention it." He caressed the top of her foot, and her toes curled under. "Let's see if the hotel gift shop has any."

"Okay." She turned off her e-reader and set it on the night table. As she swung her feet around, they brushed his hip.

That impersonal contact shouldn't affect him so much, but he was a goner. He'd make it through the day and evening, but when it came time for bed, he'd give her a good-night kiss so intense it would keep them both awake in their separate beds.

~~~

They stepped through the open door of the hotel gift shop. Vivian scanned the room. A few t-shirts and sweatshirts proclaimed the local attractions, but not a swimsuit in sight. She was surprised at her disappointment since she hadn't wanted to fork over money for a swimsuit since she had one at home.

Russ marched up to the woman at the counter. "Excuse me. Do you sell swimsuits?"

The woman's gaze darted around the room. Yeah, pretty obvious answer. "No, but the store next door has them."

Russ grinned. "Great. Thanks."

He took her hand and led her past the front desk, and to a door at the side of the building. He stepped out and stopped, and she waited while he checked the area. He tugged and she followed him across two driveways and along the side of the next building. He kept between her and the parking lot as they stopped at the corner, and he scanned the parking lots. He whisked her across the front and into the first door.

Vivian paused, getting her bearings. Men's clothes were on the left and women's on the right. She headed down the aisle and stepped between racks when she found swimsuits. The tag of a bright blue one-piece caught her eye, and she nearly gagged. The price would pay for three of her outfits. This was such a bad idea.

Russ dragged her to another rack. "Try this one. It's a clearance rack."

The sign on top read *Up to 80% Off*. Most of them wouldn't be that much off. Vivian found the right size section and grabbed tag after tag, trying to find something affordable. There. She pulled out a one-piece of the most hideous shade of fluorescent green. She shoved it back in. No way would she wear it.

A beautiful jade colored bikini appeared between her and the rack, and she stepped back. It was attached to Russ's hand.

"I'll buy this for you."

She checked the tags, a price for each piece, and added them together. She shouldn't have bothered. The price for one piece was too much. She kissed his cheek. "No thanks. But thanks for the offer."

Back at the clearance rack, she finally found some swimsuits she liked at more affordable prices. Still twice the price of the suit she'd bought at Target. The best prices were on individual pieces—that didn't have matches. She picked out three bottoms and sorted through the tops, trying to find one that sort of matched. There. One bottom was black with a splash of fuchsia. One top was mostly fuchsia with splashes of black and other colors. Good enough. If they fit.

She grabbed a couple one-pieces in the same section and headed to the changing room. It didn't take long to strip to her panties and put on the bikini. How was it that so little fabric could make her body look good? She spun and peeked over her shoulder, ran her hands over her butt. That looked good, too. Sold. No sense trying on the others if she was only buying one suit.

Back in her clothes, she hung up the rejects and headed to the sales counter. She handed over her credit card as Russ stepped up beside her, a bag with the store logo in his hand.

She narrowed her eyes. "That's not the swimsuit you showed me, is it?"

"No."

"Then, what is it?"

A pen hit the counter. "Miss, can you sign this?"

After her purchase was bagged, Russ hustled her to the door. He did his usual reconnaissance and they hurried to the hotel's side entrance where he let them in with his keycard.

He took her hand. "Let's get changed and have some fun."

In their room, Vivian rushed into the bathroom with her purchase. She stripped and put on her new swimsuit, then stared at herself in the mirror. She couldn't walk through the hotel like this. She slipped her shirt back on, and fastened two buttons.

She stepped into the room. Russ wore his swim trunks, his shirt on, but not buttoned. All the time she'd spent with him and this was the first she'd seen his sexy chest. His grin told her that he knew where her gaze had been.

He held the bag up. "Here. I have something for you."

She didn't take the bag, so he opened it and pulled out a beach cover-up, black and fuchsia, longer than the shirt she wore. "Russ, you're not supposed to buy me stuff."

His eyebrows dropped. "Why not? Viv, this is a gift."

The tag had been clipped off, so she wouldn't know how much to pay him back for it.

He stepped up to her, unbuttoned her shirt, and slipped it from her shoulders. "It's a gift." He slipped one of her arms into a sleeve, but she'd have to help with the other.

The concern, worry, sadness in his eyes made her relent, and she slipped her other arm into the sleeve. "Thank you."

He grinned. "You are gorgeous. Let's go swim."

Once they reached the empty pool, Russ shucked his shirt onto a lounge chair and dove into the deep end of the pool. Vivian took off the beautiful cover-up, and dropped it on the same chair. She made her way to the shallow end, and eased into the pool, getting used to the water temperature, although it wasn't too cool.

Long strokes took her to the deep end where she flipped and returned.

Russ waited in the shallow water. "You're a graceful swimmer."

She shrugged. "But I'm not fast. And don't ask me to race."

"That's okay. I'll match your pace."

Several times, back and forth, they swam side-by-side. His strong, slow strokes kept him even with her shorter strokes.

She stopped in the shallows. "Let me see how fast you can go." He must need more exercise than traveling at her speed.

Russ kicked off from the wall like a torpedo, and raced

underwater across the pool. His head bobbed up at the end as he flipped, returned to her end, and repeated.

He boxed her against the wall, his respiration a bit above normal. "Viv, you are gorgeous in that suit."

His kiss was every bit as exciting as the one they'd shared after he'd told her about losing his teammates. Until he pulled her closer, wet body against wet body with barely a scrap of clothing between them. Then it was over-the-top the best, sexiest kiss she'd ever had. She tried to wiggle closer and he groaned.

The door opened to the chatter of excited children. Russ released her and fell back in the water. Her eyes widened. There was no way he could leave the water in that condition. He dove under and struck out for the far end.

Vivian paddled around in the middle as two of the three children cannonballed into the pool, causing big waves to rock her.

Russ swam up behind her and grasped her hips. "You ready to go back to the room?"

She nodded and headed to a ladder. How far would it have gone if they hadn't been interrupted? How far did she want it to go?

~~~

Vivian combed out her wet hair. The bathroom mirror reflected rosy cheeks and bright eyes. She'd had fun in the pool with Russ. It'd thrilled her heart when he'd called her gorgeous. Bob had called her beautiful, but it seemed to be always followed by something he wanted. Russ meant it and didn't expect anything in return.

She sighed. After leaving Bob, she'd been determined to go it alone, but if Russ hadn't flung himself into her life, she'd be dead. It was more than that. This man who risked his life for hers on several occasions was sweet, kind, and did crazy things to her heart when he looked at her. Bob's face never showed adoration the way Russ's did.

Wearing the same clothes she'd had on earlier, she left the bathroom. Russ had already changed back into his clothes. "Give me a couple minutes, and we'll go to dinner. In the hotel, so we're not exposed again."

"Okay." The bathroom door closed behind Russ. She sat on the bed and picked up her tablet to read, but her thoughts of Russ stayed her hand. She touched her lips, recalling the kisses they'd shared in the pool. He made her feel special.

The bathroom door opened, and she yanked her hand down. Russ grinned, and she blushed. He knew what she'd been thinking about.

He held his hand out. "Ready?"

"Yes." They slipped into their shoes and headed to the elevator. As soon as the doors closed behind them, Russ nudged her against the wall and kissed her.

"Russ, it's only four floors." She wished it was twenty.

He nibbled up her jaw. "I know. It's short enough that I can kiss you and not get carried away."

She giggled.

"Viv, are you laughing at my lack of restraint?"

"Maybe."

A ding signaled they'd reached the first floor, and Russ backed away from her. His face had become a neutral mask. Not that it mattered, since anyone could look at her face and guess what they'd been doing.

He took her hand and walked her to the restaurant, stopping in front of the hostess. "Two for dinner."

The woman marked off a table on a floor plan and picked up two menus. "This way."

Vivian followed with Russ behind her. They took seats next to a wall, and the hostess handed them menus. "Your server will be Maggie."

Vivian peeked over her menu. "Are we considering this our first real date?"

Russ waggled a finger. "Uh-uh. This is our second date. The first one, we had restaurant food, sat on the couch together to watch a movie and"—he patted his cheek with a forefinger—"you kissed me before saying goodnight."

Although she wanted more of the kisses they'd shared in the elevator, spending more time with Russ in other activities would probably be better for both of them. She hadn't known the real Bob when she'd married him, and maybe spending more time together before getting intimate would have revealed his character.

Maggie came and took their orders and returned soon with their drinks.

Russ took Vivian's hand. "I need to tell you something."

She stiffened. It seemed that whenever someone said that, they had something bad to relate.

He shook his head. "It's not bad. At least, I don't think so."

Her eyes widened. It was as if he'd read her mind.

He leaned closer and stared into her eyes. "I love you."

"Y-you do? But we haven't known each other very long."

"I got to know you when we talked in your checkout line. You probably don't remember me."

She grinned. "I do. I enjoyed talking to you more than any other customer." Her heart had skipped a beat every time she saw him at the store. She'd never seen him in any line but hers, and had wondered if it was intentional. She hoped it didn't bother him that she couldn't tell him yet that she loved him. It was too new for her, and she'd already made a mistake with Bob's character.

Their server returned with plates and set them on the

table. "Can I get you anything else?"

Both shook their heads.

"Enjoy your meal."

After she walked away, Russ took Vivian's hand again. "I know this is fast for you, but the close calls we've had have shown me how much I love you. I'd do anything for you."

She believed him. Where Bob's number one was Bob, everything Russ had done was for her. She gave his hand a squeeze.

By noon the next day, the worry would be over. They could have a normal relationship without the threat of death hanging over their heads. Or she'd be dead.

Chapter 7

Russ felt a bit nervous as he escorted Vivian back to their room. He tightened his hand into a fist, when what he'd rather do is splay it against her back. It would have been easier to remain a gentleman if he could kiss her good-night at her door, but it was more important to be nearby to keep her safe. He'd just work harder at not taking advantage of the situation.

He was ready to go all in, but Vivian hadn't said she loved him, so he'd give her the time she needed. Three official weeks of growing closer wasn't enough time for most people to declare their love. She'd also been stressed about these attempts on her life and her ex's death. He didn't need a commitment yet.

He unlocked the door and stepped in with Vivian right behind him. A check of the bathroom found it empty of unwanted visitors. His gaze dropped to the floor under the drapes, checking for feet of someone hiding. It was unlikely that anyone would have found their room, but he couldn't be too careful.

He slipped off his shoes beside the dresser. "Do you want to watch a movie?"

Her gaze darted to the beds and back to him. He placed his hands on her shoulders. "We've watched movies at my house, snuggled on the couch. People have had sex on couches, and we didn't. The bed's no different—unless you want it to be different. But if it makes you too uncomfortable, you can watch from over there." His gaze flicked to the other bed.

Her eyes widened, and she studied him for a few moments, but she grinned. "So, what are we watching?" She hadn't backed away from him, but hadn't acknowledged his step to advance their relationship either.

He handed her a paper from the nightstand between their beds. "I checked earlier and circled a couple I think you'll like. Or pick another." He flipped the pillows on his bed on end and leaned them side-by-side against the headboard, hoping, but not knowing which bed she'd choose.

"How's this?" Like so many other evenings, he wanted to hold her.

"Perfect." Vivian kicked off her shoes and crawled onto the bed.

Even on top of the covers, it gave him a jolt of longing. He hoped it wouldn't be much longer before they were together in all senses of the word. He snatched the remote and turned on the TV. "Which one?"

"This one." She pointed and he flipped the channel, dropping the remote beside him.

He put his arm around her, pulling her close, her vanilla scent filling his head with all kinds of ideas. Being together like this was nearly perfect. He kissed the top of her head, and she wiggled closer. Contentment like he'd never felt before spread through him.

Three-quarters of the way through the movie, she fell asleep. Russ finished the movie, enjoying holding her even while she slept. The credits rolled, and he carefully separated from Vivian. He slid her and the pillow down then tucked the covers around her. She would probably have been more comfortable in pajamas, but he'd let her take care of that if she woke in the night.

He stared down at her for long minutes. It was the second time he'd seen her sleeping, and he wished he could snuggle up behind her all night. It'd be so easy to say he'd fallen asleep, too. But she trusted him.

His nighttime ritual completed, Russ climbed into the other bed and watched Vivian until sleep took him.

~~~

Vivian woke and stretched, surprised by the constricting clothing. She ran her hand down her body, and discovered she was fully clothed. Then she remembered the movie, and couldn't recall the ending. She'd fallen asleep, and was still in the same bed.

Russ lay with his back to her in the other bed, a t-shirt stretched across his shoulders. She itched to slip a hand underneath and run her fingers up his spine, slide it to the front and plaster herself to his back. Snuggling next to Russ had become the most important part of her evenings.

"I know you're watching me."

She jumped at his words. "How can you know that?"

He turned to face her. "I'm a Marine. I'm attuned to being watched. I heard you moving, so I knew you were awake, but you didn't get out of bed." He grinned. "So I knew you were watching me."

Warmth crept up her chest, neck and into her face.

He chuckled. "It's okay. I fell asleep watching you." He slid up in bed, and leaned against the headboard. "Why don't you go shower, and I'll call Delgado about an escort?"

"All right." She grabbed her overnight bag and headed to the bathroom, relieved she didn't have to walk in front of Russ in her night clothes. Since she used the hall bathroom in his home, they sometimes passed in the hallway while she still had on a nightshirt, but somehow, the hotel room seemed more intimate.

She made quick work of showering and blow-drying her

hair. The business suit she'd chosen complimented her blue eyes. The nearly knee length skirt hugged her thighs and emphasized her legs. She wanted to look business-like for the attorney, but she'd picked this outfit for Russ. She twisted her hair up and pinned it, instead of wearing her usual braid or leaving it down. She slipped on the short matching jacket, slid her feet into heels she hadn't worn in months, and spun in front of the mirror.

Perfect.

Two steps into the main room, she caught Russ's attention. His eyes widened. "Wow. You look so professional. And sexy."

He set his phone beside him on the bed and stood. She only had a quick peek of him in his boxers before he closed in on her. He gave her a kiss that left her wanting more.

"A few more hours and you'll be safe. Officer Delgado is picking us up out front at ten-forty-five and will return us afterward."

He snatched up his bag and she had a great view of his butt as he strode into the bathroom. She fanned her face. It might be a good thing they were leaving when he came back out.

~~~

After checking out of the hotel, Russ hid Vivian in a dark corner of the lobby, and ran their luggage out to his car. He joined her, but studied every person who came through the door. No one remotely resembled the men gunning for her. At the appointed time, Russ led Vivian to a chair not far from the door where she perched on the arm. He stood next to the door, watching for Delgado to arrive, and for any suspicious activity. A man and woman strolled past, each rolling a suitcase. The doors automatically opened and they walked into the parking lot. They paused and looked over their shoulders as a police car drove up.

After Delgado got out, the couple continued single file between cars. The officer came around to the passenger side of the cruiser, and opened the back door. Russ ushered Vivian into the car. No one seemed to take notice of her.

He dropped in beside her. "Thanks for doing this, Officer Delgado."

The man waved a hand. "My job is to protect."

A ten minute drive, with no apparent tail had Russ relaxing a bit. It was almost over, and who'd attack with a police officer present? Once Vivian got her inheritance, he couldn't imagine the two guys doing anything more.

Delgado pulled into a parking lot beside a three story building. He stopped at the corner of the building, which meant they'd still have to cross the front to the double doors in the center. "I'll drop you here. Sorry I can't get you closer, but I don't see anyone loitering. I'll come in once I park." He got out, circled the hood and opened the back door.

Russ scanned the parking lot and the street they'd come in on. No black car, no suspicious men hanging around. He climbed out, standing where he'd shield her from the street. Vivian slid to the edge of the seat, and he helped her out. The six-inch curb caught her shoe and she stumbled.

The car window behind them shattered. His heart pounded as he pushed Vivian to the ground, wrapped himself around her, and tensed, waiting for the next bullet. He'd been under sniper fire before, but never when he'd been protecting anything so precious.

He grunted as hot pain sliced across his upper arm. The bullet pinged as it hit the door of the patrol car. At least it was his left arm. He could shoot with either hand, but was a more accurate shot with the right.

Vivian wiggled. "You've been shot!"

Russ covered her head and held it down. No way would he let her get in the line of fire. "It just grazed me. I'm fine." No matter where he'd been hit, if he had a breath left in him, that's what he would have told her.

Her short, raspy breaths puffed at his throat. He wished Vivian hadn't been subjected to this terror. A simple risk free life was sounding pretty good right now.

Delgado pulled his gun and yelled into his shoulder radio. "5405. Shots fired. I repeat, shots fired. Bradley and Harmon on Birch Street." He crouched beside Russ and Vivian. "Stay down."

Russ raised his brows. "Yeah, not going anywhere right now." He was totally exposed, but he'd take another bullet for Vivian.

Delgado stood, arms extended, gun pointing at the bushes. "Drop your weapons and come out with your hands in the air. Now!"

The bushes rustled and running footsteps was the response.

Delgado raced off and yelled over his shoulder. "Get inside the building."

Russ scrambled up and helped Vivian. Those shoes she'd worn had saved her life. He'd kiss them when he got the chance. He pushed through into the office.

A woman was plastered to the wall beside the door. "You've been shot! What's going on?"

He flipped the lock on the door. "Let's leave it locked for now."

Her mouth dropped open, and she hurried back to her desk. "I saw the police here, but I'll call an ambulance."

"I'm not leaving until everything's settled for Vivian. Just get me some paper towels."

Her eyebrows rose. "You're Vivian Lirette? I'm Ellen." She bit her lip and studied Russ's arm. "All right. Let me get you something, then I'll take you to Mr. Harmon's office."

Vivian stared at the blood seeping through his shirt, then into his eyes. "You should really get that looked at."

"It's fine. I've had worse."

Her eyes got shiny. "This happened because of me."

With his good arm, he pulled her against him and kissed her forehead. "This happened because some greedy bastard wants the money your aunt intended for you."

The receptionist returned with a whole roll of paper towels and handed it to him. He unrolled a bunch of sheets, folded them into a thick pad and pressed it against his wound. He suppressed a gasp, not wanting to worry Vivian.

"I'll take you to Mr. Harmon now."

Russ gazed at Vivian. "Do you want me to stay out here?" It didn't bother him if she wanted to do it on her own.

She shook her head. "No. I want you with me."

He was glad that she wanted that. He wasn't ready to be separated from her either, but he could have done it. Maybe.

~~~

Vivian wished she could hold Russ's hand as they entered the office.

A gray haired man came around his desk and took Vivian's hands. "I'm so glad to meet you. I'm Bruce Harmon. Your aunt was a good friend of mine."

"Nice to meet you, M—"

Russ stepped to her side, and the lawyer's gaze snapped to Russ's bloody arm.

"What happened to you?"

"Got shot in front of your office. Someone didn't want Vivian to make it here." Russ gazed at her. "You're safe now. They have no more reason to hurt you."

Mr. Harmon cleared his throat. "What's this about

hurting Vivian?"

Russ turned his attention to the attorney. "They tried to hurt her several times, including just now. We believe it's the person who would have inherited if Vivian wasn't found. They killed her ex-husband."

Mr. Harmon enclosed Vivian's hand in both of his. "I'm so sorry. I recommended your aunt add another heir in case you couldn't be found. I had no idea this would happen." His eyes widened. "That's why the police wanted to know the details of the will. Marsha told me she'd refused to give out the information, but I didn't know why they wanted it. We can pass the name to them once we've finished."

He narrowed his eyes at Russ. "And who are you?"

Vivian slid a half step closer to Russ. "My boyfriend, Russ Dresher. I want him here for the reading."

Russ sucked in an audible breath, and she gave him a smile. The happiness in those eyes took her breath away.

Mr. Harmon waved behind him. "Let's have a seat and get started." They sat and Mr. Harmon opened a folder. "You do look a bit like Patricia, but I still need to verify your identification."

"I remember Aunt Pat, but I don't know why Dad never kept in contact." She fished her birth certificate and driver's license from her purse and handed them to the attorney.

He examined her identification and handed them back. "Thank you." He held out a business-size envelope. "This explains that. Your aunt wrote to you about what happened after her sister died."

Vivian's hand shook a bit as she took it. She'd spent a lot of time with Aunt Pat until Vivian and her father left. She tore open the envelope and unfolded the sheet.

My dear Vivian,

I'm so sorry I didn't get to see you grow up. It's my own fault. When your mother, my only sister, died, I insisted that I take and raise you. Your father had been devastated by Janet's death and I thought he needed time to recover.

Later, after he ran with you, I realized that you were the only part of his beloved Janet he had left, and he wouldn't have survived without you.

I should have only offered my support, and I would have been able to watch you grow up. You don't know how much I regret that selfish decision.

I wish I could have been there to love you, give you advice, and be a mother-figure for you. Now, the best I can do is provide you the means to do what you want.

Vivian, I have always loved you as my own.

Aunt Pat

She handed the letter to Russ and wiped her eyes. What would it have been like to grow up with a mother figure? Her teen years would have been easier. Her father had been wonderful, but as a man with a teenage daughter, he'd been kind of lost. Maybe she would have seen through Bob before marrying him. If they'd never moved she wouldn't have met him, but she couldn't blame anyone for that.

Vivian pulled in a long breath. "Thanks. I'm glad she left a letter. With what happened after my mom died, we all lost."

Mr. Harmon lifted a paper from his folder and handed it to her. "Now for the will. Your aunt left you everything. Her house, her stocks, bank accounts, and IRA. I had the house appraised. All told, you have just over a million dollars."

"What?" Vivian flung her hand out and gripped Russ's arm. He hissed in a breath. It wasn't his injured one, but he held the toweling over the wound and she must have jarred it. "Sorry. I didn't realize she was well off. What am I supposed to do with all that money?"

Mr. Harmon chuckled. "A lot of people would want that kind of problem."

"Viv, you could go back to school. Become a lawyer," Russ said.

While taking her paralegal courses, she'd wished she could go to law school, but now that she'd been out of school for a few years, she didn't want to go back. She wrinkled her nose at Russ. "No thanks." She turned to the attorney. "No offense, Mr. Harmon. I enjoy being a paralegal, when I've got a job."

Mr. Harmon's eyebrows rose. "You're a paralegal? We happen to need one. One of ours is pregnant and won't be coming back after the baby's born. If you think you'll be moving to your aunt's house, send me your resume."

"Okay, thanks." She didn't have family or friends here anymore. And the only friend she had in her new hometown was Russ. Now that Bob was dead, she could move back to her old town. At least there, she had friends. If she could reconnect with them.

Mr. Harmon had her sign papers, showed her information about her new accounts, and gave her a folder of documents she needed for the bank, including a copy of the will.

Mr. Harmon sat back. "There you go. Now, here are the keys for your house." He set them on the edge of the desk beside a card with an address. He held out a business card. "And call me if you have any questions. If you decide to sell the house, I can line you up with a realtor."

Vivian took the card and stood. "Thank you, Mr. Harmon." She shook his hand, then scooped up everything else and turned to Russ. "Do you want to go to the hospital now?"

He lifted the paper towel on his arm and blood seeped out. "Yeah. I probably need stitches, but we'll have to go back to the hotel for my car."

They found Delgado sitting in the outer office, chatting with Ellen. The woman leaned back against her desk with a smile. Delgado stood. "They've been arrested. Led a merry chase until they ran a stop sign, and had an accident."

Vivian gasped. "Is everybody okay?"

"Just a few bruises. Cars had to be towed. They're Phillip and Martin Andrews. Haven't said a word."

Vivian flipped open the folder and shuffled through the papers. "Here. The will says if I wasn't found that an Albert Andrews would inherit. I wonder how he's related to Phillip and Martin."

Delgado pulled out a phone. "Let me get a picture of that."

Ellen stood. "I'll make a photocopy for you."

Delgado slipped his phone away as Ellen took the page and made a copy on the machine behind her desk, then gave them their respective sheets.

Delgado took his, folded it and tucked it into his shirt pocket. "Now, I'll drive you to the hospital."

Russ shook his head. "No. Just get us back to my car, and Vivian can drive me there."

"Uh-uh." Vivian poked him in the chest. "Officer, please drive us to the hospital. We'll take a cab to the car after we're done."

"Yes, ma'am."

They settled into the back of the police car once more and she tipped her head against Russ's shoulder. He kissed her hair, giving her a warm feeling inside. This man was special in so many ways.

Finally, the dangerous part had to be over.

Chapter 8

Russ pulled into the circular driveway of a mansion. His arm hit the door as he shoved the gearshift into park, and he hissed in a breath. That hurt worse than when he'd been shot. They'd spent some time at the police station giving statements, then gone to lunch. Vivian had insisted on paying.

He checked the address again and stared at the building in front of them. He'd Googled it on his phone during lunch, but the pictures didn't convey the size. The well maintained lawn surrounded a grey brick two-story with more windows than he wanted to bother counting. Wide stone stairs led to dark-stained double doors. "Viv, do you remember this place?"

"Yes. It's Aunt Pat's house."

He gave her an incredulous stare. "This isn't a house. It's a palace."

Her gaze swept the building. "It is big, isn't it? I remember thinking it was big when I was a kid, but I figured everything looks big to a kid."

"Are you okay going inside?"

She unclipped her seatbelt, swung the door open, and turned back to him with a huge smile. "Yes. Come on."

His heart swelled with love for this woman. She hadn't been fazed by the money, but her excitement over her aunt's house was beautiful to watch. Her eyes glowed and her cheeks were flushed. After the terror she'd faced, she deserved this.

She jumped out and raced up the steps before he had a chance to close his car door. He reached her as she fumbled and dropped the house key. He scooped it up and shoved it in the lock, but stepped back, letting her open the door to a house filled with memories.

~~~

Vivian gazed at Russ and bit her lip, not anticipating this to be so hard. She blinked back the unexpected tears. "There was a gathering here after Mom's funeral. It was packed with so many people. When I walked in with Dad, Aunt Pat rushed over and gave me a huge bear hug. That day was the last time I saw her." She turned the key, stepped inside, and he followed.

The closed up odor hit her. Through the warm months, the scent of flowers filled the house, cut from Aunt Pat's garden. Even in winter, often there were flowers.

Russ wrinkled his nose. "It's kind of stale in here. Let's leave the door open."

A light layer of dust covered the table beside the door, so unlike what she remembered.

"Okay." She grabbed his hand and dragged him into the first room on the left. "Sometimes, when I visited here, I'd bring a friend and we'd race circles around the furniture." She gestured their track pattern. "It looks exactly as I remember it."

She showed him four more rooms before entering the massive kitchen. "Aunt Pat used to have these huge dinner parties. When I was six, they let me come—"

He grinned. "They let you come to dinner parties when you were six?"

She giggled. "No. My parents came, and I was allowed to come downstairs as far as the landing. I got to wear a pretty dress even though I couldn't join them. I'd sit on the landing and watch everybody until dinner was served. Then Aunt Pat would take a dinner tray upstairs to my bedroom, and I had to stay there all night." She leaned close to him and spoke in a quieter voice, pretending to be afraid someone would hear. "After I ate, I'd sneak to the railing at the top of the stairs and watch between the balusters until I got tired. Sometimes Aunt Pat would see me and come upstairs after the music started. We'd dance in the hallway for a song and then she'd tuck me into bed."

It was nice recalling the fun things she'd done with her aunt, to now know how much Aunt Pat had loved her. She also learned how much her father loved her, taking her away so he wouldn't lose her. She hadn't talked to him since she moved away. Maybe it was time to call him.

Vivian took Russ's hand again and they tread up the stairs. She peeked into each room then brought him back to the second on the right. "This is the one I used. The drapes and bed covering are different, but otherwise it's the same."

The room wasn't designed for a little girl—yellow walls, hardwood floor, massive dark dresser and headboard, and a queen-size bed—but she's loved it anyway. She'd felt more grown up when she stayed here.

She followed Russ to the window, disappointed the garden had been neglected. She'd loved that view—a fairy land of ever changing color. Here and there, various colors still peeked through the weeds and dead plants. In the fall, the garden had been cleaned and neatened, in preparation for spring. Then she could easily see the statues of mystical characters. Her favorite sat at the far end, a unicorn with a fairy princess sitting on its back. "It used to be so beautiful."

Russ rubbed her back. "I can imagine it."

The unicorn wind chime that hung from a hook over the window tinkled in a slight breeze. She'd been so excited when Aunt Pat had surprised her with it. "I can't believe she still has the unicorns."

He turned her toward him and circled his other arm around her. She stared into his blue, blue eyes. He leaned in and gave her a kiss. "Viv, this would be a great place to raise children together."

The breath froze in her throat. She'd been falling under his spell for weeks, but was too stunned to understand him. "Children?"

"Yes, our children. I love you, Viv. I want to marry you."

She saw it all in his face—the tenderness, the worry she'd say no, the hope. She hugged him, her heart almost hurting with all the love crammed into it. "I love you, too. I didn't think I could again after...Bob." She leaned back, needing to see his face. "Yes, I'll marry you."

His shoulders dropped and he grinned. The kiss he gave her was the most gentle. "Thank God."

Still in his arms, her gaze wandered the room. "But I don't want to live here. This place is too big, and I don't have ties here anymore. It would be nice if we could live close to your family." She hoped he hadn't fallen in love with the house. She'd loved visiting it, but her own room at her parents' house had always been the most comfortable.

"I agree it's too big. I'm not much into giving parties."

She poked the crazy man in the chest. "Then why did you suggest it?"

"You had good memories here. I didn't want you to lose that."

If she didn't already love him, this would have pushed her over. He would have lived in this monstrous house if that's what she wanted. She kissed him. "Thank you. I lost it a long time ago. I'd like to keep some of the furniture and mementos, but sell the rest. Maybe Mr. Harmon can help with that, too."

~~~

Vivian moved into her old bedroom at Aunt Pat's house, and Russ took the one across the hall. Her house now. Living in it convinced her she didn't want such a large home. She'd labeled furniture she wanted to keep, and they boxed dishes, pans, lamps, and a few knick-knacks. Together, they picked out books. It would take years to read through them all. Russ helped her take down pictures, and they gathered them, the boxes and smaller pieces in a corner of the foyer.

They also talked to Officer Delgado and a detective about Phillip and Martin Andrews, the sons of Albert Andrews. The two were being sent back to face murder and attempted murder charges. Later, they might also be charged with the two local attempted murder counts. As far as anyone could tell, their father, Aunt Pat's cousin, was blameless. Patricia had told him of her placing him as a contingency in her will, but he hadn't told his sons. Maybe they'd overheard. She hoped the sons hadn't planned on killing their father, as well.

On day three, Vivian's cell phone rang. It had been quiet since they left home. "Hello?"

"Vivian, my dear. It's Bruce Harmon. I have a buyer for your house. He used to attend parties there and fell in love with it. He'll pay the appraisal price plus add on for any furniture you're leaving."

Vivian danced a little jig, and Russ grinned at her. She wouldn't have to wait months for a buyer to be found or figure out how to sell everything she wasn't taking. "Does he want to come see what we're leaving behind?"

"He can be there tomorrow, if that's all right."

"Perfect. We'll be leaving the morning after that. Thank

269

you so much, Mr. Harmon."

"I'm doing this for Pat as much as you. I'm glad I could help."

She pocketed her phone and threw her arms around Russ. "We have a buyer. When we go home, we'll have everything wrapped up here."

"I like how you say that." He kissed her.

"Say what?"

"Home. You haven't been in my hometown long, but you called it home."

"It's not the town." She gazed into the eyes she'd grown to love. "I lived in my apartment for months and it doesn't feel like home the way your house does. That's where I want to be. So, um." She glanced over his shoulder and back at him. "Would you mind if I give up my apartment and move in with you?"

"I was going to ask, but I wasn't sure if you were ready. You can continue to stay in the guest room or move into my room."

"I..." She'd made Bob wait until they were married. Maybe if she hadn't waited she would have found out before marrying him what type of man he was. But that didn't really matter with Russ. He was so far ahead of Bob in every way that mattered. She felt comfortable with him, but with just the right look or a kiss, she wanted so much more.

"Hey, you don't have to decide right now. No pressure. It happens when it happens."

She hugged him and laid her head on his shoulder. "Do you know how much I love you?"

"Almost as much as I love you?"

She didn't know someone could make her feel so happy. "Yeah, almost."

~~~

The itch was starting again. Their lives had calmed down, and Russ needed to amp up. Vivian was safe with her inheritance, and the Andrews brothers were being held without bail. Unbelievably, the house had sold for cash, and Mr. Harmon had drawn up the papers, then helped Vivian invest the proceeds. He'd listed his house for sale, and they were house hunting together.

Then that stupid itch had come back. He'd gotten nervous and twitchy. He'd reach for something on a high shelf and imagine reaching for that next hand hold. He craved the cliff face. He'd started dreaming about scaling it. Before, the risk, the high, was all that mattered, but now, he had Vivian to consider. It would devastate her if he fell to his death—as much as it would him if he lost her. He couldn't do that to her.

He gulped down some coffee. It was Saturday morning. He could climb the mountain and be back by noon. The sun streamed in the window. A perfect day for a climb.

Warm arms came around him and soft hair tickled his bare back. Vivian's engagement ring sparkled in the light. "Good morning."

He set his cup down, spun around and wrapped his arms around her. He held her tight so she couldn't see his face. He was sure it was contorted in anguish.

She struggled to put distance between them and gave up. "Something's been bothering you. I've noticed it for days. It's like you're pacing in your head."

"I need to climb."

"Climb what? A mountain? A roof? A flagpole?"

"A cliff face."

She pushed back, and this time he let her. "You mean like ropes and spikes?"

He couldn't meet her eyes. "Not exactly."

She grabbed his face. "What exactly is it?"

271

He glanced at the concern on her face then stared at her hair. "It's called free solo climbing. It's like what you see when someone scales a cliff, but without all the gear."

She tipped her head. "What gear do you use?"

"None."

She whacked his chest with her palm. "None? So if you slip, you plunge to your death?"

He shrugged. "It hasn't happened. I'm good."

She backed away and rammed her fists onto her hips. "Yeah, and so are the mountain climbers who have all that gear and still sometimes die. Are you crazy?"

He rubbed his chest. There was only one way to get rid of the itch. He needed the adrenaline that coursed through his veins when he climbed. "Sometimes I need to do it." He ran shaky fingers through his hair. "It's building up inside. I need to take action, and then I can breath easy again."

Her eyes widened. "You're an adrenaline junky. Is that what being a Marine did to you? Instead of PTSD, you need to risk your life?"

He didn't want to be psychoanalyzed by her, but she hit so close to the truth. A small part of him wanted to push away. The rest wanted to hold her tight.

She glared at him, and he looked away. She'd probably break up with him. Who'd want to marry a man who risked his life for the high?

She touched his arm. "Can't you become a policeman or an EMT or some professional where you get that adrenaline burst and you're actually doing something good for people?"

His mouth dropped open. She understood him. Why hadn't he thought of that? It might work. Delgado must have gotten a shot of adrenaline when the Andrews were shooting at them. The same for the other officers who'd helped. It wouldn't be every day. He didn't need climbing every day. "That might work."

She grinned. "Of course it will." Her smile disappeared. "Maybe you could talk to someone, too."

"No!" He closed his eyes and tipped his head back. "Maybe." He'd never talked to anyone about it before. He'd never thought of it as a problem. Until Vivian came into his life. Leave it to his smart woman to pinpoint a possible solution. "I'll find out what I have to do to become a police officer. But I'm on edge. I have to climb today."

"Can't you use ropes and stakes? Please." The worry on her face nearly gutted him, almost wiping out the pressure in his chest. Almost.

"They're called pitons." He dropped his hand onto her shoulder. "All right. I'll use my gear."

Her shoulders dropped, and the tension around her eyes disappeared.

She wrapped her arms around him. "Thank you." She gave him a nudge. "Now, get going. We have houses to look at this afternoon."

~~~

Russ stared at the cliff face, mapping his route. He clipped the carabineers to his harness and picked up the coiled rope. Most of the gear had been in his garage, but he'd had to buy a new rope and pitons. The urge to free solo had tugged at him, and he'd driven past the store. A block away, the image of Vivian's grief stricken face tore out his heart. He couldn't do that to her. He'd promised. So, he'd turned back.

He was still surprised Vivian hadn't left him once she learned his risky secret, but she understood him, was there for him.

He glared at the dark clouds in the distance. The storm wasn't supposed to hit until early evening, and he'd be done before lunch. With the stop at the store, and a talkative sales guy, he was starting an hour later than he'd originally planned. He'd considered buying gear for Vivian, but figured he'd have to talk her into climbing.

The Marines had required ropes for climbing, but whenever he had the chance, he'd done without. Some of the guys had thought he was crazy, and now he could see why. Those were the ones with wives and girlfriends back home.

He studied the cliff face, figuring out his route. At the twelve foot mark, he'd place his first piton. He wasn't concerned about a fall before that. He placed his hands in natural holds and started climbing. At the predetermined spot for his first piton, he clung with his feet and one hand while he shoved a piton into a crack then hammered it. He glanced up the wall, so tempted to keep climbing. No. He promised.

He attached the rope and climbed higher. The gentle breeze had turned into a stronger wind, but nothing he hadn't experienced before. It cooled the sun's rays beating down on his back.

At his next handhold, a piton was already in place. Testing it, he found it solid. Further up, he tested another piton and it pulled free. He shoved it in his pocket and used one of his in a nearby crack. Halfway to the top, clouds rolled in and rain started. Not a gentle mist, but a downpour. Russ couldn't see the top any longer, or the ground below. He worked his way up twenty more feet when a foot slipped, sending a surge of excitement through his system. Not surprising since the blowing rain had saturated the crevices. It added some excitement to a climb that had less than his usual risk.

The rain and wind offered an exhilarating climb, despite the safety gear. This was exactly what he needed.

He regained his footing, placed a piton, and attached the rope. With the sun hidden, the rain chilled him. With more care, he climbed higher. His foot slipped again, and each time he tried to place it he couldn't get traction. He found new hand holds to the left, secured his dangling foot where the other had been and stretched his other foot to a new spot.

He stretched a hand higher and both feet slipped out, yanking his hands from their holds. He plunged. His heart pounded, blood surged, and fingertips tingled. The rope played out, and he jolted to a stop, slamming against the wall, bounced away and hit it again, knocking the wind from his lungs.

Russ stared above. He'd dropped about ten feet. His heart beat erratically as he struggled to pull in the first breath. He leaned his forehead against the cold, wet stone. Finally, sweet, damp air filled his lungs. He should be dead. One more time he'd cheated death, but the adrenaline rush this time left him nauseous and shaken. His shoulder ached, and his fingers were raw, but it was nothing compared to the pile of broken bones and flesh on the rocks below that he should have been. If not for Vivian's pleading and divine intervention, he'd be dead. This rope had been his lifeline. So he could return to Vivian.

He rappelled down and landed on shaky legs then sunk to his knees. He ran a hand over the ground. Some poor soul would have found his broken, lifeless body on the rocks. Maybe it would have been Vivian when he didn't come home. A full body shiver shook him as he imagined her crying over what was left of him.

He pushed to his feet and leaned his back to the wall. Once his legs steadied, he removed his harness, shaking hands taking twice as long as it should to unfasten. He rolled up his rope, and headed to the car.

The drive home calmed him, made him feel nearly normal. He rushed through the door and found Vivian on the couch with her eReader in her hands. He dragged her up and hugged her so tight she grunted. He didn't care that he'd gotten her all wet.

She pushed back. "Russ, what's wrong?" She cupped his face between her hands.

He grabbed one hand and kissed her palm. He couldn't tell if the wetness on his face was from the rain or tears, but it didn't matter. "You saved me. That damn rope saved me. If not for you and your love, I'd be dead today."

Tears filled her eyes and she tightened her arms around him. "Your love saved me, too."

~~~

Darrah smiled down on the happy couple. Russ deserved this happiness. He'd still have to battle his need for an adrenaline rush, but Vivian and this experience had tempered it.

She glanced behind her. Another discouraged soldier needed her help.

THE END

Books by Deborah Wallace

Wounded Warrior Hearts Series
Wounded Warrior Hearts: Steven
Wounded Warrior Hearts: Amy
Wounded Warrior Hearts: Russ

Rawlins Series
Kathleen's Legacy
Forbidden Woman
Jamie's Trials
Adam's Redemption
Kristy's Puzzle – *Spring 2020*

Other Books
I Shot the Sheriff
Second Choice
New Memories
Only My Love

Check out my website for details on these books and where to find them. You can also sign up to receive emails when I have a new book. www.DeborahWallaceBooks.com.

About Deborah Wallace

Someone suggested I try writing, and stories started populating my brain, begging to be put on paper (or my computer screen).

I have been called a Jane-of-all-trades, from seamstress to house and furniture designer/builder to computer programmer to technical writer and bookkeeper. I even do car maintenance. I've also guided a team of 'Future Problem Solvers'.

I grew up in Michigan, but Massachusetts has been my home for more years than I care to think about. I love the history here, the museums and antique houses, the seacoast and hiking trails.

My three children have grown and scattered, but my husband is by my side, encouraging my writing.